EVERY COUPLE'S FEAR

JOANNA WARRINGTON

Every Couple's Fear

Joanna Warrington

All rights reserved

The moral right of the author has been asserted

Copyright 2025 Joanna Warrington

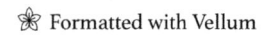

❀ Formatted with Vellum

One of the themes covered in this story is the possibility of a link between thalidomide and second-generation birth defects. Scientists have consistently asserted that deformities caused by thalidomide cannot be passed on. However Dr William McBride, the obstetrician in the early 1960s who discovered the link between the drug and birth deformities, believed there is a link, but because of his flawed claims over another anti-nausea drug, Debendox, his theories weren't deemed credible and were widely rejected.

There were around 10 children born in the 1980s to thalidomide survivors with similar defects to their parents. Their stories received extensive media coverage, and affected families set up a group to publicise their plight. Surely, their children were proof that deformities could be passed on, but sadly their claims were greeted with scepticism by the thalidomide charities and they were unable to claim compensation.

I had the privilege of meeting one such family and we have become good friends. Characters Sally and Martin mirror some of the challenges this family went through. I would like to give my heartfelt thanks to them for their help with this book. Their names will remain anonymous.

The long-term implications for such families has been devastating, with some having IVF treatment for subsequent children for fear they might have another child with deformities, and some worrying about a third generation as they await the birth of grandchildren.

St. Bede's, the school that Toby and Sue attended and where Bill works as caretaker, is loosely based on Chailey Heritage School in East Sussex, the first purpose-built school for disabled children in the UK. It was founded in 1903 and is

DISCLAIMER AND BACKGROUND

Every Couple's Fear is part of a series, 'Every Parent's Fear'. You can read this as a standalone novel, but I hope you will enjoy the series. Here is the link to the whole series available in Kindle and in paperback. My Book

All characters in this publication, other than those who are known public figures, are fictitious, and any resemblance to real people, living or dead, is purely coincidental. All opinions are those of the characters and not my personal opinions or the opinions of real people.

This is a fictional story based on the thalidomide disaster, one of the blackest episodes in the annals of medical history, which had devastating consequences for thousands of families across the world. Thalidomide was used to treat a range of medical conditions. It was thought to be safe for pregnant women, who took it to alleviate morning sickness. Thalidomide caused thousands of children worldwide to be born with malformed limbs, and the drug was taken off the market late in 1961.

where many of the British thalidomide survivors were cared for and educated. There are various schools around the UK called St. Bede's. The name is coincidental and bears no relation to any of these schools.

The story reflects the situations and experiences that families and thalidomide survivors might have faced, draws on real-life events and real experiences, and has been thoroughly researched. I have spoken with many thalidomide survivors at various events and in private, and I worked with a survivor as a personal assistant for ten years.

The story of Sheena is a tribute to my incredible friend Sheena Pollock. She had spina bifida and tragically died at age 37 following complications in surgery for dystonia. She worked at Coutts and one day in the 1980s she fell in a crowd at Charing Cross Station, a very scary experience.

This book is set in the 1980s when the terms 'handicapped' and 'handicap' were still very much in use, but I've tended to use the more modern terms, 'disabled' and 'disability' more frequently as we progress in this series.

PROLOGUE

2nd January 1986.

DEAR TOBY,

Congratulations on your forthcoming wedding!

This is a wonderful time in your life, and we sincerely wish you all the happiness in the world as you prepare for your special day.

As 1986 marks the 25th anniversary of the thalidomide disaster, the *Horizon* team is producing a documentary to commemorate this important milestone. We would be honoured if you would allow us to film your wedding ceremony as part of this project.

We believe it could offer a meaningful insight into your life and experiences in your 20s, showcasing not just the joy of your celebration but also the inspiring journey you and others have taken.

If you would like to explore this opportunity further, we would be delighted to discuss it in more detail.

Thank you in anticipation for considering our request, and again, heartfelt congratulations!

Wishing you all the best,

BBC Two *Horizon* Team.

1

SUMMER 1986

Jeremy was in the middle of getting ready for his daughter's wedding when the phone started ringing. He dashed down the stairs, buttoning his shirt as he went, yelling for someone to pick it up. He snatched the receiver just as his wife emerged from the kitchen, holding a tube of mascara and a small mirror.

On the other end of the line was a parent of a thalidomide survivor, their voice sharp and hurried.

'Jeremy, it's Tim, I won't keep you, I'm sure you're in the middle of getting ready, but what's this about the BBC coming to the wedding?'

Jeremy went quiet. They'd informed everyone about the media's presence today, so why had this family slipped through the net? This was most disconcerting; how many others weren't aware?

'I thought Toby had told everyone, I'm sorry you didn't know.' Toby should never have agreed to allow the BBC to film the wedding. It was utterly foolish. He'd sensed trouble from the beginning.

'It's not my daughter getting married, so I don't want to

interfere, but I like to think we're one big family. Our children's weddings should be private affairs, not another media circus. The last thing we need is the press barging into our lives yet again. I'm worried for everyone's sake. The media are only interested in making money and they will make it as sensational a story as they can.'

Tim's concern was palpable, his words laced with worry and protectiveness—anxiety built from past intrusions. Jeremy felt the weight of his worry, a reminder that love and joy could easily be eclipsed by the shadows of a history that threatened to ruin their special day.

'I hear what you say and I'm sorry you've only just found out.'

'Look, I know this isn't what you wanted to hear, but we've decided we won't be coming.'

Jeremy was speechless. How many others would boycott the event? 'I'm really sorry you feel you can't come. I think in many ways this could be a positive for everything we've achieved over the years. Our children will always be the focus of attention throughout their lives, and as you know, Toby's his own boss and has become a key protagonist of his peers.'

'I wouldn't be happy about the media being at the reception. Fine if they're just filming the speeches, but it wouldn't be right filming our kids eating. Have you considered that? Some eat with their feet. While it might have been acceptable to film them eating as toddlers, it doesn't feel appropriate as adults.'

'As far as I know they're only filming the ceremony.' He was cross with himself. He was footing the bill but he felt like a spare part. Why hadn't Toby and Sue discussed the details of the day with him and Pearl? At times Sue was a silly girl, far too impetuous and so wrapped up in planning her wedding dress, he wouldn't be surprised if she'd overlooked all these issues. What troubled him most wasn't the world seeing how they ate, but the embarrassment of his close friends witnessing their table manners, though he wasn't going to admit that to Tim.

When he came off the phone, Pearl and the twins were eager to know what had been discussed. Jeremy headed back upstairs to continue getting ready, his family trailing behind him. Pearl wanted to know the exact details of the call, but Jeremy didn't want further disruptions to the day, and he certainly wasn't going to tell Toby and Sue that Tim and his family wouldn't be attending.

Jeremy had become tired of Pearl's demands, she'd only make a mountain out of a molehill. The less said, the better. He had no intention of spoiling Sue's day and getting it in the neck, then having to spend the rest of his life regretting it.

2

Sandy was sitting in the front row of the church as she waited for the ceremony to begin. She was a bag of nerves. Here was her son about to be married to his sweetheart but everyone only knew her and Jasper as friends of the family. Bill was effectively Toby's father, he'd raised him with unwavering love, yet the family secret weighed heavy on her heart. The burden of the secret still rankled, and keeping it hidden had become almost unbearable. She smiled at the complications, secrets, and skeletons of all their lives.

The secret felt like a massive gulf between them and yet it was what bonded them as a unit. But oh, how she longed to tell the world that he was her son, the relief she'd feel, but she couldn't, it was a vow she had promised not to break. Toby was standing at the altar next to Dave, looking so smart, sharing a joke with his best mate. She felt so proud of what he'd become and how he'd coped with life's difficulties, but she realised what an anxious, fussing, clucking mother hen she'd become in recent weeks. All the worry, wondering how they'd cope and what if it didn't work between them once the veneer wore off? And she felt sad knowing she wouldn't be seeing Toby as much now that there was someone else taking care of him and occupying his time.

Her thoughts turned to Sue. Sandy pitied Sue, her upbringing hadn't been easy. She was such a lovely girl, and she wanted to get closer to her as a mother-in-law, but Sue would never know the truth. Holding back emotions was sometimes the hardest thing to do. And then there was Sue's mother, Pearl. What a difficult woman she was. She noticed how she looked down her nose at Bill. "How can he drive such a scruffy van?" she'd said. What a snob she was. Sandy didn't like stuck-up people who thought they were somehow better than others. She glanced over and saw the tension on Pearl's face. Today was clearly more an ordeal than a pleasure for her. She noticed how few relatives and friends there were on that side, which wasn't surprising given they weren't very nice people. All that high society living and mingling with the churchy lot, while keeping Sue very much in the background of their lives––it was unforgiveable. You couldn't wash away the sins of the world by going to church. Church gave her the appearance of respectability but didn't turn her into a nice person. Pearl was the biggest hypocrite alive. There was no love lost between them, they were never going to become good friends, marriage or no marriage.

Pearl's life seemed to be about keeping up appearances, a façade of respectability, but what lay beneath the surface? How had they reacted when Sue was born? They didn't seem to want to have much to do with their child, as if they were embarrassed and living with the shame that she was imperfect.

Something niggled as she sat waiting for the ceremony to begin, then she realised what it was.

Lucy.

In a flash, she knew.

Lucy was gazing straight at Toby almost in a trance with a look of love on her face. Sandy's instinct told her this was more than just admiration and friendship. It reminded her of how she'd felt about Jasper all those years ago. The yearning, the longing, that sudden realisation, the intensity of the feelings, unspoken love. Then Toby turned and looked straight at Lucy.

Sandy's heart flipped.

She saw it.

That instant connection between them that words could not express. Had something happened between them? Toby had always been close to Lucy, but just how close were they? Did they have an intimate connection and had Sue ever picked up on this?

Her thoughts were broken by Jasper shuffling along the pew and plunging down next to her. He leaned in and whispered, 'I've just met the young lady who's coming to stay tonight. The German lass. You didn't tell me she's one of Toby's friends.' All the time he was rambling on, her focus remained on Toby and Lucy.

Jasper and Sandy had been running a bed and breakfast for several years. One night, while filling up the car with petrol, Jasper met an American couple who were touring the area. At the checkout they asked the cashier if he knew of lodgings. Jasper stepped forward and offered them a bed for the night as it was getting late. The next morning after cooking them a full English, Jasper said to Sandy, "That was fun, why don't we run a B&B?" Her husband loved their new venture, he was in his element, meeting new faces and engaging with guests from all corners of the globe. He delighted in the stories the visitors shared and sometimes they became the focus of his photography, and he would arrange them into poses in his garden studio. And if the photos turned out well, he submitted them to competitions at his local photography club.

Just then the music started, and everyone rose to their feet. Toby and Dave stood to attention like two soldiers on parade and Bill's chest was puffed out with pride as he looked from Toby to the back of the church to see the sight of Sue walking down the aisle. A feeling of intense happiness washed over her.

Toby, the child she thought she'd never see again all those years ago, was getting married.

3

Sue squealed in delight when she saw the shining pink Cadillac arrive outside her flat. The roof was down, and her dad was lounging in the back, arm draped across the seat and looking dapper. Tears welled and she sniffed them back, not wanting to ruin her make-up. This was her dream, to ride in one of these gorgeous 1950s cars on her wedding day, and until now, she wasn't sure it would come true, but Toby had promised he'd do his best to make it happen. He hadn't stopped teasing her though, throwing out all kinds of ideas to get her to the church, from a dust cart to a Reliant Robin, or Bill's van.

As she tottered towards the car on her new prosthetic legs, her dad and the chauffeur hurried over to assist her. Her dad was an impatient man. She wanted to take her time getting into the car on her own, but he was glancing at his watch before he bent down and lifted her into the car.

'Dad,' she protested, 'I don't need your help.'

'We'll be late, you don't want to be late for your own wedding.' He tutted and winked at the chauffeur in the mirror.

'It's the bride's prerogative to be late.'

'You don't have to keep proving everything to yourself. You're a stubborn miss.'

Her long dress was billowing around her like a tempest, there was so much fabric, and she didn't like to admit it; it would have been a struggle getting into the car without his help.

Before pulling away, the chauffeur slid a cassette into the tape deck and hearing the song, Bruce Springsteen's 'Pink Cadillac', Sue started to sing.

'Wow, this car is amazing, I can't believe Toby managed to hire such a beauty.' She felt a sudden rush of love for her husband-to-be.

'He didn't.'

Sue turned and stared at her dad.

'It was that fella that lives next door to you. He did all the ringing round, he booked it.'

'Norman, really?' Her heart plummeted and she felt a stab of disappointment. Maybe Toby had been happy to delegate but it just seemed that everyone was taking over. Norman wasn't even family.

'Of course.' She hated the way he said it so matter-of-factly, as if it were obvious that Toby wouldn't be capable of ringing round. It saddened her to think her dad had so little faith in him.

'You should have married Norman, ma girl,' he jested. *They don't even like Norman, but they'd just rather I married an able-bodied man, anyone would do.*

Sue tried not to let the comment get to her, but she'd always sensed that whoever she married, he wouldn't be right for their disabled daughter. It went deeper than that though. From a young age, her parents had never missed a chance to remind her she'd never find love or marry. For a long time, she'd believed them. They'd instilled that thought and it was hard to shift. Their words still echoed in her mind. Each remark had chipped away at her self-esteem, casting a shadow on her hopes and dreams. And it was only when her thalidomide friends started dating, marrying, and even having children, that she realised she could embrace love and happiness too. Their collective joy inspired her to dream beyond the hateful words of her childhood. She too could have a fulfilling life.

She was grateful for the wonderful family she was marrying into. They were kind and welcoming and couldn't do enough for her. How lucky she was. So different to Andrew's family. It would never have worked with him and thank God she'd realised weeks into the relationship. It made her cringe when she thought about the first time she met Andrew's mother. She was always a bit nervous and wary when she met someone for the first time because of their reaction to her. They always saw her in a wheelchair and couldn't see past her disability. She'd waited round the corner of the house while Andrew pressed the doorbell and spoke to his mum. "I want you to meet Sue," he'd told her. "Why are you going out with a girl with no legs?" she'd asked him. "You'll end up doing all her personal care. Life will be very difficult for you. Why would you choose to take on all that? Why don't you go out with that nice girl from college?"

Saddened to overhear her tirade, Sue had emerged from around the corner. She desperately wanted this woman to like her, but it was hopeless, the miserable cow wasn't going to give her a chance. She just stood on the doorstep and sneered down at Sue as if she was a bit of dirt.

They hadn't been dating long before it became apparent

that Andrew couldn't cope with all the family pressure. Keeping his parents happy and not rocking the boat was more important to him. He couldn't stand up to them. Still, Sue mused, they'd got what they wanted. He eventually went out with that girl from college, and they were now married. It was his loss; he'd freed her to be with someone much kinder, Toby. Being with Toby gave her a warm glow, she'd always felt that way, even when they were just friends at St Bede's, though she'd never acknowledged it, even to herself. In the last year of school and at a loose end on Saturdays, they'd started meeting in the grounds to chat. She found him funny but intelligent too. He was just great company, and they'd stayed in contact over the years, only getting together three years ago. She couldn't imagine him not being in her life. He was the man of her dreams and her best friend.

They turned into the lane leading towards the church where she saw Gill waiting.

'Gill's brought a wheelchair for you,' her dad said.

'Yes, for the reception.'

'No,' he said, glancing at her. 'To get you into church.'

Sue was taken aback. Gill was her volunteer helper through the CSV programme. They were a similar age. Gill was going to be Sue's paid carer after the wedding and had agreed to come in twice a day, an hour each visit to support Sue. Gill had helped her for several years and they had become close friends. She, of all people, understood the importance of Sue walking into church unaided. She refused to be pushed in a wheelchair. What had this been for otherwise? Roehampton had made her prosthetic legs especially for this moment, and the TV crew were here to film it.

'Dad, you know how important this is to me.'

He scoffed. 'It's ridiculous. It'll take you all day to walk up that bloody aisle, the vicar will get tired and give up waiting. Think how embarrassing that would be. And what if you fall and break your teeth like you did as a child? That would ruin everything. Is that really what you want? Another hospital visit? Because I know your mother won't want that. Hours sitting in A&E.'

His words struck deep, overshadowing the joy she longed to feel on this momentous day. 'These legs were made specially for me.' Her voice was rising. 'I'm going through with this, whether you like it or not.'

'Calm down, you sound like a petulant child.'

Her head jerked round to face him. She was furious. 'If you don't want to walk me up the aisle, just say. I'm sure Bill or Jasper would be happy to step in.'

'Now you're just being stupid. It's thirteen years since you last wore limbs.'

She'd gone to the effort of contacting the limb-fitting centre at Roehampton Hospital. They were brilliant and had started work on her limbs immediately.

'You've got to realise, Dad, I've spent twenty-six years doing everything on my own because you and Mum weren't there for me. Toby's lucky, his family rallied round. I wouldn't be where I am today without their kindness and support. You couldn't wait to get rid of me and you never wanted me to marry. You and Mum aren't going to spoil our day, so if you can't handle it, or can't support me, I'll walk up the aisle on my own, and after today, you and Mum can get on with your own lives, I'll be somebody else's responsibility.'

'Don't be so obstinate and be grateful for once. This

wedding cost me a fortune, a lot more than your cousin's wedding did last year.' Sue couldn't comment on her cousin's wedding since she hadn't been invited, likely due to her parents' embarrassment over her disability or her cousin's lack of consideration for accessibility.

'That's typical, all you think about is money. It doesn't cost anything to show you care. I wonder how you'd all feel if you had a disability. I'm determined to make a life for myself and my darling Toby.'

'I'm just being realistic. You don't have the balance like you did when you were young.' He had a point, but she refused to listen.

In one sense, he was right, it had been touch and go. It wasn't just a case of making the legs and putting them on. She'd needed lots of physio and practice walking in them. It had been years since she'd worn prosthetics. It was like learning to ride a bike. As the limbs neared completion, she was still struggling to master her balance. She remembered sitting down between a set of parallel bars which were used to help steady artificial limb users while they learned to balance. Lacing up the legs, she'd closed her eyes and prayed for God to help her. She'd gently lifted herself off the chair and steadied herself before walking through the parallel bars and over to the limb technician and doctor. The doctor had been amazed and told her that her balance was perfect. Her confidence had grown by the second. She'd walked into the corridor, and the staff on reception who had been at the hospital for years and knew her well, all clapped and cheered. She'd been so delighted, but her parents' response was, as usual negative.

'You'll be amazed, I'll show you. Roehampton were brilliant, I am going to do this.'

He tutted. 'I'm surprised you could bear to go back to Roehampton, you hated it there when you were a kid. I remember your whining. Soon as we saw Buckingham Palace, that's when you'd kick off.'

'I hated the journey, and I hated staying up there.'

'The fuss you made. Those nurses on the Leon Gillis Ward were lovely, they couldn't do enough for you. I think your problem is, you've been spoilt rotten and pampered too much over the years. You won't be able to walk up that damn aisle and that's the last of it.'

Sue was fuming. 'That's where I'm going to prove you wrong, and all the other doubters.'

His words were like a red flag to a bull. *I'll show them.*

He hadn't seen her practising for hours, her sheer determination to succeed. He wasn't interested and wasn't bothered about the importance of her doing this. How little her parents really knew her. His only concern was that she didn't make a fool of herself in front of his friends. He'd never wanted this wedding to go ahead, and he was determined to ruin it for her.

As the car pulled up, she leaned over and yanked the door open, and Gill hurried over with the wheelchair.

Determined not to let her dad make her feel disheartened, she put on her best face. 'Hi,' she gushed, glancing from Gill to her married friend, Sally. Sally and her husband Martin were trying for a baby. In the lead-up to the wedding, Sue had been worried about Sally getting pregnant and no longer being able to fit into her bridesmaid's dress. But she needn't have worried.

Gill and Sally were her bridesmaids and Angela, Toby's sister, was the chief bridesmaid. 'You look stunning, both of you.'

Sally and Gill had been over to Sue's flat earlier on to

help dress, apply her make-up and put the finishing touches to her hair, before scooting off to get themselves ready.

Gill glanced nervously at Sue's dad before gently nudging the wheelchair in Sue's direction.

'I won't be needing that,' Sue said. 'Not till after the ceremony.' She hoped and prayed that she could cope with the legs just long enough to get to the reception, she'd be happy with that.

Gill looked sheepishly at Sue. 'Well, that's what I thought,' she said tentatively, 'but your dad insisted.'

Her dad got out and shot round to join them, ready to lift Sue from the car into the wheelchair.

'No, Dad, you won't change my mind, I am walking.' She shuffled along the car seat and lifted her legs out of the car before standing up. It wasn't easy and the prosthetics were pinching her skin.

'She's in one of her stubborn moods, girls.' Her dad tutted and looked resigned––it wasn't a battle he was going to win.

She linked his arm. 'Be thankful I won't be in my wheelchair. You're always telling me I use it as a battering ram.'

'There is that, I suppose.' As they turned and smiled at each other, she saw a look on his face she'd never seen before. 'I know I don't say it often, but your mum and I, we do love you. You look beautiful today by the way––you really do.'

Her dad was normally such a stiff, stoical man, she instantly forgave him and felt suddenly overwhelmed with emotion. She couldn't remember the last time her parents had told her they loved her, they probably hadn't.

The photographer approached to arrange them for a group photo by the lychgate and then in front of the church.

Sue could predict what was coming. Her dad, a keen

amateur photographer with a high-end camera, couldn't stop himself. When he jumped in to instruct Sue and her bridesmaids on where to stand, suggesting a range of poses, she wasn't at all surprised.

'Dad, you're so embarrassing, bossing the poor man around. You're trying to do his job,' she whispered through gritted teeth.

'He lacks imagination,' he replied, not bothering to keep his voice down.

She could sense Gill and Sally cringing too, but Angela, still a kid, just laughed. 'I'm surprised my dad's not out here taking over too.'

Sue laughed. 'Jasper's too polite, he wouldn't dare.'

After the photographs, Sue turned towards the church entrance.

I'm going to marry the one I love and no matter what happens, nothing will change that.

She'd found someone who had no expectations of her. Toby was happy to just spend time with her. How she wished her own family were as kind and loving as Toby's.

She hoped she would be able to walk down the aisle. It was worth the pain. This was going to be the only time she would wear the prosthetics.

After today, Toby will have to get used to calling me stumpy.

For the first time, she felt truly good about herself, like a princess. She was sure as hell going to enjoy the day like no other. One thing she did know, she could take anything that was thrown at her.

Beyond the challenge of walking down the aisle, her biggest fear now was taking all her clothes off in front of Toby and sharing a bed with him. In all those months of dating, they'd never been intimate. He was a true gentleman and had the utmost respect for her, so hadn't pushed it.

Sometimes she wondered if he was too shy to make a move, but tonight? Tonight was their wedding night, there was that expectation things would go further. She wasn't expecting fireworks, the first time was bound to be awkward and clunky. But she felt excited, also nervous, like a kid before a rollercoaster ride.

4

Standing rigid before the altar all trussed up, a bowtie around his neck threatening to garrotte him, Toby was as nervous as a tightrope walker in a sandstorm. Even a penguin would be proud of him. Every few seconds, he glanced over at his best man, Dave, for moral support and to check if he still had the rings. The pint at The King's Head had given him Dutch courage but now it was his own head, not the king's, on the chopping block.

In that moment all eyes were on him as everybody—including the TV cameras which were poised and ready—braced themselves, ready to turn their heads for her grand entrance.

He was terrified, for her, for them both. If something went wrong, if she had an accident, he'd never forgive himself. They'd spent a lifetime in the spotlight, the butt of jokes, the laughing stock. What had he been thinking, agreeing to be filmed for a documentary on this most personal and intimate of days?

It meant so much to her to be doing this, walking up the aisle on artificial legs, and to be filmed doing it. It was the choice she'd made, but it was not going to be easy. He wouldn't have thought any less of her if she'd backed out. He tried to think of an analogy. It was the equivalent of him being in a boxing match, and he knew that was outside his capabilities.

From the car, through the lychgate, navigating the uneven Yorkstone paving, often treacherous, slippery, and mossy, with cracks to dodge. Fortunately, it hadn't rained this past week. At the end of the path, there was a small step into the porch, then another step into the church.

This journey, so brief, so simple for many, yet an odyssey for her.

This wasn't just any journey; it had been planned and practised meticulously. The rehearsal had left her sore and in pain, and that was before the real event.

She was making this journey for him.

She had her reasons. They didn't matter to him.

And for that, he loved her all the more.

He could hear whispering, people speculating how she was going to do it.

Out of the corner of his eye, he spotted Norman, that annoying prat, buzzing round and making sure everyone had a buttonhole. He was acting like he was some sort of usher, which was just typical.

Oh God, what's the plonker up to now? He was shuffling people around, rearranging them like chess pieces. Toby couldn't believe this idiot, full of his own self-importance. He had managed to insert a role for himself, yet again. Hadn't he done enough meddling? The thought of living next door to this creep filled Toby with dread, and his frustration threatened to boil over as he desperately tried to catch his eye and signal for him to sit down and stop this chaos. *Dear, oh dear, I hope he backs off after we're married.*

Suddenly the music began, Mendelssohn's 'Wedding March', and everybody rose and looked to the back of the church with anticipation.

At his first glimpse of her, his breath caught in his throat. He gazed down the aisle in admiration, watching as his bride-to-be slowly advanced towards him, her arm linked in her father's.

His eyes welled with tears. He couldn't help it, he was choked with so much emotion. His young sister Angela was behind her, in a shimmering peach gown, but he barely registered her or the other bridesmaid. He couldn't remember a time when he'd felt more nervous.

He noticed Dave casting a not-so-subtle gaze at the bridesmaids, with all the concentration of a cat watching a dance of butterflies. It was classic Dave, the perpetual flirt who treated every wedding like his personal dating game show. He had a grin that could charm the pants off a statue and was completely unaware that his behaviour screamed, "I'm a dirty sod". If there was an award for bottom pinching, Dave would be the reigning champion, proudly accepting the trophy while blowing kisses to an awestruck audience.

Toby was momentarily distracted by a mother perched at the end of a pew bouncing her whining baby gently on her knee. He saw the flicker of panic in her eyes as she feared the soft whimper turning into a full-blown scream. The baby was clutching a colourful rattle and waving it around.

It happened so fast.

Too fast for anyone to act.

All he could do was stare on in horror, watching as the rattle soared through the air right in front of his bride, then clattered to the flagstones.

His body tensed.

A second later, he let out a sigh.

She wasn't fazed, her smile unwavering, determined not to lose her balance, not to trip.

She was okay, he could breathe again. She was nearly by his side, had survived the ordeal, hadn't toppled in the prosthetics Roehampton Hospital had made especially for her big day. Once it was all over, she could collapse in her wheelchair and lob those pesky prosthetics into the nearest dust cart.

But the ordeal wasn't over yet.

In an instant everything shifted.

The rattle had bounced into the pathway of Jeremy, his soon-to-be father-in-law, whose face a moment ago was filled with pride, his feet on the flagstones, a purposeful stride. His bride-to-be let go of her father's arm as time seemed to slow. He teetered, arms flailing. Gasps filled the air, all eyes widened in horror as Jeremy stumbled forward, then a jarring thud as he crashed to the ground, the rattle spinning ominously beside him.

Sue stared down at him. 'Dad, are you okay?' Then her mum was beside him helping him up.

He got up and brushed himself off, like a knight rising from the battlefield. 'I'm fine. If my daughter can get to the altar without a hitch, so can an old geezer.' He laughed and everyone clapped.

As the last notes of the music faded, Toby's breath caught in his throat as he gazed at his bride standing beside him.

Sue.

He was so used to looking down at her sitting in a wheelchair. Now she had a pair of legs. His equal.

She's the same height as me.

Wheelchair or prosthetics, this was his Sue, the woman

he'd proposed to on Bognor Pier two years ago. The world around them seemed to fade into a blur, all the worries faded, leaving just the two of them locked in this sacred moment. He couldn't lift the gauzy veil covering her face, but Angela stepped forward to do it. He could see her eyes properly now and they sparkled with joy and tears and a hint of nervousness. The softness of her smile made his heart swell, and he felt an overwhelming gratitude for the journey that had brought them together.

This, they would remember forever, and this was witnessed by thousands at home on the TV.

The first televised thalidomide wedding.

There were so many people here to support them. He looked at Sue's side of the church. They were few in number. And only one aunt. That was because her parents kept Sue at arm's length as if they were ashamed of her. But a group of friends had come to support her from school and college. There were still a couple of families that hadn't arrived yet and he just hoped they didn't arrive in the middle of the ceremony.

He smiled warmly at his family—Jasper, Sandy, his parents, and Bill, his adoptive dad. Bill had spontaneously decided it was a bright idea to invite Patsy, one of their old neighbours from Blackpool. Toby couldn't remember the woman. To his knowledge they hadn't stayed in touch since the Great Fence Dispute of 1978 and yet here she was.

There were far too many people here, all thanks to Jasper inviting a small army of their work colleagues from the newspaper. Sam was lurking at the back, still hanging on to his editor title like a stubborn mule, refusing to step down and seeming to think that retirement was just a conspiracy to keep him from free coffee. He had no intention any time soon of being put out to pasture.

Having his work colleagues at his wedding felt like inviting the cast of a sitcom to witness the live taping of Toby's most embarrassing moments.

Then his gaze shifted to his other family, the thalidomide community, fifteen members were gathered, their presence a powerful testament of support and connection. Sharing their special day felt like the culmination of all the fun moments they'd spent together—holidays in Jersey, Tenerife, Switzerland, and countless other adventures. Dave had gathered stories from every escapade, all the essential pieces of their shared history and soon he'd be raising a glass in their honour.

The ceremony whizzed by. And then the vicar was inviting the congregation to voice any legal reasons against their union before proceeding with the vows. 'Does anyone know of any lawful impediment why these two persons should not be joined in holy matrimony?'

Sue's head twisted round, a smile playing on her lips. This was always an amusing part of the service, and nobody ever expected a hand to shoot up. That only happened in the films. In that fleeting moment as the vicar waited, Toby's eyes were drawn to Lucy, and he noticed Sandy gazing at them both. Lucy was sitting with her parents. She wasn't in a relationship. There had been a string of idiots come and go over the years. There was a certain type she was attracted to. The wrong type, the type that let her down, the ones you couldn't change, and were never likely to commit and give her the love she needed.

Something swooped inside him as their eyes met. He couldn't breathe, it was as if she'd stolen all the oxygen from the air.

Was she remembering that moment they'd shared? One

move could have changed everything that evening. He still had no idea, how or why it had happened.

He quickly regrouped and looked into Sue's eyes, but he couldn't shake what he'd started. The ache that lingered just beneath the surface, a longing as vast as the ocean, a feeling that nestled in the corners of his heart, never daring to break free.

The tinkle of the ring hitting stone snapped his thoughts back to the moment.

'Shit,' Dave whispered.

'Mate, what you doing?'

The ring rolled off under the pews and several people were kneeling on the dusty flagstones looking for it.

'I see it,' a child shrieked. 'It's down there.'

Sue's parents went over and crouched next to the child, peering into a vent in the floor. Her mum cried, 'I can see the glint of gold.'

'The caretaker will get it out later, but for now, can someone lend their ring?' the vicar said, addressing the congregation. He surreptitiously glanced at his watch and Toby could see his mind ticking over, observing this circus, thinking *just another day on the church conveyor belt—one wedding, another funeral, toss in a christening, and pray for a snack break.*

Clambering to her feet, Sue's mum went over to Dave and fumbled in her pocket. 'I've been putting up new curtains in the lounge,' she said with a laugh, handing a curtain ring to the best man. Then she turned to the congregation. 'Ladies, always bring one as a back-up.'

So many tasks, simple for most people, weren't easy for Toby because of his birth defect. He had shortened arms. His hands came out of his shoulders. This was caused by the drug thalidomide which his mother had taken in pregnancy for morning sickness.

He'd practised for ages putting the ring onto Sue's finger, but never tried slipping on a curtain ring. Why would he? Finally, after some comical manoeuvring and an unintentional game of "ring toss", he flicked the ring onto her finger, a move that would have made a magician proud.

He leaned forward and kissed his bride, and the vicar declared them man and wife. Or was it husband and wife? He remembered Sue insisting on modern phrases.

Sue had walked up the aisle on her artificial legs—but now this was his moment. Everybody smiled and laughed as he lifted his leg, took the pen between his toes and signed the register.

The deed was done. No going back now. Joined together for eternity—at least for now.

5

NINE MONTHS EARLIER

Bill stood quietly at Rona's gravestone, the familiar chill of the coastal breeze wrapping around him. The sun was low in the sky, casting a golden glow over the headstone. He traced the engraved letters of her name with a trembling finger. It was that time of year again––his annual pilgrimage to Blackpool. He'd returned every year since her passing twelve years ago.

He closed his eyes for a moment, took a deep breath then turned to where his heart lay under six feet of soil. 'I promised you I'd be back, love,' he whispered. His voice was thick with emotion, and he reached into his pocket for a hanky to blow his nose. He remembered how she'd always made sure he had a freshly laundered hanky. She'd looked after him, the perfect wife, but these days his pockets were full of scrunched-up supermarket receipts and crumpled loo roll.

He knelt beside the grave, gently placing a small bouquet of wildflowers––her favourite––at the headstone.

She was down there.

Forever.

Right now, it felt as if he was in a deep hole like the one they'd dug for his wife, and he had no idea how he was going to climb his way out.

Will grief ever end? He felt so lost and alone. The unfairness of it all gripped him like a vice.

'I miss you every day. Even more today. I've some news, love.' His voice wobbled and his eyes filled with tears. 'It's our boy, he's getting wed.' Choked up, his voice wobbled. 'I just wish you were here to share his special day. He's grown into such a lovely lad. All that hard work from the early years, it's paid off, you'd be proud. I'm so glad you brought him home, but I wish I could have been more positive back then. I wouldn't swap him for the world.'

His chest heaved as the emotion spread across him. He thought about her every day. It was harder as time went on, now that Toby had left home, the coming back to an empty house, the silence, time on his hands to dwell. That old saying was so true. You never realised what you'd lost till it was gone.

His cheeks were wet, and he could barely see through the tears of grief. They came on suddenly with no time to prepare.

The waves of sorrow subsided. How he wished he could be stronger, braver. Stumbling, he put one hand on the cold grey stone. And in that moment, the unfairness of it all slammed into him.

What am I supposed to do now?
How the hell do I go on?

Turning and walking slowly back to the car, he saw a figure in the distance. He squinted against the sun, recognising the person. He stood for a moment observing her, not wanting to intrude. She was talking to her loved one and kneeling to place flowers into a vase beside the headstone. When she'd finished, she rose and turned towards him.

'I thought that was you, Patsy.' She looked up at him, tears flowing down her cheeks.

'Hello, Bill, didn't expect to see you here today. Oh goodness, of course it must be the anniversary. How are you?'

'Well, I'm surviving, I'm still here, but I miss her. And what about you?' He looked towards the grave she'd been attending to. It was too far away for him to see the inscription on the headstone. 'Why are you here?'

'My Arty, he passed away two years ago. I come up here every week to have a chat and freshen his flowers. Still can't believe he's gone.'

Bill felt sad. 'Oh my God, Patsy, I'm so sorry, I had no idea. As you know, I'm terrible about keeping in touch. What happened, had he been ill?'

'No, he was healthy up to six months before he passed, then he was diagnosed with stage four aggressive cancer. There was no warning, no symptoms until he had severe pain. But then again you men always bury your heads in the sand when it comes to aches and pains. We tried to make the most of those last six months, but he lost a lot of his strength and then he was gone. It's funny, Bill, we had such big plans for when we retired, but life can be very cruel, those plans were snatched away.'

They stood silently for a few moments.

'Still, I have my family, and they're all fairly local. Gemma's in Cumbria, Michael's in Manchester. They visit when they can, but they're very busy. I've got three grandkiddies now.' She perked up at the mention of her grandchildren.

Bill remembered Michael being a handful at around ten years old, and he wondered what he was like now. Gemma was the quiet one and always seemed to have her nose in a book.

'How lovely.'

'I'm just grateful for the Women's Institute, that's what keeps me going. If you don't have to rush off, we could go for a coffee and have a catch-up. I'd love to hear how Toby's getting on. Bet he's all grown up now.'

'He's getting married soon. I was just telling our Rona. She'd be proud of him.'

He remembered when Toby and Sue had popped over to tell him they were getting married. Sue was such an easy-going lass, and he'd warmed to her instantly. "Make sure you keep him under control," Bill had quipped. "Cos I can't." "Well, Dad," Toby had replied, "she's my arms and I'm her legs. We make a great combination. At least we've got one good set of limbs between us".

'Oh, that's lovely, I'm so pleased,' Patsy said. 'I bet you never expected that. Are you still in Surrey?'

'Yes.'

'You staying over?'

'Yes, I always stay over the night I come up.'

'Well, if you're not doing anything this evening and don't fancy eating alone, you're more than welcome to come round for dinner, it's nothing special, just meat pie and a few veggies. Be nice to have a bit of company.'

He turned and smiled at her. 'I'd love to. Much more fun than grabbing fish and chips and eating it in the hotel room. Are you still living in the same house?'

'Yes, I can't bear to move, it's been our marital home for years, it feels as if his spirit is still there with me.'

'I know exactly how you feel. It was hard when we moved south, I felt as if I was leaving part of myself behind.'

'You like it down there though?'

He was caught off guard by the unexpected question. He'd been so busy juggling work and raising Toby, he hadn't stopped to think about whether he liked it or whether he was happy. The past few years had left little room for self-reflection. It had proved the right move for Toby, though, after the bullying he'd endured. He wondered if he'd ever move back to Blackpool, if he'd be happier up north. It felt strangely comforting to be near to Rona's resting place, to be able to visit often like Patsy visited Arty, but being back here was always overshadowed by the memories that lingered, and those memories always turned to sadness.

Maybe he needed to explore his feelings and work out what he wanted from the future. Now that Toby didn't need him, he realised he could go anywhere, do anything. The thought should have been uplifting, freeing, but he found it wasn't. It just left him numb, confused, and lost.

'It's a job, Patsy, but they're a funny lot down south, folk are friendlier up here. All that popping in and out of each other's houses, doesn't happen in Surrey. I miss all that.'

She laughed. 'I'm not sure it's like that anymore, you'd be lucky to find a street like that these days. The old crowd have moved away. The Pickhursts, Williams and Meads, they've all gone.'

He shook his head. 'I've not stayed in touch with any of that lot.' Rona did the Christmas cards. He hadn't kept up the Christmas card tradition and regretted it now, but that had been Rona's domain.

'Can I give you a lift?'

'No thanks, I enjoy the walk after I visit my Arty, but come round when you're ready, I'm not going anywhere, wish I'd known you were coming, you could have stayed in the spare bedroom.'

After saying goodbye and before checking into his hotel,

Bill slipped into Marks & Spencer to buy himself a new pair of trousers and shirt as he only had old clothes with him and hadn't planned on going anywhere special.

He showered and spruced himself up. He couldn't remember the last time he'd bothered to make an effort for anyone, but it felt good to have a reason and he owed her that at least. But it also made him feel a little self-conscious. He remembered how he used to dress nicely for Rona in those early days of courting and he missed those times when he actually cared about how he looked. He couldn't remember when things had changed. Perhaps he'd fallen into a routine where comfort trumped style or maybe he'd just become resigned, lazy even, believing that his appearance didn't matter much anymore. But now, as he looked in the mirror and adjusted his new tie, he realised this visit was a chance to step it up a bit. It made him wonder if putting in a little effort could help him feel better too.

Bill made his way over to Patsy's house. As he stepped out of the car, he looked around at the red-brick terraces. This road was like so many across the country, he could be anywhere. But this was where he and Rona had spent their married life and raised Toby during those formative years. Memories stirred. Children used to play ball games in the road and run round chasing each other. Women scrubbed their doorsteps, sat outside in the street smoking and chatting. All that had long gone. The sound of kids playing had been replaced by the hum of passing cars. A few more vehicles lined the street than he remembered.

He could picture Rona strolling along the pavement, pushing the pram, while neighbours leaned in to peek at the baby. They were all surprised, of course they were. "How on earth didn't I notice your pregnancy? You must have had a tiny bump," they said.

He remembered how some had hurried away when they saw Toby's hands. The expressions of shock on their faces, or, the opposite reaction, a pity-filled gaze.

The thought of what Rona had done all those years ago still sparked a flame of guilt, but the guilt had softened over the years. It was such a long time ago.

About to knock on her door, he was suddenly overcome with nerves, which was silly, this wasn't a date, it was just a catch-up with an old neighbour. It was completely daft at his age, but he realised how out of step he was around women. Maybe it was the socialising in general that he found difficult. What would they have to talk about after all this time? Would the conversation be awkward and stilted? After all, it wasn't as if they'd bothered to stay in touch.

He looked down at the flowers he'd bought, maybe they were a bit over-the-top, but it was too late to ditch them. He'd hesitated about whether to buy her flowers in case she misconstrued it as a romantic gesture, but at the last minute he'd thought, damn it, women liked flowers and after all, she was going to the effort of cooking for him.

He needn't have worried though, because from the moment she flung the door open and welcomed him in, he felt completely at ease. She was very appreciative of the flowers and told him off for wasting his money on her. He followed as she bustled through to the little kitchen at the back of the house where she'd laid the Formica table. Pots of veg were bubbling on the stove. She reached over the sink to open the window, apologising for the steam before opening every cupboard in a fluster to find a vase. He noticed a couple of cupboards had missing doors and another was wonky.

He glanced through to the lounge while she was busy dishing up. 'Didn't the walls used to be green?'

Her comforting presence reminded him of Rona, standing there in her pinny and slippers. Rona had always said, "people can take me as they find me," she was true to herself, just as Patsy was now. Neither woman stood on ceremony. He liked that.

'Blimey, you've got a good memory. Yes, but that was years ago. Shows how long it's been since you were last here.' She laughed and put the plates on the table. 'It could do with a freshen-up. The wallpaper is scuffed and peeling in places and it's a bit dated. These decorators though, they charge a small fortune.'

Wallpapering was one of Bill's favourite jobs and Rona had always said it was his forte: measuring and cutting sheets precisely, applying the paste with care and smoothing out every crease achieving the perfect flawless finish. He even took care around radiators.

'What a shame I'm not local, Patsy, I'd gladly help you.'

She blushed and passed him the condiments. 'That's sweet of you. Rona was a lucky woman, my Arty wasn't so good with his hands.'

He spotted a lamp on the worktop and remembered the broken fluorescent strip lighting. He was surprised Arty had never got round to fixing it. How she coped, cooking in such dim lighting, he didn't know. The more he glanced round, the more jobs he saw needed doing. The lino had worn in several places, the tap had a persistent drip, and his chair was slightly wobbly. He found himself making a mental list.

'I wonder if I know of a handyman. I'll have a think and if anyone springs to mind, I'll give you a buzz. Remind me to grab your number before I go.'

He tucked into his dinner.

'That would be good but there's no rush, I've come to

accept the way things are because I can't really afford a handyman, not on my wages.'

His heart went out to her, there was so much he could help her with. Her comment made him feel even more frustrated about living so far away.

'Sometimes I think about moving to a brand-new house. That way I don't have to worry about things going wrong, at least not for a while. They're going up all over the town, it's very tempting.' She paused, her fork mid-air. 'But I don't know, Bill, this has been my home for so long.'

'Don't move to a new build. They're awful, the walls are paper thin, and the gardens are tiny. These big building firms, they put them up in a hurry and cut corners.'

'I suppose.'

'This is delicious, best pie in ages.'

'Glad you like it. It's just so nice to have someone to cook for. I hope you like apple crumble, there's some in the oven.'

'You know how to spoil me, that's my favourite. Rona used to make it a lot.'

'If I remember correctly, she added raisins and cloves to the apple, and porridge oats to the crumble. I prefer a plainer recipe.'

He started laughing and soon she was laughing too. The type of laughter that was infectious and prolonged. 'I never liked to tell her I preferred it plain, she could be a bit sensitive to criticism,' he confessed.

'It's funny isn't it, the things we do to keep the peace? Arty used to fill the hot water bottle, then wrap my nightie around it. He was very kind and thoughtful like that, but the bottle was never warm enough, so I'd nip down to refill it while he was in the bathroom. He never found out. This must have gone on for years.'

'You want to be careful, Patsy, you could burn yourself if it was to split.'

'That's exactly what Arty used to say. And probably why he always made it lukewarm.'

'But that's nothing compared to some of the things that go on. What about people who take up hobbies just to keep the other happy. I heard of one poor fella taking up golf. It was only after he died, everyone found out he hated the sport and had only played it because his wife was an avid golfer.'

She took the crumble out of the oven, the apple and buttery aroma filling the air. He'd forgotten the delights of homemade cooking. Ever since he'd bought a microwave, he'd got lazy. Most evenings he had a meal for one from Tesco. Cottage pie one evening, fish pie the next.

'Do you remember our Wednesday evenings at the Empire? You enjoyed a game of bingo, didn't you?' she asked out of the blue as she dished up the crumble. 'I don't think Arty was too fussed about going, I'm sure he only really went for the cheap beer.'

'I miss all that, they were fun times.' He dug into his crumble and custard, and before eating his first mouthful, he let his mind drift, lost in thoughts about the past.

'I always thought bingo was more of a woman thing,' she mused.

'Not at all. But I don't think Rona was too fussed when we stopped going.'

'I wish it was still going.'

'Do you ever go up to Morecambe? That's somewhere I've not been in years. Has it changed much?' he asked.

'Not much, it's full of students, it's quieter than Blackpool, but not the same without Arty, nothing's the same when you have to go to places alone.'

'Tell me about it.'

'Listen to us, two old miseries.' She laughed. 'Tell me about your Toby. You said he's getting wed.' She sounded chirpier.

They talked for some time like two excited sparrows, often chatting over each other in the way that people do when they're catching up after a long period of time. When he took out a recent picture of Toby and Sue from his pocket, her eyebrows arched as if in surprise and she stared at it thoughtfully.

'It was taken at Butlin's last year. A group of us went for the weekend.'

There was a beat of hesitation before she spoke. Her face furrowed with concern. 'Her mother took the drug too?'

It was an innocent question but felt loaded, like an accusation, and he was surprised how he felt in that moment—fiercely protective of all those mothers who'd suffered but also proud of how they'd coped. He also felt proud of his soon-to-be daughter-in-law. He'd grown very fond of the girl. She was upbeat, fun to be around and didn't let her disability faze her. She was good for Toby, they were a great team.

A dull sensation moved across his chest as he braced himself for the negative comments he feared would follow.

'Yes.'

'They'll struggle, won't they?'

'Struggle? They aren't training for the Olympics.' He laughed, trying to lighten the mood. 'They're just getting on with life, like every couple starting out.'

'They won't be able to have children though, will they?' She looked sad.

This was something he'd thought about but hadn't broached with Toby. It wasn't his place, it was too private a subject. And besides, they were still young. But it didn't stop him worrying about their future. He wondered if they'd discussed having children.

She frowned. 'She's very pretty, I can see why he likes her. And he's a good-looking lad, tall.' She hesitated, a dark look came over her face. 'But they'll always need help.'

'We all need help, Patsy.' In a bright tone he added, 'Tell you what, if you can put me up for a couple of nights, I'll sort your jobs. I'm a dab hand at wallpapering. Write me a list, I'd love to help.' He slipped the photo back into his pocket and with it the worries she'd stirred in him.

'Oh, Bill, do you mean that? I don't want to put you to any trouble, it's such a long way for you.'

'Nonsense. I'd drive a thousand miles to eat your crumble.' He scraped his bowl before wiping the crumbs from his lips. 'We could even go to bingo, if you're up for it. The Empire might have closed, but there'll be other places.'

'And a stroll along the pier, if the weather's good.'

'Okay, you're on.'

They smiled at each other.

It had been years since he'd lost Rona, and the idea of female company felt like a breath of fresh air. Already he was looking forward to the laughter they'd share while tackling her DIY projects and the simple comfort of conversation. He realised the trip wasn't just about helping her with home repairs, it was a chance to reconnect with life and embrace the companionship that had been absent for far too long.

With a hopeful heart, he thanked her for a lovely evening and returned to his hotel, excited about rediscovering the little joys that came from friendship.

6

From her pew, Lucy watched as Toby and Sue exchanged vows. She wiped away a tear, both pleased for them and heartbroken for herself. Seeing how happy they were made her reflect on her own life and her failed relationships. A wave of sadness washed over her, and her heart ached. Despite her best efforts, she hadn't met anyone who made her feel the way she imagined love would feel. Time was slipping away, and her body clock was ticking. She couldn't shake the feeling that she was missing out and wondered if she'd ever find happiness. All her friends were marrying and having families, but here she was, still on the shelf.

Why do I always end up with losers? Toby is so nice. She remembered all the fun times with him. Toby looking after her rather than the other way round.

I wonder if we could have had a relationship, would it have worked?

She recalled a conversation with her mum a few years back. "You're getting too close to Toby," she'd warned. "You shouldn't play with his feelings."

"I'm very fond of Toby," she'd replied. "He's like a brother, but more than a brother."

"You stop that, there's no possibility of a relationship, so don't you string him along. Meet someone your own age that's got all their faculties. I know he's a nice boy, but he's hardly marriage material. Why on earth would you want to saddle yourself with someone like that?"

Lucy had felt so hurt and so ashamed that her own family harboured such awful thoughts.

As she looked over at him, seeing the love and admiration in his eyes for his bride, a fierce pang of emotion hit. She'd seen that same look in his eyes––for her––and she'd ignored it, swept it away, flattered by his obvious schoolboy crush. It had been amusing and maybe she'd toyed with his feelings, teased him, knowing how smitten he was, and she had enjoyed the attention. For a long time, he was just that, a schoolboy she could wrap around her fingers. He was thin, lanky, spotty and had a lot to still learn about life. A lovesick puppy, eager to please, always looking to impress her, and for years she'd found this entertaining. But things were different now. The Toby standing at the altar was all grown up.

He's a man.

Her heart ached and she realised then, she did love him.

There had been opportunities in recent years before Sue when things could have got intimate. She'd always pushed him away and now he was marrying someone else. She didn't know how she felt: both hollow and happy. The ten years since they'd first met had flashed by.

He's always been there for me, but today, that changes.
I'm alone, all alone, they have each other. They're so lucky.

She thought about all those times when he'd been there for her. Helping out when that prick had broken her arm, there when she was at a loose end, bolstering her when no one else had. And all those times when she'd got drunk, that concert in Hyde Park and many other occasions. What a fool she'd been to take him for granted, not to appreciate his friendship, automatically reaching for that next glass of wine, the alcohol clouding her ability to talk normally, to be normal, and those hangovers from hell. It had taken years to work out that alcohol was not her friend.

Bang, she was starting to realise the feelings she had. She wanted to shout, "Toby, I love you". All those idiots she'd dated couldn't hold a candle to him. Why had it taken this long to realise how she felt? Her chest heaved and her heart felt heavy, and the intensity of those feelings made her want to get up and leave.

She stared at the stone floor unable to look at their happy faces any longer, it only highlighted the emptiness of her own life. An ache settled in her heart. Was this what it felt like to witness someone you cared for find true happiness, knowing it wasn't you? Was it really love that she felt, or was it just jealousy creeping in? It was confusing, she hadn't wanted him before, but now that he was about to marry someone else, she found herself wishing they weren't so damn happy. A tear trickled down her face, her heart was screaming. She remembered all the rebuffs, her words to him not so long ago. "Toby, I'm flattered you're always there for me, I hope you realise how much I appreciate you, you'll always be my special friend". She'd seen the sadness in his eyes, knowing that was all they were going to be, but the fact was, she couldn't cope with everything he came with and especially the thought of all that family criticism.

Now, all she felt was shame. She recognised the ugly side to herself, one she'd seen in some of her friends. They'd end relationships but weren't happy for their exes to move on to someone new, especially if they looked happier than ever. It made Lucy wonder if she was falling into the same trap. Here she was, grappling with feelings she hadn't truly acknowledged, feeling a twinge of possessiveness over a guy who, just a while ago, was just a friend. She didn't understand what the feelings really meant, but it was powerful.

She looked up to see camera flashes and the congregation rising to follow the bride and groom out of the church. The atmosphere buzzed with excitement as guests mingled, exchanging hugs and handshakes, reconnecting as friends and families came together to celebrate. Among the chatter, she could hear the usual sort of comments. "Wow, hasn't he grown? He was just a baby the last time I saw him," one guest exclaimed, gesturing towards a young lad who was now nearly towering over her. "It's great to see you, how have you been?" another voice chimed, followed by a chorus of friendly updates and laughter. "You keeping busy these days?"

Toby and Sue's love story was the talk of the day and compliments filled the air. "Didn't Sue do well?" "Doesn't she look beautiful?" "What lovely flowers".

The buzz of happiness was suddenly hard to cope with. It felt like a distant melody, a reminder of what she yearned for, and it cast a long shadow over her loneliness. She was still waiting for her own love story to begin.

Her mum must have noticed her glum face as they rose and inched their way towards the aisle. Before turning to Lucy with a concerned glance, she asked her husband to go on ahead and then whispered, 'Come on, cheer up, love, you should be happy for them.'

'I am,' she said stroppily. The comment made her bristle, and she quickly adjusted her face, not wanting others to notice how glum she was.

'Toby's a friend, remember that. It's a bit late for regrets.'

'I don't know what you're on about,' she snapped. It was typical of her mum, always interfering, she could never keep her thoughts to herself.

Her mum glanced round and leaned in. 'There are a few nice young fellas here, I see.' She winked at her. 'It's about time you found yourself someone decent for a change. I don't know what it is with you, Lucy, you're a pretty girl, you could have anyone you want, but you will keep going for all the yobs.'

She followed her mother's gaze. There were so many yuppie types here, as well as geeks. It was safe to say she wouldn't be making a move on anyone, but why would she? This was Toby's wedding. She didn't want to make a fool of herself and ruin their big day. She'd decided to be on her best behaviour and that meant not touching a drop of alcohol either. It always loosened her tongue and led to sticky situations. God knows, Toby had been witness on more than a few occasions.

As they reached the end of the pews, she glanced up to see Toby's best man Dave beaming at her as he made his way to the exit. 'I'll expect the first dance with you, Luce,' he said with a wink.

'But it's traditional for the best man to dance with the chief bridesmaid,' she replied.

'Angela's only ten.' He gave her a playful smirk, and, in that moment, she forgot about her feelings for Toby as she enjoyed the thrill of this man's attention. She'd only met him twice, so she didn't really know him at all. One of those times was when she'd broken her wrist and was in agony. Toby often talked about him, sharing stories of the fun times they had at the Young Conservatives. She'd heard all about their mischievous role in the 'Piddle on Pedley' campaign, the canapé parties at conferences, and the time Dave, his mouth stuffed with caviar and crackers, was introduced to 'Onyerbike' Tebbit, spluttering crumbs all over his shirt.

'Erm, point taken.'

As he strolled towards the exit to join the throng of well-wishers, her eyes traced his confident stride. He had a swagger about him that made him look confident and appealing. The way his slicked-back hair caught the light added to his allure. Why didn't he have a girlfriend? she mused. Maybe they were like-minded souls, seeking fun and adventure, not taking life too seriously, and always avoiding the types that might tie them down.

She followed her parents out of the church and into the bright sunshine for photographs, and already she was feeling more positive, excited about the upcoming dance with Dave and the attention he'd show her. His charm would cheer her up and take her mind off Toby.

As long as she stayed off the booze, she wouldn't be in any danger of making a scene. But she had a feeling Dave might entice her to have a drink.

7

At last, Norman settled into his seat just moments before the bride made her grand entrance. He'd squeezed in along the front row next to the bride's family.

Well, as far as I'm concerned, I am practically family.

He'd known Sue for over five years—people served shorter terms for burglary. Their friendship had grown so strong. God knows, he spent far more time with Sue than her own parents did. While her parents rarely made the effort to visit, Sue and he were frequently in and out of each other's flats. From what he could gather, her parents had always been distant figures in her life. It was a strange and strained relationship. He couldn't understand their lack of support. A lot had happened in the lead-up to the wedding—he was honestly surprised her parents were even here at all—but it now seemed to be water under the bridge.

Sue's mother looked a bit disgruntled when he sat down but shuffled along the pew, and her twin brother looked over and glared. Surely, they must have realised he would be sitting here as he'd unceremoniously dropped his Sainsbury's carrier bag and satchel on the pew to save a space for himself. It was clear to everyone whose they were. Norman took these bags everywhere, as if they were his loyal companions. Inside, were a jumble of books, providing him with a makeshift support system, helping to keep his balance. People said he reminded them of a tramp.

Feeling hot and sticky, he wiped his glistening brow. He had been so swamped with organising everyone, including the TV crew, and, as for the wheelchairs, he'd made sure there was ample space and easy access for them. He was now sweating profusely. *Good grief, this bunch couldn't organise a piss-up in a brewery.* If he hadn't been here to take charge, he shuddered to think. They were very lucky he was here to save the day.

As the congregation rose to their feet, the music swelled around them, and a deep sense of despair washed over him. He turned to watch Sue heading up the aisle and, in that moment, it hit him hard––from today he was redundant. She no longer needed him, and the weight of that heart-breaking realisation settled heavily on his chest, leaving him feeling utterly lost.

He glanced over at Toby standing at the altar in his bespoke suit from Simmonds in Tunbridge Wells. They'd altered the sleeves and done a fantastic job. He could see why Sue had fallen for him. He was quite a hottie and looked immaculate today in his dark suit, peach bow tie and a matching hanky poking out of his breast pocket. His shoes were shiny patent. He couldn't shake the jealousy and resentment that gnawed at him. Toby was exactly the type of guy that women gravitated towards. He wished he could be like him: charismatic, charming and that magnetic smile that drew people in. He oozed confidence. Norman was tired of stumbling awkwardly through every social situation, and no matter how hard he tried he could never compete with the effortless allure that Toby possessed.

And then she was there, at the altar, standing beside her soon-to-be husband, both looking so happy.

His breath caught in his throat, and he nearly lost his balance at the sight of her. She looked absolutely stunning, he'd never seen her so radiant. Her hair gleamed, and he thought back to the previous day when she'd asked him to nip into Boots for strawberry shampoo, telling him a magazine claimed it made the hair shine. He gazed lovingly, wistfully wishing it was him.

He remembered her moving into the ground-floor flat and being instantly struck by how positive and capable she was. They'd met during her first week there when he'd opened the front door for her. Her huge grin and sparkly eyes drew him in. She radiated happiness and was always so jolly. She never looked miserable. He'd seen the person not the disability and wanted to make a difference to her life. Over the years, he'd grown fond of her. She was the most perfect woman he'd ever met and even though Toby was now in her life, she was still his Sue and always would be.

The fear of losing her was beginning to overwhelm him, as it dawned on him just how much he loved her. She had become such an integral part of his life, and she was running off with another man. Tears welled in his eyes as he listened to them exchanging vows, thinking it should have been him. When it reached the part where they say *I do*, he had to look away. As he regained his focus, he saw Sue's mother staring at him with daggered eyes. If looks could kill he'd be dropping into his coffin right now. The hardest part for him would be dancing with Sue later on at the evening reception, something he had to do but it was effectively the last dance for him.

After the ceremony, he was the first to arrive at the reception. Then Sue's parents arrived and took up position waiting to receive the guests. He gingerly approached them as they stood in the foyer.

'Where are the ramps? They're supposed to be out.'

Sue's mother spun round, startled frantically looking around.

'How do you think these people in wheelchairs are going to get up the steps? I'll have to sort it. I need to speak with reception immediately. They'll be arriving shortly. I knew I couldn't leave it to you. My girl needs a perfect day and I'm going to make sure she gets it because no one else seems capable.'

He marched over to reception and banged the bell even though there were two staff standing there and it gave them a blast. 'Where are the ramps? They're supposed to be out.'

The receptionists looked at each other. 'Oh my God, I'm sorry,' one of them said. 'We forgot to put them out.' She looked all flustered. 'I'll sort it immediately.'

He strutted back to Sue's parents like a peacock and took great delight in saying, 'I've sorted it, I've saved the day, yet again. I wonder what else I'll need to sort before the day is out.' He shuffled round and muttered, 'what an incompetent family.'

'Thank God she's married Toby, that will get you out of our lives once and for all, I don't know what she sees in you,' Pearl said indignantly.

'I'm a damn sight closer to her than you are, I'm more like family. You're supposed to be her parents, when did you last come to visit? When have you ever cared about her? To you she's just an inconvenience.'

'Go away, you stupid little man,' her father said with a

sweep of his hand as if swatting a fly. 'I will not be insulted and let you ruin my day.'

'It's not your day, it's Sue's day. That's the trouble with you two, you only ever think about yourselves.'

The other guests were starting to arrive, so he sped round to ensure the ramps were where they should be. Finding this sorted, he prowled round checking everything in sight, trying to find something out of place. Once he was satisfied everything was in order, and feeling smug with himself, he headed into the lounge area where he was served a glass of sherry.

8

As soon as Norman was out of earshot, Sue's mother turned to her husband. 'Why did that idiot have to be the one to identify that error? I can't trust you to do anything, all you're interested in is getting a scotch down your throat and getting back to the wrestling.'

'Stop your complaining, woman, why's everything down to me? All you do is carp on, this wedding's cost a bloody fortune. It's money we saved up to spend on ourselves. We never expected to fork out for *her*. She wasn't supposed to get wed, it's just ridiculous,' he spat. 'I don't know what they're playing at, and I still think it's doomed to failure, then we'll have missed out on our world cruise for nothing, you mark my words, but what do I know? I'm just the general dogsbody round here.'

'Well, you couldn't even walk down the aisle without falling flat on your face, could you?'

'Yes, and my knee's still sore, those church slabs are very hard.'

'Why is it when something goes wrong, it's always that

idiot that steps in? There's something about that obnoxious weasel that gives me the creeps. He's been muscling in and pandering to Sue ever since she moved to those flats. I'm surprised Toby puts up with it, but he's hardly going to punch him on the nose, is he? I think there's going to be three in this marriage. Thank God Norman's not becoming our son-in-law. I'll be glad when today is over, then Sue won't be our responsibility. I must say, it is a bit of a relief we don't have to worry about her anymore.'

'Well to be honest we've never had to worry about her, have we? We've done our best to palm her off.'

'Hello, dears, poor Sue won't notice any difference then, will she? You've never taken an active interest in your daughter right from the moment she was born.'

'Marge, where did you appear from?' Marge was Pearl's sister.

'I was the first to arrive. I've just been to the ladies to put a bit of lippy on.' She was a glamorous woman, but she'd never been married and as she didn't have children, what did she know about raising them?

'I see your tongue's still as sharp as ever, Marge,' Jeremy said.

'Try making today special,' Marge said, leaning towards Pearl. 'Poor girl deserves that much,' she said as she whipped round and marched off towards the bar.

When she was out of earshot, Pearl whispered, 'At least we won't have to worry about grandchildren, that will be a blessing in disguise.' Then she smiled and smoothed her hair as the first guest headed towards them.

'God forbid, grandchildren,' Jeremy muttered while extending his hand for the guests approaching.

He hadn't thought about Toby and Sue having children until now, and the idea terrified him.

9

A wedding was hardly the right occasion for business talk, but that didn't stop Sam from pulling Jasper aside as soon as the wedding breakfast and speeches were over. He'd wandered over to the top table, congratulating the bride and groom before offering his congratulations to Bill who was chatting to Jasper and Sandy. He heaped praise on how beautiful the occasion was, before turning to Sandy with his apology. 'Forgive me, I need to borrow your husband a moment, there are a few matters I'd like to discuss.'

Sandy shook her head in disbelief. As Jasper started to rise to his feet like a proper lackey, Sandy pulled him back. 'Hold on a sec. This is a wedding, not a corporate event. Save your boardroom meeting for the office unless you want me to throw a bouquet at you both.' She laughed, but her hand was planted firmly on his knee to stop him from getting up.

Jasper looked up at Sam. 'Sorry, mate, looks like I'm on a short leash today. Business is off the agenda, wife's orders.'

Waiters and waitresses were busy clearing the tables and offering more coffee. There was now a two-hour interval between the wedding reception and the start of the evening's entertainment, providing the guests with the opportunity to explore the hotel's gardens, mingle on the lawn and reconnect with friends and family. With so many people from work here, Jasper had expected a bit of shop talk at some point during the day.

Sandy pushed her chair back. 'You boys have five minutes.' She raised five fingers. 'I'm off to powder my nose.' She skittered off, pausing to chat to guests en route.

'What is it, mate?'

'Let's go outside to chat, shall we?' Sam raised an eyebrow.

'Sounds ominous, I'm not in any trouble, am I, boss?' He laughed, feigning a nervous glance around.

'Not yet,' Sam replied, chuckling as he led the way out of the room and along the corridors to the garden. 'But if you keep reporting on my terrible taste in music, you might be.'

Some of the guests were mingling in the garden in the shade, and some had decided to go out the front of the hotel and across the road to the beach. Bognor Regis had clearly become a top spot for Toby and Sue, as they frequently visited for day trips. Jasper couldn't help but smile at the idea of Toby choosing to propose on Bognor Pier. Anyone else would have chosen a quiet romantic moment, but it had been in the middle of the day and during the crazy Birdman of Bognor event when hundreds of day trippers flocked to the town to watch people dressed up in strange costumes queuing to jump off the pier. It made perfect sense why Toby had picked The Royal Norfolk Hotel for their reception. The hotel, perched at an angle and overlooking the sea, had a pleasant ambience with a large lawn at the front for the photographs and plenty of space for parking. The décor was tired though and needed an update, its faded elegance betraying its former glory.

'Who doesn't love a bit of Michael Jackson? You've not seen me on the dance floor yet.' Jasper did a little shimmy as they stepped outside.

'Oh, I have, at the last retirement do. You'll have to be careful, I can see tomorrow's headlines.'

'Very funny, but on a serious note, you're itching to share something with me.'

'Well,' Sam said leaning in, 'I was thinking we could write a piece on wedding disasters. You know, the things people would rather forget but end up being legendary stories.' Sam pulled out a hefty cigar and lit it, and Jasper watched the thin wisps of smoke as they curled into the air. The scent was comforting, a familiar one that Jasper had come to love, reminding him of the many lively discussions in Sam's smoke-filled office back in London over the years.

Sam was puffing away while gazing across the lawn at a cluster of Toby's friends who looked as if they were enjoying themselves. Some he'd met at school, others he'd connected with on Thalidomide Society holidays and events. There were a few in wheelchairs and they'd expertly manoeuvred through the short grass, while others leaned on crutches. They animatedly chatted and joked. It was a lovely setting. The sunlight filtered through the trees, casting dappled patterns on the grass, and there were pretty flowerbeds around the lawn.

'It's desperately sad, isn't it?' Sam said, his eyes lingering on the scene.

'Yes, but look at them, they're enjoying life. They weren't expected to live, yet here they are, proving everyone wrong and beating the odds. And they have such drive and ambition too. A few are married and starting families of their own.'

'We were wrong about lots of things,' Sam said in a sombre tone as he puffed on his cigar.

Confused, Jasper looked at Sam. 'How do you mean?'

'We thought it was just a dark chapter in history, a mere blip in humanity's timeline.'

Jasper wondered where the conversation was heading.

'When the drug was banned, we thought it would never see the light of day again.' He paused, took a deep breath. 'It hasn't stayed banned though. That's the worst part of the story. Ever since then, doctors and scientists have tried to find more uses for it. It seems almost unimaginable that a drug that caused so much human misery and suffering could be taken and used again, as if it's a necessary evil.'

'Is that what you wanted to talk to me about?'

'There's so much you and Toby can investigate. I'm looking at a double-page investigation piece, you can be the insight team. I want you to explore some of what's going on and with your usual human tragedy stories to tug at the readers' heartstrings.'

'Are you talking about leprosy?' He knew that thalidomide had been used widely in Brazil where leprosy was ravaging the population, and this was leading to a new generation of babies born with birth defects.

'That's just for starters. This drug isn't going away anytime soon.'

A wave of disgust washed over him, and he practically spat out his next words. 'Don't they ever learn?'

Sam rubbed his fingertips. 'Big bucks are involved. That was the case back then, still is today.'

Jasper felt pure revulsion. 'Profits before humanity, it stinks.'

'It's not all doom and gloom. Thalidomide is a potent weapon against some illnesses. Should it be banned because of a tragedy that happened thirty years ago? Science is more informed now and strict regulations and procedures are in place.'

'That's debatable,' Jasper scoffed. 'They did know better back then, but there was so much corruption and plenty of shady dealings. Remember, money talks.'

'You get my drift though. This story isn't dead yet, it's just waiting to be written.'

Just then, a sharp voice interrupted. They swung round to see Sue's mother standing there, her face a mixture of anger and disbelief. 'Excuse me, this is my daughter's wedding. How can you discuss such a painful topic here?'

Heads were starting to turn as people stopped their conversations and looked round. Sue's mother had a voice that carried, and she was making no attempt to keep it down.

Caught off guard, Sam and Jasper exchanged glances.

'We didn't mean to upset anyone,' Sam said, dropping his cigar butt and grinding it with his heel on the paving slab. 'Besides, you shouldn't be eavesdropping on private conversations.'

She crossed her arms. 'You might not think it affects you personally, you're just greedy journalists looking for the next story, but my daughter lives with the consequences every day. Can't you just give us this day, free from reminders of the past?'

'Where's all this concern suddenly come from? I've never seen you championing the cause like other parents,' Sam quipped.

Jasper snorted, then said, 'You're right, Pearl. We're sorry. We'll change the subject.'

As Pearl turned on her heel and sailed back into the hotel, Jasper whispered to Sam, 'We'll talk on Monday, she's right, now isn't the time or place.'

Jasper, priding himself on his sensitivity, knew he'd let himself down and he didn't want to make an enemy of Toby's in-laws. After all, they were now all related even though Pearl didn't know it.

10

TOBY

Toby sat at the head table surveying the room, about to give thanks to everyone for coming. A lump formed in his throat. This was the culmination of months of planning, and it had all come together nicely. The table decorations looked classy, and the chairs had gauzy peach bows tied around them. There were posies of peach-coloured roses, coral-toned carnations, white anemones and orange tulips adorning each table, their soft hues complementing the pristine white linen underneath. Gold bowls had been placed on the tables, glittering under the light of the chandeliers and piled with fresh peaches. It was a scene he'd dreamt of, but seeing all the special people in his life gathered here made every moment feel surreal. There were people from all walks of life and many with interesting stories.

How he wished his mum had been here.

He glanced over, and seeing Bill's demeanour wondered if he felt the same.

Toby polished off his coffee and rose to his feet. He hadn't eaten much because his nerves had taken away his appetite. He'd become quite an accomplished speaker, but this was different, it was more personal. He was standing before friends and family. His stomach was twisting in knots with worry leaving him more anxious than hungry. It seemed better to have the speeches before the food because everyone could enjoy it more. He hadn't planned a long speech, it was simply a few words giving thanks to all the key people, but he felt self-conscious and preferred the focus to be on his bride––this was her day.

He signalled to Dave to clink a glass for silence.

'Ladies and gentlemen,' Dave said, 'pray silence for the bridegroom.'

A big chuckle went out followed by cheers.

Once silence had fallen Toby started by expressing his gratitude to everyone for being there today––especially the beautiful bridesmaids in their peach gowns, his trusty best man, and his dad, looking suave and sophisticated in his suit, and his mother-in-law Pearl for miraculously producing the emergency wedding ring. He then turned to his beautiful bride.

'And of course the most important person here today, is my wife.'

Everyone whooped and Dave whistled.

'I'm a lucky man, Sue, you look so beautiful, you make me very proud, and I promise to make you the happiest woman alive.' With tears in his eyes and overcome with emotion he suddenly choked up. He quickly introduced his best man. 'I'm not normally lost for words but I'm going to hand you over to my best man, Dave.'

Dave stood up to a chorus of cheers as Toby sat down.

'Ladies and gentlemen, if I can grab your attention for a minute,' Dave began as he clinked a glass with a spoon.

Toby looked up at Dave, sniggered and wiped his brow. 'Over to you, mate.'

'Hey, Toby, I've never known you say so little, so I'm going to have to make up for it.'

Normally Toby could speak for England having spent years honing his public speaking skills and aspired to make a career in motivational public speaking. For now, he was working with Jasper covering news stories. He'd worked very hard since joining the team and had passed his journalist exams.

'Hello, everybody, I'm Dave, definitely the best man here, apart from Toby of course,' he said when everyone was quiet. 'Toby's best man and partner in crime. I still can't quite believe Toby actually convinced someone to marry him. It really is a pleasure to give Toby away so that someone else can look after him. I've done my bit over the years to keep him on the straight and narrow, so it's with great pleasure to hand him over to you, Sue. And my advice, for what it's worth, is to keep an eye on him as he can be quite a cheeky chappie when he wants to be.

'I could share loads of stories but have been told to keep it clean. And as for mother-in-law jokes, I've plenty. Sorry, Pearl, only kidding. I have to say, Sue, you look absolutely stunning today, and you, Toby, brush up well too. You're a very lucky man. It's not every day your woman puts on a pair of legs to come and meet you, definitely a case of putting your best foot forward and we can't accuse her of being legless at her own wedding! And I do know you, Toby, would love to give her a hug if you could.'

There was a cry of groans, aws and ahhs.

'But seriously, everybody, cheesiness aside, it's so wonderful to see this lovely couple tie the knot. They've had their struggles and it's great to see them achieve this. I'm really looking forward to bouncing kids on my knee in a few years.'

He noticed Pearl tut to Jeremy at this comment.

'As best man I'm duty bound to share with you a few things about Toby. Some things are too funny to keep to myself. As some of you know, I first met Toby at college when we were studying for our A levels. We were always playing pranks on each other. I fooled him into thinking we were off to a fancy dress party. So my old buddy, Tobe La Rone, dressed as a tart and I went as a vicar. But in fact we were going to listen to a talk by the MP Michael Heseltine. As we walked into the hall, you should have seen Toby's and Heseltine's faces. It was a classic. But fair dos, they both took it in good part.'

He glanced over at Pearl and Jeremy, as if taking inspiration from their embarrassed looks, then went on to say, 'Toby once threw up all over his mother-in-law's cream settee and carpet and if that wasn't bad enough, the family dog licked it all up.' Dave started laughing uncontrollably. 'It must have been something in her cooking.'

Why was he ad-libbing? The story wasn't even true. But he was on a roll, he loved seeing Sue's parents squirm.

Everyone gasped and turned to look at Pearl, who was shaking her head and cringing. She looked as if she wanted the floor to swallow her. 'Okay, Dave, that's quite enough, move on.'

Dave chuckled. 'I've got a few more stories about you two, but I won't.' He paused. 'As you know, it's traditional for the bride to wear something old, something new, something borrowed and something blue. Here's my version of those four. The something old is her parents.'

Toby shot him a look of embarrassment. He leaned down and gave him a nudge with his shoulder. Dave lost his balance, and his glass of red wine teetered dangerously before crashing over.

Time seemed to slow as he watched the wine arch through the air and splatter right onto Toby's mother-in-law's lap.

Her pale peach silk dress, ruined. Her face a picture of horror.

A gasp rippled through the guests and then silence fell, eyes wide as Pearl looked down at the dark stain spreading across her dress. All Dave could do was stammer his apology, his face as red as the wine.

'Pearl, I'm so sorry,' Dave apologised. 'I'll pay for the dry cleaning.'

'You won't have to,' she hissed under her breath. 'Because it's completely ruined.'

This couldn't get any worse, Toby thought. He saw tears welling in her eyes and in that moment, he just wanted the floor to swallow him whole. But Dave wasn't going to be fazed. He carried on with his speech.

'Talking of dresses, Sue's dress was the something new. The borrowed are her pair of legs or my wallet because Toby can never get his out of his pocket, and the something blue is from our favourite club, a blue rosette which says, "Maggie In". We wore them at the last election. I understand that Sue has this pinned to her undies.'

With this comment, Pearl shook her head and gave up mopping her dress. She slid out of the room looking angry and flustered while Dave carried on with the rest of his speech.

'Toby and I had some great times in the Young Conservatives, and we met many top politicians. Toby was elected chairman of Guildford Young Conservatives and did a brilliant job. When we had the honour of meeting Margaret Thatcher, she pointed out Toby's loose bow tie and playfully adjusted it for him, saying he needed a young lady to help dress him. On another occasion, we invited Tory grandee Michael Heseltine to a dinner, but he didn't like the wine and sent us off to pick a better one. After that, we affectionately nicknamed him, "Heselprat".

'Now it's often said that the best man has his eye on charming the chief bridesmaid, but she's already spoken for and the other bridesmaid, Angela, is too young for me. So I'm hoping my first dance of the evening will be with the lovely Lucy. For once she's free to enjoy herself and not on stage. So how about it, Lucy?'

Cringing, Toby looked over at Lucy and gave her a wry smile, but his heart was banging as his mind jumped to how he felt about her.

A sudden thought hit.

Oh my God, it could be Lucy sitting next to me.

He wasn't sure what his face had given away, if it was betraying him, but he was suddenly aware of Sandy studying him with a curious expression on her face. He quickly adjusted his own expression and smiled at her, but something had clicked between them.

It was hard watching Lucy with other men. And now it looked as though he was going to have to watch his best man and beloved friend get together, almost flaunting it in his face. But maybe Dave would be good for her. He'd never thought about them as a couple, not until now. Sue coughed in the background, and he wondered if she knew more about his feelings for Lucy than she'd let on. She'd always been jealous when Lucy was around. Lucy was his closest female friend, and he didn't want that to ever change. They went back years. He hoped Sue would always accept her as his friend and hoped Lucy wouldn't back off now that he was married. Since they'd told her they were getting married, she'd been quite happy to fuss around the both of them.

He looked around and saw Mandy, her red hair a beacon in the crowd. She was grinning from ear to ear. She'd also had the ability to make his heart race. She was a bundle of fun and had so much energy, she was positively effervescent and great to be around. How lucky he was to have so many great friends. Mandy had instilled an inner confidence, and he'd never forget that, how even in his darker moments she'd dragged him out and forced him to have fun. She was the only person to tell him off and he didn't mind because she always dished out positive criticism. He puckered his lips and blew her a kiss.

Dave was rattling on. 'Sue was sent to Coventry but now she's completed her penance and returned to come to be with her man in Surrey. I've met some amazing people through Sue and through Toby too. Watching her friend Veronica who has no arms trim a poodle with her feet was amazing and such an eye-opener, and just goes to show how resourceful Toby and Sue and all their other disabled friends are. And Sue's friend, Sally, she needs a mention too.' Everyone turned to Sally. 'Sally put Sue's make-up on and did her hair. How is that even possible using your feet, I'll never know. I'm in awe of some of the things you guys can do.'

He paused. 'Ladies and gentlemen, please could I ask you all to stand and raise your glasses to Toby and Sue and may they have many happy years together.'

Once the wedding breakfast was over, Toby spent the next couple of hours mingling with the guests. It was interesting to see how they'd all retired to their respective groups. He desperately wanted time with Sue alone but that would come later. He wondered why they hadn't got married later in the day, then there wouldn't be this time gap. The room was emptying, and he spotted people heading for the bar, the garden and over to the beach. There were kids playing ball on the lawn.

When it came to the evening, other friends arrived. There was a buzz of anticipation and excitement as the first dance started. Mandy kept pushing her to change into the dress she'd made for her, but Sue was adamant. 'I'm going to stay in my wedding dress as long as I can,' she told her firmly. 'I want to give the evening guests a chance to see it.' It seemed fair enough.

She didn't want to disappoint Mandy after all her efforts, so she agreed to change after the first few dances.

She went to her room before the first dance and put her prosthetics on again. Sally rearranged her hair and make-up. Sally was a trained beautician and being thalidomide-damaged, worked with her feet.

THE FIRST DANCE was a surreal experience, and Toby felt conspicuous with all eyes on them, but then they settled into a pattern. After he'd seen Sue safely back to her chair she said, 'I'm just going to take my legs off now and I'll be glad to get out of this wedding dress.'

'About time,' Mandy said, laughing. 'I can't wait to see you in the dress I made. Took me long enough to make.'

'It's so hot in here.'

Toby couldn't believe how stunning Sue looked in Mandy's dress. It was fabulous and really suited her. He'd always known that Mandy would come up trumps, she was very talented and would have stayed up late to get it finished on time.

'I wish I'd put it on earlier,' Sue conceded.

'What did I tell you?' Mandy smiled.

After half an hour, Toby gave the nod to the DJ to slow the music down.

He saw Dave heading over to Lucy for a dance so before he had the chance, Toby dived in.

'Take My Breath Away' by Berlin was playing and he knew it was one of Lucy's favourites.

As he turned to Lucy and asked her for a slow dance, he felt Sue's eyes on them. The smile had faded from her face and was replaced with a look of disdain.

11

As Lucy threw her arms around him drawing him in, he stole a glance at Sue. She wasn't at all happy, glaring across at them with Dave by her side. But Toby so wanted to dance with Lucy and besides, he had to include everyone. He'd be dancing with other women afterwards. He wasn't just singling out Lucy.

As they started to dance, he noticed Sue was still watching them, forcing herself to smile, but her eyes betrayed her. They were shadowed with something deeper—jealousy. It struck him suddenly that this day, which was meant to be filled with joy, was stirring up insecurities in both of them hidden just beneath the surface. After this song, he'd pull Sue close, make her feel as cherished as she truly was. But for now, he remained swept up in the dance and in the moment.

There wasn't much chance for a chat with Lucy while they danced but they managed to exchange a few words.

'I know Sue now comes first, but I hope you'll always make time for me,' Lucy said. 'You'll always be my special friend.'

His gaze locked on hers, and for a fleeting moment, he caught a glimpse of hurt in her eyes. It tugged at his heart.

'I'll always love you, Lucy.'

The air felt bittersweet as the words hung between them. He could see the way her smile wavered slightly, mingled with sadness. It felt like a complicated web they were tangled in, filled with shared memories and unspoken feelings, yet he was committing to another—one who deserved his full attention. Navigating this friendship through the changes ahead was going to be challenging but he hoped their bond would endure.

'Don't be daft.' She laughed. She was being her usual flippant self and he felt deflated.

'Seriously, Luce, you'll always be my first love, but I knew I wouldn't be good enough for you.'

Holding his shoulders she leaned away and studied his face with a puzzled expression. 'God, Toby, I never knew you felt like that.'

He looked away. 'I'm sure you did.' He was starting to feel embarrassed.

'What was the point? I was never going to make a move, I couldn't give you the life you have, you're way out of my league.'

'Don't you put yourself down.'

'It's just the way it is.' Why did he feel suddenly flat? This was his wedding day, it was supposed to be the happiest day of his life.

'How does it feel marrying your childhood sweetheart?'

'She's not my childhood sweetheart.'

She looked away awkwardly.

'I've always carried a torch for you, Luce. You were the first person there for me, I loved being around you. I would have treated you like a lady, not like those pricks you've been out with. You're everything I wanted in a girl, I love you, Lucy, I always have.'

'I'm really flattered, you'll always be special to me, Tobe, you know that.'

She gazed up at him, her eyes pools of undeniable emotion, and in that moment the world around them faded into a blur. Her fingers tightened around him and her breath hitched ever so slightly as their bodies swayed. They were subtle gestures, but he recognised the truth, she felt more for him than she had ever let on. He was shocked and couldn't let Sue see his face.

'Why didn't you tell me all this years ago?' she asked. 'Or are you teasing?'

He looked at her, but feeling the heat rise to his face, he quickly glanced away. 'I'm being serious.'

She flung her arms around him, squeezed him, and gave him a big smacking kiss on the cheek. 'That's so sweet, I never knew.' She paused before adding, 'We've had some lovely times together, haven't we? Sometimes you don't realise until it's all gone.'

And then, it's too late.

Lucy was rarely reflective, she preferred living in the moment.

He suddenly felt very nostalgic, a desperate longing for the past welling inside him, but this was ridiculous, he couldn't think like this, be like this. Sue was the girl he'd just married, and they had their whole lives ahead of them.

'Why do you always go out with pricks, Luce? I just want to see you happy.'

So consumed was he with his own thoughts, he almost missed Sue glaring at him from across the room. In that moment, he wanted the floor to open up and swallow him whole.

Not looking at all happy, she turned and steamed out of the room.

Great, I've succeeded in making my new wife miserable on our wedding day.

Making his apologies, he abandoned Lucy and hurried after Sue.

She was zipping off down the corridor and he ran after her. 'Wait.'

She twirled round, her face filled with hurt and anger. 'How could you do that on our wedding evening?'

'I can't help it. Everyone loves me.' His mind was still full of Lucy. He should have told her years ago how he felt.

'You're such a bighead. It should be the bride getting all the attention not the groom,' she said huffily.

He felt embarrassed. He hadn't meant to sound bigheaded. Under the spotlight, he saw tears glisten in her eyes.

'Babes, I had to get in there before Dave.' He laughed, trying to make light of it.

'We've only been married a few hours and you're off dancing with an old flame.'

'She's not an old flame, she's my Lucy.'

A flicker of pain darted across her eyes. 'What do you mean, *your* Lucy?' Her voice rang out in the narrow corridor like a spoon against glass. She looked insanely jealous.

'You've got Norman,' he quickly retaliated.

'I'll dance with him then, see how like it, dancing with your trollop.'

'Lucy's not a trollop.'

'You only have to look at the men she goes out with.'

'It's up to her who she goes out with, she's a grown woman, she can make up her own mind.'

Sue scoffed.

'Why are we bickering? This is supposed to be our

special day. I don't want to argue, come back and dance with me, people will wonder where we are.'

She looked at him with sadness. 'I know you love her, Toby, just admit it, I could see it in your eyes. What were you talking about? Reminiscing about old times?'

'You're being paranoid. I love her as a friend, but not like that.'

'I think in a few years' time, you're going to regret marrying me. I'm just boring old Sue.'

He sighed, irritated. 'That's your lack of confidence talking. I can't fix your past, but it's you I love. I chose you. If you don't know that by now, you never will. You daft bugger.'

She was crying now. 'I can't go back in there.'

He leaned down and kissed her face. 'Come on, cheer up, poppet.'

'I feel so inadequate. I wish you hadn't invited Lucy.'

'You're feeling a bit sensitive, that's all, it's been an emotional day.'

Just then Sally came trotting along. 'Everything okay with you two lovebirds?'

'Can you fix my make-up, Sal?' Sue asked.

'Course I can, let's go in the ladies.'

Leaving them to it, Toby returned to his friends and decided to stay away from Lucy for the rest of the evening. It wasn't worth upsetting Sue. But going forward, he realised he needed to find a way of seeing Lucy. He valued their friendship too much and didn't want to stop seeing her, but he didn't want to upset Sue either. How he'd get to see her, he didn't know. He wasn't going to resort to being sneaky about where he was going. That game couldn't be played for long, it would be far too wearing. It was better to be up front and honest and not get into lying, but he just couldn't see Sue being comfortable with that.

12

It was past well midnight when the wedding day finally came to an end. Gill offered to wheel Sue back to their room to help her wash and undress, while Toby lingered at the bar for a quick whisky with Jasper, Sandy, Bill and Patsy.

He was exhausted yet exhilarated, his heart still buzzing with the magic of the occasion as he took a warming sip of his drink. He'd thought about their wedding night so often over the past weeks. In his dreams there were no physical restrictions, and he'd imagined them rushing off to their room, tearing their clothes off and making mad, passionate love. But it was never going to be like that. He'd always known that. What he saw in his dreams didn't match the stark reality of their situation. He was in love with Sue and committed to her, but the fact that she needed care and support weighed on him. He didn't like to admit it to himself, but it bothered him. How could they be spontaneous, natural, how could they truly be unbridled?

He reflected now on how different his life might have been if he'd married Lucy. Sue needed a carer to help her wash and dress while he could do most things for himself, thanks to Bill's adaptations. Whilst she was quite independent across the day, there were still tasks she could not do, and he wasn't able to help.

He thought about all the issues they hadn't discussed or even considered. Perhaps family and friends were right when some had asked, how will you manage?

Toby was pleased though that he got on so well with Gill. She was friendly, good company in fact, and Sue relied on her a lot. She would be around when he was away working and so at least it was one worry that was taken care of. He felt daunted though by his new responsibilities. Sue depended on him now, far more than he depended on her. His mind raced about the sudden change in his life. It had been such a romantic day, but now real life was kicking in, could he cope?

He gave it twenty minutes, then tottered back to the room.

'Wow, what a day. I can't remember a time when I felt so knackered.' Toby flopped onto the bed like a ragdoll, completely spent. He let out a sigh, feeling the soft mattress embrace him as he sank into its comfort. Fatigue washed over him, but a smile tugged at the corners of his mouth as he replayed the highlights of the day in his head.

'At least we don't have to dash off on our honeymoon till Tuesday,' he said.

Sue still had boundless energy and was chattering away. She seemed to have forgotten about Lucy. He honestly didn't know where she got all her energy from. He chuckled to himself seeing her propped up in bed, her dressing gown tightly wrapped around her. He had observed Sue's clever way of climbing onto the bed. She had strong and agile arms and managed to swing her torso up, using her upper body to propel herself, a bit like a monkey in a tree. She was still very shy about being naked in front of him. Even with their closeness, they had arrived at this day without having shared any intimacy apart from kissing.

'Thought you would be desperate to get out of that penguin suit.'

She slid over and tugged at his tie. 'Come here, you,' she said with a cheeky glint in her eyes.

He felt a bit uncomfortable and embarrassed. Was she going to undress him like his mum did when he was young? He'd been so independent for years, this was going to be hard, or was this part of the lead-in to intimate relations? He hadn't a clue. He had so much to learn. He'd listened to hours of Dave's exploits. Whether they'd happened or not was a different matter, or just made-up bragging. He struggled to get his mind around the logistics of making love. He'd have to use his foot to touch her. He used his feet for everything. It did seem inelegant. She would have to guide it in though. She had the hands. It would be fun trying but tonight was not the right time.

Just then, she flung her dressing gown off and tossed it aside. He gasped in surprise. She looked gorgeous in a new nightie.

'That's not the type of thing you normally wear.' It was a black silky babydoll nightdress.

'I wanted to look nice on my wedding night,' she said coyly.

'You look beautiful.'

By the way she'd just folded her arms, he knew she was embarrassed and self-conscious. 'Is it a bit over the top then?'

'Wow, it's a bit revealing,' he said with a cheeky grin. Her breasts were threatening to flop out and his eyes were popping out of his head. 'Where did you buy *that* from?'

'The Army & Navy. Norman bought it for me, he said, "I know just what you need for your wedding night".'

He was aghast. 'Oh my God, has he been involved in choosing that too?' Was that how Norman saw her?

'You're looking at me as if I'm a slut.' She pulled the sheet to cover herself. He couldn't look at the nightie. 'Is nothing sacred?'

'He's been a good friend to me, always making sure I'm okay. He means well.'

'Choosing your underwear is not at all appropriate.'

'It's a nightie, not a bra. And don't you think, if I'd actually fancied him, we'd be together? Besides, what about Lucy? I haven't forgotten about that dance.'

'Yeah, yeah, okay.' At the mention of Lucy, he just wanted to close down the conversation. He didn't want this on their wedding night. The mood for romance had gone.

She leaned towards him and started to unbutton his shirt and kiss his neck, but the moment had passed. His whole body went limp. 'Sorry, Sue, but you've killed it dead.'

She looked affronted. 'Cheers, thanks for that. I've gone to all this effort.'

'Don't worry about it. I've got a headache and besides, I feel a little tipsy so not sure I would function as I should.'

'You can't have a headache on your wedding night.'

He stood up, but as he undressed, he felt sad that the romance of the day was fast evaporating. 'Well, Mrs Murphy, have you enjoyed your day? Was it as special as you'd hoped?' he said, trying to stay bright.

'Apart from you womanising, it was wonderful.'

He ignored the comment, hadn't she made him feel guilty enough? 'I think it was better than wonderful.'

He had undressed to his underpants and sat down again. 'I've been looking forward to this moment all day,' she whispered as she planted kisses on his shoulders.

'If I had the energy, I'd ravish you, but I'm sorry I'm completely done in. I don't even have the energy to brush my teeth.' He felt bad, she'd made a real effort to look nice for him. He gazed down at his crotch looking for movement, but there was none. Maybe it would be different in the morning. His energy levels would peak, but it didn't get over the looming issue of him having to make the first move. How and what to do?

It bothered him that he couldn't get aroused. It was more than just tiredness. How come jack sprang to attention when Lucy was around, but nothing was happening now? Why didn't it fire up for Sue? He gazed lovingly at her, but his body just wasn't responding. A slight sense of panic set in. He always felt so aroused around Lucy. And yet he did find Sue attractive. She had a marvellous pair of boobs, and a beautiful face.

'Isn't it just nice to have time to ourselves without everyone fussing round? And all those photos. I'm stuffed, there was so much food. And all the conversation, talking too much, it drains me.'

She laughed. 'You don't have to make excuses. I'm tired too, don't worry, Toblerone,' she said with a chuckle.

Tonight was his stay of execution, but he knew come tomorrow, he'd have to make the first move. What move though? Sex was like painting by numbers. He didn't have a clue where to begin, but maybe he was overthinking it. Making love was supposed to be the most natural act in the world. It was meant to be exciting, not difficult. Yet as he sat on the edge of the bed, doubts crept in, filling his mind with questions about whether he'd be able to meet her needs and be truly intimate. He took a deep breath and reminded himself that it wasn't about perfection, but about connection. All he needed to do was let go, embrace their vulnerability, and remember that love itself was the greatest guide.

He was normally lively and full of energy and didn't mind late nights but now he just wanted to go to sleep. Perhaps it was the alcohol singing in his head and different conversations whirling through his mind.

They lay in bed grinning at each other, Sue with her arms wrapped around him. It didn't feel real to be here, married and sharing a bed. It was completely surreal, the start of a new chapter in his life. He couldn't help but reflect at how far they'd come and how shy he'd been to ask her out.

She was on the same wavelength as him, had a knack of thinking the same thing and it showed in her next comment. 'I thought you'd never make the first move.'

'Well, I haven't, not yet.' He sniggered at the double meaning.

Sue sidled up to him. 'Come on, Toby. We're both in this together.' Her eyes were puppy-like as she leaned in and kissed him. 'Do you remember that magic moment at the conference when it all started? We mustn't let go of that.'

Of course he remembered it. They were the last to leave the bar and it was getting late. He recalled the rain pattering against the windows and a playful discussion about Monty Python's *The Meaning of Life*. He hated Monty Python, he just didn't get it, but she loved it.

The conversation was buzzing and turned into heartfelt confessions.

'I remember our conversation in the bar after the disco when I said I felt there was something really special between us and I couldn't put my finger on it.'

'And you asked if I felt something similar.'

He remembered it all so clearly, the world around them faded and all he saw were her bright eyes like pools staring into his and the laughter they'd shared leading to a kiss.

'Oh my God that means I'm responsible for all of this. What have I done? I hope I've made the right decision. What would you have done if I'd said no?' She was grinning from ear to ear.

'Oh well, I would have had plenty of other women queuing up.' He laughed.

'I'll never forget the time you took a detour just to see me. That was the nicest thing anyone has ever done for me. I knew then you meant more than just a friend to me.'

He watched her as she gently drifted off to sleep, and it wasn't long before he joined her.

13

The next morning Toby woke to a knock on the door. It was Gill coming to help Sue.

Damn, I was hoping for a lie-in and cuddle.

Was this how their life would be, the interruption of carers, no flexibility, and governed by a set routine? It meant never being spontaneous and always having to clock-watch.

He gazed lovingly at his bride as she stirred. She looked so angelic with puffy cheeks.

'Looks like we'll have to wait till Florida for the magic moment.' He gave her a wink before sliding out of bed and unlocking the door for Gill before legging it to the bathroom and grabbing his trousers on the way.

'Hang on a tick, I just need to put my trousers on,' he called.

He heard Gill chuckle to Sue.

It felt strange. This was the first time he'd been woken by a carer wanting to wash and dress her and he wasn't sure how he felt about that. It felt like an intrusion into their privacy, but it was something he was going to have to get used to. How was he now going to lie starkers in bed or walk around the flat in his undies? Sex would have to be to a prescribed timeline. It was these day-to-day challenges that were starting to emerge, and they'd given no consideration to. It felt as if their independence was being eroded, they weren't in control of their lives, and it took him back to school days.

He emerged from the bathroom and Gill said brightly, 'Morning, Toby,' grinning from ear to ear. 'Did you have a good night?'

'You caught me with my trousers down, whatever you do, don't tell Sue.' He laughed.

Sue overheard, and they all burst out laughing and the awkwardness of the moment was defused.

Later that morning after they'd breakfasted, they got into Sue's car and with tin cans attached to the exhaust clattering behind them, they set off to Haslemere. They had been invited to lunch at Jasper and Sandy's. They were looking forward to catching up with their German thalidomide friend, Heidi, who had come to the wedding and was staying at the bed and breakfast.

It was wonderful, Toby thought, to have formed friendships over the years with so many people affected by thalidomide—not just here in the UK, but in every country across Europe. They'd met people at different events and shared and compared stories of the difficulties they faced with their governments and the pharmaceutical companies that had made and distributed the drug. It had been enlightening, and he had bonded with many, including Heidi when they met in the Black Forest on a European thalidomide holiday a few years back.

14

After the day's celebrations, Jasper and Sandy collapsed into bed late. Jasper could have used more sleep, but they needed to be up early to prepare breakfast for their two guests. He heard pots and pans clattering as he descended the stairs and entered the kitchen, where Sandy was already up and gathering utensils, ferreting for food, grabbing eggs and bacon from the fridge and slicing crusty bread. She'd bought extra sausages because the butcher insisted that Germans had a serious sausage obsession. 'Best not take any chances,' Jasper had jested.

Sandy coped so much better than him with these early starts. She was always the first to bound downstairs, looking immaculate, her face made up, her hair in a bun. Adjusting his body clock was tough, he was used to weekend lie-ins, but this venture had been his idea, he couldn't let her do all the work. They'd developed a routine. She cooked, he laid the table, served the guests, and did the washing up. While Sandy made the beds and cleaned, he skedaddled off to a local coffee shop to read the weekend papers. Sandy always complained about this, but keeping abreast of world news was essential. That was his excuse and he was sticking to it.

'Whatever you do,' Sandy said as she put on her apron and tucked a few strands of hair behind her ears, 'do not mention the war, and none of your *Fawlty Towers* shenanigans.'

He quickly broke into his *Fawlty Towers* routine. 'Yes, Sybil, no, Sybil, three bags full, Sybil dear. I'll be on my best behaviour, but what do you want me to do with the dead body? A guest died in the night. I don't want anyone to turn up in the gas cupboard.'

Sandy tutted.

Jasper carried the plates into the dining room and gave the guests time to eat before popping back in to ask if everything was okay.

Back in the kitchen, he complained to Sandy, 'They want more sausages. Can you believe it?'

'Shush, keep your voice down,' she scolded as she whirled round, a wooden spatula in her hand.

'And they want more toast and more coffee. What do they do with all that sausage?'

'You get more like John Cleese every day. Do they really want more?'

'No, you're fine.'

'Honestly. Stop your teasing, I was about to throw more sausages into the pan. Your turn to cook breakfast tomorrow.'

'Hey, no chance. Unless you want our guests to be poisoned.' He laughed. 'Don't I get any sausages?'

She flashed a smile and playfully whacked him on the shoulder with the wooden spoon.

It was going to be a busy day because Jasper had invited the German guests and Toby and Sue for lunch.

They finished serving breakfast and the guests went out for a walk while Sandy made their beds. They were staying for three nights before heading down to Dorset to visit friends.

Just then Toby and Sue arrived, and Angela rushed down the stairs to open the door for them. They joined Sandy and Jasper in the kitchen. It was a big kitchen, otherwise it would have been a tight squeeze.

'How are you, Basil?' Toby asked as he goose-stepped across the kitchen. 'Isn't it about time you played the part and grew a moustache?'

'You're as bad as Jasper,' Sandy said, turning from the hob and sniggering. 'When are you two planning to grow up?'

'Hopefully never,' Jasper said, laughing. 'I'm sure young Sue will whip Toby into shape. But she might decide to join in the childish fun. Sue could be Polly. And Toby could be Manuel with Bill as the major.'

Sue laughed. 'He'll definitely need his sense of humour living with me, watching some of my daily challenges, like my ongoing battle with the vacuum cleaner. My life is one big comedy show.'

'So is mine,' Toby said. 'I can see us doing a sketch.' They laughed.

Jasper admired their ability to see humour in their everyday challenges. It was refreshing, given all the able-bodied people he knew who grumbled about the small inconveniences in their lives.

Angela had slept in and was making breakfast when she accidentally spilt her cornflakes.

Sandy wheeled round. 'For goodness' sake, child, I've got enough to do without clearing up after you as well.'

Angela climbed down from her bar stool, flicking milk

from her nightie before grabbing a tea towel and dropping it onto the puddle to soak up the liquid.

'I'll have the health inspector onto us before long. We've got cloths under the sink for the floor.' She pointed to the cupboard.

'I hate all these different people in the house, having to be quiet, tidy and not being able to run round in my own house.'

Jasper, having made coffee for Toby and Sue, was now checking the bookings for the coming week. 'I think we may have overbooked.'

'No, that's not possible, I'm very organised, I know exactly who's staying.' Sandy didn't look at all perturbed and must have guessed his game.

He looked at Angela with a grave face. 'I think you'll have to sleep in a tent in the garden for the night, pet.'

'I don't want someone sleeping in my bed,' she whined. 'How can I sleep in it again? It won't be my bed anymore. And they'll mess up my teddies. Toby, tell them.'

Toby hadn't guessed that Jasper was just teasing. He looked aghast. 'Surely you don't let out Angela's room. At least pay the poor kid.'

'I don't need any money.'

'I'll remember that when you ask for pocket money,' Jasper said with a laugh.

Angela burst into tears.

'Now look what you've done.' Sandy was all flustered. 'I'm trying to cook. Angela, go and get dressed, it's nearly lunchtime.'

Toby, Sue and Jasper left the kitchen and busied themselves laying the dining room table. Jasper put the last placemat on the table, then looked from Toby to Sue with concern.

'I know what you're going to say.' Sue laughed. 'Stop worrying. We'll be fine. We have to prove we can do it, for ourselves, not for others.'

Jasper couldn't help worrying. They were flying all the way to America for their honeymoon and while they had support at the airport and on the plane, they were going to be alone for a fortnight without any assistance.

'They have support workers if we need help. We've checked it all out.'

Toby looked relieved when Heidi and Claudia returned from their walk because it brought the conversation to an abrupt end.

In heavily accented perfect English, the women raved about how charming the village was. One compliment led to another and soon they were sharing stories of their travels across Europe, from bustling cities to tranquil pine forests.

Everybody headed into the lounge and the conversation carried on. As Toby and Heidi caught up, Jasper listened to and studied the German women. Heidi was a tall willowy blonde with a very short bob. She wore a sweatband on her head, an interesting accessory Jasper thought. Her sharp cheekbones and chiselled features made her look stern. Her eyes had a certain hardness and detachment, as if she was carrying hidden scars within. There was visible tension in the way she carried herself and Jasper couldn't help feeling intrigued to know more about her life. He surreptitiously glanced at her short arms which were about half the length they should have been. She had four fingers on each hand, and some had fused. She'd inherited none of her mother's warm features, for Claudia had a round, ruddy, mumsy type of face and unruly auburn hair. In fact, the more Jasper studied the two, they didn't look at all like mother and daughter. Maybe Heidi took after her father. He wondered, had they left him at home or were her parents divorced?

Over a simple lunch of quiche and jacket potatoes and a generous helping of Sandy's homemade coleslaw, he gathered his nerve and asked Claudia what it had been like to give birth to a thalidomide baby.

She leaned back and smiled. 'Didn't Toby tell you? I'm Heidi's foster mother.' She put her arm around Heidi.

Jasper's eyes widened in surprise, and he glanced at Sandy, who had also stopped eating, clearly astonished. It was a shame they hadn't invited Bill to join them, he would have been intrigued by this, but he was otherwise engaged with his lady friend, Patsy.

'I can tell you're a journalist, Jasper.' Heidi smiled. He wondered if her comment was a way of closing him down and stopping him from asking more questions.

'You know me, I've always had an inquisitive mind. I don't know much about German survivors though.' He decided not to comment on the noble, selfless act of fostering a handicapped child, it felt patronising.

'I've had a lifetime of journalists, and one of them wanted to write my story because it's so unusual.'

Claudia stared at her in shock. 'Really? You didn't tell me that.'

'Yes, last year. Some guy from *Der Spiegel*. I thought it might upset you, so I told him I wasn't interested.'

Claudia looked hurt. Since Heidi hadn't asked for her opinion, she felt excluded—at least, that was Jasper's guess.

Jasper was intrigued. He wished they'd trust him enough to share their story, but he was careful not to appear too eager with a barrage of questions. If they wanted to tell him, they would.

He kept his next comment general. 'It's sounds as if you've had an interesting life.'

'We both have, Claudia more than me, but I don't want my story glorified and it would only sensationalise it and single me out.'

He glanced at Toby, who was looking down at the tablecloth with a look of slight embarrassment, and he wondered how much he knew about Heidi's life. If he did, he'd not said.

'My story is sad, but I'll always be grateful to Claudia.'

Claudia cleared her throat and patted Heidi's hand. 'One day we're going to find your parents.'

'The records are lost.'

'Your parents haven't abandoned you. If they could be reunited with their daughter, they would, but it's not possible, we both know that.'

'You don't know that. Maybe they considered it a lucky escape. Why would they have wanted me, looking like this?' She flapped her arms.

'They loved you. I know it. I saw their love first-hand.'

'I doubt I'll ever find them and even if I did, I might be disappointed. As far as I'm concerned, you're my mum.'

Sandy glanced over at Toby and gave him a smile full of love. 'I'm sure they'd be very proud of you and sad too, all those lost years.' She sniffed and Jasper sensed she was stifling tears. Old wounds were being opened.

'All the while that bloody wall separates the city, I'll never find them. Will I get to meet them before they die? The GDR is so corrupt, rotten to the core and has little regard for lives and families.'

Jasper's curiosity had been piqued. This was becoming more intriguing by the minute, and he was finding it hard to hold back. 'If I can help you in any way, please bear me in mind. Journalism is a double-edged sword, a powerful tool for truth and sometimes a weapon of misinformation. My reporting of the scandal a decade ago led to a successful campaign to raise money for the survivors and set up the UK Thalidomide Trust to manage the funds for each of the beneficiaries, and we succeeded in our compensation claims against Distillers.' There, he'd said it, now it was up to her to decide.

'Thank you,' Heidi said.

'Maybe I can use my connections to help find your parents.'

A look passed between the women. The shutters were down.

Claudia patted Heidi's knee then turned to Toby. 'You're lucky, young man.' She smiled. 'Your mum must have really cared, and you were lucky to grow up in a country not experiencing political upheaval.' She started to ask him about his parents, but Toby was suddenly sheepish, and Jasper and Sandy stayed quiet, guarded and on edge in case something came out. There were so many skeletons in their own cupboard. As much as he longed to say that Toby was in fact his son, he couldn't.

'What you have to appreciate is the struggles our country went through,' Claudia said. 'Attitudes towards the handicapped were deep-rooted and inherited from Hitler's regime, and they changed very little in the decades after the war when Heidi was growing up. That mentality lingered on for many years, especially in rural communities. People are more tolerant now, but there are still things that go on.'

Jasper dropped his fork and it clattered to his plate. 'My God, of course, I didn't think about that. The Jews.'

They fell silent. Then Heidi said, 'I thank my lucky stars I wasn't born during the war.'

'Would they have sent you to the gas chamber?' Toby asked, his eyes wide with intrigue.

'Thousands of handicapped children were experimented on, sterilised and murdered as part of the Nazi *Kinder* euthanasia programme, Aktion T4. I remember when I was a kid, the occasional older person came up to me and said things like, "Hitler would have gassed you".'

Claudia added, 'Tragically, the killing of disabled children continued for months after the war ended, until the occupying forces discovered what was happening.'

Claudia cast him a look that hinted at guilt for her country's actions. 'We weren't the only country to have such beliefs,' she defended. 'There were American and British doctors who admired the Nazi programme. 'One of them said, "they're beating us at our own game".'

Sue stared from Toby to Jasper. 'Can we save the heavy stuff for later? Right now, I just want to enjoy this delicious jacket potato.' She was adding extra butter and mashing it in. 'Have you made your yummy lemon meringue pie, Sandy?' She gave a cheeky grin.

Sandy beamed. 'Yes, especially for you.' She turned to the women. 'It's Sue's favourite dessert.'

'I don't think I've eaten that, but it sounds delicious,' Claudia said.

'The wedding cake was amazing, Sandy. Thank you so much for making it,' Sue said. Jasper was disappointed the conversation had moved on, but he didn't blame Sue. She was cheery and he knew she'd make Toby happy. She was such an upbeat lass, positive and bubbly.

He was just glad the wedding was over. Countless hours exiled from the kitchen while she crafted all those dainty and intricate decorations and embellishments, fretting and stressing, aiming for perfection. It looked amazing though, but whether it was worth all that aggravation, he did wonder. In mere minutes, the cake was reduced to a pile of raisins and icing, calories waiting to be heaped on hips, but the photos of Sue cutting into it, Toby beside her, would forever stay in their memories.

Jasper smiled to himself. All those hours spent making the cake reflected Sandy's love for Toby and symbolised a bridge over the lost time when she wasn't there for her son. Similarly, Heidi's parents had missed out on her upbringing. He looked around the table, only half listening to the discussion they were having about their plans for the honeymoon as the poignancy of a thought hit. They were all connected by their similar circumstances.

A deep sadness settled in his chest as he considered the countless parents separated from their children for different reasons––whether through choice, circumstance or time, each story unique yet hauntingly familiar. It was a heavy reminder of the many ways families could be torn apart, leaving a void that echoed in their hearts.

15

The German ladies were heading off to Devon but would be returning to Jasper and Sandy's for their final night in England before flying back to West Berlin.

Jasper waved them off and wished them a lovely trip to Devon while Sandy cracked on, stripping beds, and throwing laundry into the machine. She was just trotting down the stairs with her hands full, as Jasper came back into the hall.

'I found this while I was stripping Heidi's bed.' She held out a silk scarf while heading to the utility room. 'They'll be back though, so it's not a problem.'

Guests were always leaving belongings behind, but this felt different somehow. Jasper stared at the silky scarf, a sickening shiver sweeping over him as if someone had just walked over his grave. It was just a scarf, yet in that fleeting moment he knew that it represented so much more. He reached to touch it, noticing how fragile and threadbare it was. The colours were dull and muted, brown and greens, not the sort of scarf a young woman would wear. It looked decades old, as if it belonged to a different time and place, much like a forgotten melody that lingers in the air evoking memories of a world long past.

Over the next few days while he waited for the Germans to return, his mind became preoccupied with the scarf and its history. There was something about those two women. How he wished they'd share their story.

His chance came unexpectedly, a few days later when they returned. It was shortly after breakfast when Heidi slipped off for a walk alone and to explore the village. Claudia popped into the kitchen to thank them as it was their last day. She lingered, perching on the bar stool as she chatted to Sandy while Jasper loaded the dishwasher.

'Thank you for finding Heidi's scarf, she didn't sleep well in Devon without it.'

That sounded babyish. As if Claudia had read his mind she added, 'It was her mother's. She's slept with it ever since her mother left.'

Once again, Jasper found himself desperate to learn more. He guessed that Claudia, a recently retired nurse, was in her mid-sixties. 'What did you specialise in?' he asked as Sandy went to hand him a dirty plate.

'I trained in midwifery—it was during the war. I delivered one of the first thalidomide babies.'

The shock of her words sliced through the air and made Sandy drop the plate. It clattered to the floor, shattering into shards.

He glanced at Sandy, saw the horror on her face and knew that her mind had wheeled back to the night of Toby's birth, and Rona the midwife's actions. An eerie stillness seemed to settle over the room as they stared at the globules of egg streaked with ketchup splattered across the tiles.

'I'm distracting you, I'll let you get on.' As Claudia turned on her heel to go, Jasper threw Sandy a silent plea.

I need to talk to her.

'Why don't you make Claudia coffee and sit outside. It's a beautiful day.'

He had an incredible wife who always knew what he was thinking and rooted for him, and right now, she was completely right. With Heidi gone, perhaps Claudia would open up.

It was as if the weather was proving to their guests that Britain could deliver sunshine and warmth. The air smelled of freshly cut grass and the scent of peonies and lavender.

Jasper put the coffee tray on the patio table and offered her a chair.

'You have a lovely garden.'

He was proud of the garden. It was immaculate and his recent efforts had paid off. He told her about all the work they'd done to improve it and after a time casually asked, 'Did you deliver Heidi?'

'No, by the time she was born, I'd moved into paediatrics at a top children's hospital in West Berlin. The hospital had been struggling for years to recruit good surgeons and specialists. All the highly skilled physicians were forced to retire in the thirties.'

He turned and stared at her. 'Why?'

'They were Jews.'

A chill swept over him rendering him speechless as he stared at the distant greenhouse at the end of the garden where his tomatoes and lettuces were growing nicely, and for one awful moment he wondered what part she'd played in the war.

'I don't know how it was for Toby's parents, but in Germany where that dreadful drug was created, we faced our own unique situation. I think you need to know how it was back then, and maybe it's a story you might want to explore.'

She briefly closed her eyes, looking up at the sky and taking in the sun's warmth before beginning to speak.

16

CLAUDIA

7TH AUGUST 1961

My breaks are very short, my work is demanding, and the hours long. I need to make the most of this scrap of free time. I walk fast along the brightly lit corridor, my heels clipping on the hard floor.

Although I love my work and it's very rewarding, there's always a heavy ache in my heart. The fragility of each child's life is a delicate dance between courage and vulnerability. Sometimes I make a difference, yet there are moments when my efforts fall short and a child departs for the angels, leaving behind two heartbroken and stunned parents.

I dread those days. No parent should ever have to lay their child to rest.

It has happened far too often lately—the tragic loss of tiny souls, born with tangled and missing limbs, and God only knows what other issues are happening inside their broken and frail bodies rendering them unable to survive.

As I hurry to the quiet room to eat my sandwiches, I glance into wards full of brave little soldiers, sad eyes wide above glistening cheeks, laughter echoing in some quarters from those over the worst, happy now to be the centre of attention, the cause of so much worry and pain. It always seemed to be someone's birthday in one of the wards, bringing with it the cheeriness of the occasion—balloons, cakes with candles and presents.

This is the life of a children's nurse and it's hard, I will admit that. The never knowing if the children in my care will reach their next birthday.

I turn on the small television and the face of Khrushchev in a cream suit and glasses fills the screen. Listening intently, I learn that the Soviet Union will soon assist East Germany to stop the number of people fleeing the country. What does this mean? I'm confused. The man's talking in riddles.

As I sip my tea and look out of the window at the bustling street below, a fellow nurse joins me.

'Look at all these people,' she says with a pointed finger. 'They must be utterly desperate to leave the East. But we don't have the space for them here. There aren't enough homes for any of us and it'll just force up rents. They're high enough as it is.'

I ponder their circumstances, what it must be like to leave your home, your worldly goods in a bin liner, and start a new life from nothing.

After lunch, I return to the unit where I'm caring for an underweight baby girl born at the Charité in East Berlin. She arrived via ambulance soon after birth because we are better equipped to deal with babies with abnormalities. These days, the Charité just doesn't have a clue because all the skilled doctors worth their weight in gold are leaving East Berlin in their droves and transferring to hospitals in the western part of the city.

Once I've carried out all the vital checks on baby Heidi, looking for rashes and jaundice, checking her eyes, ears, nose, and mouth, there isn't much to do. Apart from feeding her regularly and checking her vital signs, she's like any other newborn—she sleeps a lot and feeds a lot. She has short arms which are half the length they should be, and she has four fingers on each hand, some fused, but apart from that, she seems otherwise well. In fact, she's better than well, she's thriving. Every day this week, she's gained in weight, and I've noticed her cheeks are filling out. I don't know what more we can do. But because of her deformity, we don't know what we're up against and the doctors are keeping her in, under observation for a few more days, just to be on the safe side.

The way I see it, the only thing this child needs is love. To be cuddled, cosseted, and shielded from the cruelty of the outside world, from those who are sure to look on in revulsion and pity and blame the parents' blood.

If only we knew what was causing these deformities. Some have said it's something in the water and others are speculating a drug that some doctors prescribe for morning sickness is causing it. It continues to be a mystery.

At that moment, as I'm gazing into Heidi's cot and stroking her downy head, her mother rushes in, looking flustered and breathless, complaining about the long wait at the border. She has another child at home and it's challenging finding a friend to look after her.

'How is she? Can't I bring her home?' she pleads as she heads to the cot to pick up her daughter. She kisses her on the head. 'It's such a performance coming here and it's getting harder, all the people at the borders, it takes forever for the queues to clear.'

'The doctor wants to keep her in for one more week. How will you cope when she comes home?' I've only been with this poor child a few days; I'm not her mother and yet I feel fiercely protective towards her.

'She needs to be with me, I'm her mum, poor love, she can't help how she is, we'll get through this. And I'm breastfeeding.' Her eyes plead and I wish the decision was mine, but it's not and I must follow the doctor's wishes. Tears trickle down her face as she cradles little Heidi in her arms, nuzzling into her, and my heart tugs.

'Very few breastfeed in this day and age.'

'I know she looks like damaged goods, poor mite, but she's my damaged goods.' She bangs her chest. 'No hospital can fix her,' she continues to plead. 'She just needs her family. I don't want my child to become a study case being poked and prodded in the name of science. Why can't we just be transferred to the Charité? It's just a ten-minute walk from where we live and she can be treated there.'

17

CLAUDIA

13th August 1961

A shout coming from outside stirs me from my sleep. I sit up, my bones creaking into gear after yesterday's long shift. There is it again, a cry ringing through the early morning air. Adrenaline courses through me, dissolving my tiredness, and I throw the covers off, haul myself out of bed and go to the window. Sunlight is streaming through the gap in the curtains, and I tug them open and peer down at the street below.

Something is going on in the streets, I'm not sure what. It's typically a quiet season in the city, especially on a Sunday, with many Berliners spending time at their countryside summer homes. So why are there so many people out there?

I'm almost fully dressed and ready for work when there's a sudden knock at the door. It's my neighbour, Karin.

Her eyes are wide, and she can barely get her words out quick enough. 'Have you heard the news, there's something big going on, something about a wall going up. We need to get down there.' She turns and dashes off down the stairs shouting for me to hurry.

Out on the street, I'm scared when I see a group of Vopos in peaked caps, each with a short stubby machine gun. Armoured troop carriers are flooding the area. I weave my way towards the main thoroughfare and at the bottom of the road a crowd several lines deep has gathered. Ahead there are signs.

Halt Zonengrenze.

Closer, I crane my neck above the sea of trilbies, and notice people have hastily dressed, their pyjamas poking above their trousers. Construction workers are tearing up the street as far as the eye can see in both directions. Men wielding powerful pneumatic drills rip into the concrete, excavating holes for heavy posts which are lifted by crane and driven into the earth. The sharp roar of machinery echoes through the air, mingling with the heavy thud of debris as posts fall to the ground creating clouds of dust and grit, causing children to cough and splutter.

Horrified, I watch on as men working like ants carry huge reels of barbed wire and begin to unravel it, stringing it between the posts like fairy lights. They are sealing the divide, the crossing between East and West is vanishing before my eyes.

Angry words from people in the crowd are tossed and left to float in the air.

'You said no wall. Liars.'

It is true, Walter Ulbricht, East Germany's Communist leader, had stood in front of the press and announced, no wall.

'This is illegal, you can't do this.'

'It's not a wall, it's an anti-fascist protection barrier,' one soldier shouts back.

Laughter rises from the crowd, then raised fists, anger simmering.

'This isn't right.'

'Good,' someone shouts. 'That'll stop them coming here and taking our jobs.'

The soldiers are starting to look uneasy in the face of so much chanting and anger. They are young boys, what do they know about politics? They have no perception of history, they were running round in nappies and playing with toy guns during the war years.

And just then, one of those young boys clad in uniform stares at me from across the mess of barbed wire still being erected. His face looks defiant, there's resolve about him, and with a swift leap, he sails over the menacing spikes. Below, the wire seems to writhe like a serpent, but he soars above it, arms extended, legs straddling, and then he lands in a heap next to me and scrambles to get up and as far from here as he can, ready to confront whatever lies ahead.

I keep walking, I'll be late for my shift, but this is hard to take in. How are people going to travel between East and West? I'm pretty sure the Soviet Union had pledged, years back, no interference in free travel. Those Ruskies can't be trusted. The leader is a loose cannon, but also weak, the whole politburo is. This is about the desperate measures of a weak bureaucracy, even I can see that and I'm only a humble nurse. They are embarrassed by the daily haemorrhage from the East.

I pass a newspaper stand, glancing at the eye-catching headlines.

Blockade uberost Berlin verhangt.

Sowjet Panzer a den Grenzen.

Nach West Berlin

Ostberliner Rotten Sich Zusammen

As I approach the hospital entrance, it suddenly hits me.

Baby Heidi.

Her mother hasn't been in to see her these past couple of days, but that's not unusual, she has Heidi's older sibling to look after and her elderly mother is not well. The poor little mite. Heidi is a special baby, she needs more than just care, she needs warmth, love and affection, and if her mother can't come for another few days, I will be there for her.

Every Couple's Fear

I whisper softly, 'I'm here, little one.' As I lift her, her scent calms me, a mix of baby powder and milk, but I'm also anxious. What's going to happen? Is her mum going to be able to cross the border?

I carry out my checks, look at the clock, glance into the corridor. She's probably on her way. It's taking her longer with all the commotion, but she will come. No mother can keep away from their child. She will find a way.

When the doctor does his rounds, I update him. He's satisfied with Heidi's progress, but he still won't release her.

'The paediatrician wants to do further checks and there's the physio sessions. She also needs a brain scan at some point.'

'I realise the Charité isn't the best of hospitals, but surely being close to home is more important and family can visit. The situation outside is so uncertain, we don't know what's going to happen. They say a wall's going up within days. Will she even be able to get across?'

'Of course she will. She has a child in hospital.' He seems so certain, but the expression on his face contradicts his words.

A week passes and there's still no sign of Heidi's mother. I'm starting to get really concerned. What if something's happened to her? The doctor has tried to contact her, but to no avail.

Another week slips by without any news. As I spend more time with the baby, I can see her beginning to form a bond with me. In turn, I'm experiencing a growing attachment to her as well. A sense of urgency to shield her from the world overwhelms me. I know she will face challenges and opposition that could threaten her well-being. In this uncertain landscape, it's my responsibility to protect her.

An overwhelming and powerful feeling washes over me. I realise that I've stepped into her mother's shoes.

'What do you think has happened to her mother?' I ask the

doctor one day. 'Heidi should be going home now, it's been weeks. Or why can't we transfer her back to the Charité?'

'She'll be jumping through hoops, I expect, going from one authority to the next trying to get permission to cross the border. It will be up to the Minister of the Interior. She must have applied for a permit to visit and been refused.'

I imagine her at the border crossing, pleading with the guards. I picture the stony-faced soldiers and their attempts not to engage with the hordes of people shouting at them, demanding answers and begging for passage.

A grave expression comes over him. 'It's time to make decisions about this baby's future. We need the bed.'

'We can't make that decision, we're just medical staff, we aren't her parents.'

'She can't stay here indefinitely. I shall be making arrangements for her transfer to a long-term institution.'

'But what about her parents, they won't know where she is?'

'I'll write and tell them.'

'Can't you phone them?'

'They aren't on the phone, but the city's phone lines have been severed anyway.'

'There must be something we can do.' It feels such a hopeless situation.

'The restrictions will be lifted, I'm sure of it, maybe she'll have to wait a few weeks, I can't see the situation running into months.'

'Weeks, months, that's still too long for a mother to be separated from her child.'

The very thought of where the baby might end up sends a chill down my spine. I can't help but worry about the kind of environment she will be placed in, and more importantly the level of care that awaits her. Will she be nurtured and loved, or neglected and overlooked? The uncertainty fills me with dread, as

I think about the worst possible scenarios for her well-being. I'm panicked imagining her vulnerabilities in the hands of strangers.

She needs her mother, and her mother needs her.

Is it possible for me to smuggle the child out of here and across the border to be reunited with her mother?

Everything is in such turmoil, nobody seems to know what the future will hold. Half the staff from the East haven't come in for the past week and it's rumoured they won't come back. We'll just have to do the best we can.

18

Toby and Sue chose Florida for their honeymoon after hearing about the modern disability-friendly facilities at Disneyland from several thalidomide survivors who'd enjoyed a holiday there. Bill and Jasper dropped them at Heathrow and helped them into the terminal and across to the check-in desk. Once they were checked in, they were given priority assistance. On the one hand, special assistance allowed them to bypass the queues, but on the downside, Sue's wheelchair was immediately whisked away to be stowed in the hold. She transferred to an airport wheelchair designed specifically for boarding the plane.

'Have an amazing time, and don't do anything we wouldn't do,' Bill said with a wink and a laugh before awkwardly patting Toby on the back. Although Bill was always reserved with emotions, Toby saw the softer side of his dad. He worried about him, even though Toby was now an adult and capable of taking care of himself.

'And if you run into problems, just give us a shout and reverse the charges,' Jasper added with a big grin.

Bill raised an eyebrow at Jasper, feigning horror. 'Reverse the charges? Are you kidding me? They'll bankrupt us.' He laughed. 'If they're in trouble, not much we can do from across the pond. You're on your own now, kiddos.'

'We'll be fine,' Sue said. 'Stop worrying, both of you.'

JASPER AND BILL LEFT THEM, and a member of staff pushed Sue's wheelchair in the direction of security. 'Got your passports?' he asked in a voice devoid of warmth.

Sue didn't like his manner at all. There was a brisk efficiency to the man, his service wasn't at all personal and he didn't attempt conversation. It felt almost mechanical. He didn't even bother to make eye contact, his focus was entirely on manoeuvring Sue's wheelchair through the busy terminal. It saddened her to encounter people like this who overlooked her as a person and left her feeling invisible. To this man, they were just handicapped people in need of assistance, a problem to be solved and a reminder that society prioritised convenience over compassion.

Through security, the man whisked them through the bustling duty-free, leaving little room for pause.

'Wait a minute,' she called out, glancing at the perfume counters with longing. She just wanted to browse and choose something nice for her holiday. The bottles looked gorgeous—all colourful and cute. She'd put some money aside especially and wanted to treat herself.

She tried again. 'Can we stop, please?' But from her low vantage point in the wheelchair, her voice barely rose above the din of the airport, the constant announcements echoing through the tannoy blending with the rhythmic squeak of shoes on the polished floor, and he barely heard her. He was a man on a mission to deliver her to the gate as if she was a parcel.

The flight passed without incident, aside from the challenges of using the toilet. The cubicles were cramped, barely big enough for Toby, and Sue required the assistance of two staff members but was permitted to use the first-class facilities. Thankfully she was lightweight which made the process a bit easier, but beyond their honeymoon, she didn't imagine they'd be going on another flight. Cruising was perhaps a better idea and more suited to her needs.

The tannoy crackled into life with the announcement they'd soon be landing and the instruction to put their seats into an upright position. Sue leaned over and adjusted Toby's seat. She also checked he was buckled in properly. She noticed how much she was now doing for him and felt a bit uncomfortable about it. She didn't want to be mummy to him. She knew how much he valued his independence and didn't want to take that away from him, but today for instance, it was proving easier for her to step in and help rather than wait for a member of staff.

As the plane began its descent into Orlando airport, the cityscape unfolded beneath them, bathed in warm sunlight. The landscape was flat and dotted with lakes that shimmered next to swathes of green and lines of housing.

'Look,' she gasped. 'I think I see Disney from here.'

'I can already hear the Disney theme tune in my head.' Toby chuckled.

'Ha, ha, that's just the plane's engines, they've got a certain beat.' The rhythmic hum of the engines filled the cabin. They glided lower, the long runway and a straggle of buildings, and beyond—they were in Florida, gateway to the sun-soaked adventures that awaited.

As soon as they were on the ground, one of the cabin

crew stepped forward to assist Sue into the wheelchair and they were the first off the plane, even before the other passengers had risen to grab their bags from the overhead lockers. Sue was glad they weren't going to get caught up in all that kerfuffle. Everything appeared to be going well, which was a huge relief after weeks of worrying that things might go awry. However, as they waited in the terminal for her wheelchair to be retrieved from the hold, a sense of unease started to settle in.

She glanced at Toby. 'Where's my wheelchair? It's taking a long time. I hope they put it on the plane.'

19

Their flight assistant went to find Sue's wheelchair and they waited in the terminal. Toby frowned and looked around him. 'It shouldn't be taking this long. Wheelchairs and prams are the last to go on and first to come off.'

The special assistant hurried back, and grabbing the handles of Sue's wheelchair, steered her towards the carousel to retrieve their luggage. 'We'll probably find it down by the carousel.'

Arriving at the carousel, they looked in dismay. Their suitcases were the last ones still trundling round the conveyor belt, but there was no sign of Sue's wheelchair. The assistant loaded the cases onto a trolley and called for extra assistance while he guided them to a help desk to locate the wheelchair. The woman behind the desk made a couple of phone calls and it all seemed to take an eternity.

'We've got transport waiting for us,' Sue said, visualising someone standing at arrivals holding up a placard with their names on.

Neither the lady behind the counter or the special

assistant made any attempt to reassure her, but Toby leant down and gave her a kiss. 'It'll be okay, babes, they'll wait for us, and if they don't, I'm sure they'll sort something.'

Toby was his usual unruffled self, which wasn't always reassuring. Sometimes she found him far too mellow. 'What if they don't?'

She was beginning to feel panicked. How were they going to get to the resort and what if they'd lost her wheelchair? She didn't want to consider that prospect, it was just too awful to contemplate. Her heart sank. Why hadn't they listened to Bill when he'd suggested honeymooning in Devon or Cornwall?

Just then, the woman came off the phone. 'I'm so sorry but we think your wheelchair ended up on the wrong flight. We think it's gone to Miami.'

A jolt of panic shot through her. 'What do you mean, it's on a different flight?' Her voice was all shaky and she was fighting to keep the tears at bay. This felt completely overwhelming, it was her worst nightmare.

Fortunately, she had Toby with her, and he remained calm and practical. 'What will happen next?' he asked.

'I'm going to take the details of where you're staying, and have it delivered there as soon as it's arrived here.'

'When will that be? I need my own wheelchair, it's what I'm used to.' Her eyes were watering.

'Don't worry, madam, you can borrow the chair you're in and the delivery guy will swap it over. It shouldn't be any longer than three days.'

'Three days!' Toby and Sue said in unison, aghast.

'Why that long?' Toby asked.

'I'm hoping it won't be as long as that.'

The thought of three days in this narrow and uncomfortable chair filled her with horror.

Able-bodied people just don't understand what it's like for us. They had choices. They could switch chairs, change shoes and just about any freedom they wished for.

It wasn't just the narrow width of the chair that concerned Sue, or the saggy back. It was the small wheels. How on earth was she going to propel herself along? Her chair had large wheels. Toby wouldn't be able to push her.

She peered up at the lady behind the counter whose blank expression told Sue all she needed to know––she had already moved on, satisfied she'd solved their problem. 'And how will I get around? My husband can't push me in this.'

The lady craned her neck to look down at Sue with a puzzled look on her face. 'Sorry, I don't understand.'

'My husband can't push me.'

She turned to Toby, and Sue watched the realisation hit her when she noticed his missing arms.

'My wheelchair has large wheels. I'm able to get myself around.'

This completely flummoxed the lady, and Sue could see that she hadn't a clue how to solve this one.

'Look, if you can just see us onto our minibus, I'm sure we'll cope––somehow.' Toby looked bewildered and she could see he was getting impatient but there was a resigned air. He'd been here before with people's attitudes. They both had. He just wanted to get out of the airport and safely to their hotel. 'If you can get the wheelchair to us within a couple of days that'd be great.'

Safely on the minibus, they soon forgot about the wheelchair saga as they gazed out of the window in awe, excited by the bright lights, tall neon signs and palm trees swaying gently in the breeze.

They found a way of muddling along over the next couple of days, staying close to the hotel, rather than trying to be too adventurous. Languishing by the pool during the day, sipping cocktails in the evenings at the hotel's bar. Very quickly they bit the bullet, asking for help and accepting help when it was offered. Mostly it involved simple tasks like wheeling Sue into the dining room or lifting her out of her chair and onto the sun lounger. The hotel staff were brilliant.

One older lady in particular kept rushing over to help and even offered to take Sue to the toilet. 'Lovey, it's no trouble at all,' she said in a thick Liverpudlian accent. 'I was a nurse for years. I'm used to helping people.' The woman seemed very eager to help.

'That's very kind of you,' Sue said. 'It's just nice to have someone who knows what they're doing and isn't fazed to help. Do you still work?'

'Not anymore, I'm retired, but I can't seem to shake off the instinct to help others. It's in my nature.'

Sue sensed deeper layers to this woman and then on the third day when they were in the ladies' toilets, she suddenly revealed that she'd almost had a thalidomide baby. Her doctor had prescribed the drug for morning sickness but fortunately she hadn't taken it. She took out a photo of her daughter from her purse and showed it to Sue.

Sue stared at the photo of the woman, a similar age to herself, standing on a beach, and tried to imagine what she might have looked like had her mother taken the drug.

'Why didn't you end up taking it?'

'I was going to. I was desperate. I'd been throwing up morning, noon, and night but my husband wouldn't let me take them. He flushed them down the loo. "Me mam managed without drugs, and her mam before her and so can you". He was old-fashioned and often railed against progress. He wouldn't rush to buy a telly, not till the whole street had one, even though we could afford one. He was even wary of taking paracetamol.'

'His attitudes saved your daughter.'

'Yes, thank God, but they didn't save our marriage. He was very controlling. I eventually left him.'

For the rest of the day, Sue couldn't shake the woman's story. She thought about her own mother's situation and wished someone had prevented her from taking the drug. As she lay in the sun sipping a cocktail and resting her eyes, she found herself daydreaming about all the possible scenarios that might have stopped her mother swallowing those tablets.

THEY WERE in the bar after a day spent by the pool. It had been a baking hot day and neither of them was used to such intense heat. But their scorched skin had given them a healthy glow.

'You look rather hunky with a bit of colour.' She leaned over and kissed Toby. They'd had a couple of mojitos, and the alcohol was singing in his head. When she put her arms around him, he felt stimulated.

'To us,' he declared, nudging his glass towards hers so that it clinked. 'To our adventure.' Their happiness seemed to shimmer like the bubbles in their glasses.

'I can't believe we're finally here,' Sue said above the lively chatter around them.

'We've talked about this trip for so long.' The gentle glow of fairy lights cast a warm halo around them.

Glancing round to check nobody was watching them, she slid her hand up his shorts and squeezed his thigh.

'What are you doing? You're making me all hot and

bothered.' He laughed and leaned over to tickle her. 'Love you, babes,' he whispered, gazing into her eyes.

Just then, three drunken English lads staggered by, their raucous laughter slicing through the moment like a jagged knife. 'Look at them,' one scoffed, slurring his words. 'A pair of freaks.' Laughter erupted fuelled by ignorance and alcohol.

Toby's heart sank and he instinctively moved closer to Sue. Her eyes met his, a mix of hurt and fear flaring within them. In that moment, all their triumphs felt overshadowed by the nasty words of strangers. Just as quickly as it began, the lads moved on, their laughter fading into the darkness, leaving them ensnared in a moment that shattered the fragile illusion of acceptance.

They were silent for a few moments, the air between them filled with a deep sorrow that people could still be so cruel, and then Toby said, 'Come on, time for bed.'

20

Toby and Sue had entered into marriage determined to be as independent as they could be. Instead of bringing a carer or a family member, they wanted to go on their honeymoon alone as a newlywed couple, believing in their strength to face whatever challenges came their way. The accommodation was well-equipped for those in wheelchairs, and ramps, wide doors, a large modified bathroom, and accessible transport across the site would help to make their holiday a smooth and enjoyable one. And they knew they could ask the friendly hotel staff if they needed help with anything. Neither felt daunted, because they had each other. And whatever challenges they faced, they faced them together and with humour.

They headed towards their block of apartments where they had a ground-floor suite.

'Do you need any help?' Toby asked as he watched Sue fly into the bathroom.

She giggled. 'You can help me get undressed, but I'm fine using the bathroom. It's perfect, it's got so much space and I love this big shower with the chair. If only we had this at home. I can actually turn my wheelchair around in here and it will be easy to transfer to this shower seat.'

Ready for bed, they climbed in. 'You're not wearing those in bed, they're awful,' she said, looking at his underpants and laughing. 'You can take them off for a start.'

'Maybe we should turn the light off, that way neither of us will be embarrassed,' he said, feeling his cheeks burn.

'You'll do no such thing. I've waited long enough, I want to see you, all of you.' Her eyes were wide as they drank him in. 'And besides, Toblerone, since when have you been embarrassed?'

They settled down, facing each other.

'I've dreamt about this moment.' She swept her fingers through his hair and gave him a light peck on the lips, like the brush of a butterfly. 'I've never seen a naked man before in all his full glory,' she whispered, blushing. She wrapped her arms round him and started to giggle. 'Maybe you've been dreaming of this too. I never actually imagined I'd get married. Marriage was for other people, not for people like us.'

His heart was pounding loudly. He was aware of every cell in his body being highly sensitised to her pretence. His desire shimmered just below the surface.

SUE HAD long thought about sex with Toby and decided that she would have to be the one to make the first move because she had arms, and he didn't. It felt daunting. In her head, it was the man who initiated the act, although where that idea came from she didn't know. It was something deep in her psyche. The prospect of Toby reaching for her with his teeth, or his toes seemed bizarre. It made her aware of their contrasting bodies and their capabilities. He carried out so many tasks using his feet, it was natural for him, and she wondered if he'd use his feet in making love.

As she wrestled with her thoughts, a wave of doubt washed over her. Had she made the right choice in marrying Toby? The very notion filled her with shame as if she was betraying him. Yet in that turbulent moment of reflection, she couldn't help but think about all the challenges they'd encountered and overcome over the years. She chastised herself for her fleeting uncertainty, their love was a journey, learning and adapting and ultimately growing closer. She'd just have to take the lead and maybe they'd create their own Karma Sutra. It was going to be a struggle, but they'd have fun trying. It would be a trial-and-error thing, scary yet exciting too.

How difficult could it be to poke a toad in a hole?

She let out a hysterical laugh. 'I've no idea what to do but I think we'll have fun trying, we'll find a way, and you know what they say, practice makes perfect.'

He was kissing her neck and whispered, 'One thing's for sure, you're going to have to help me out. Everything I do is with my feet, so I know I'll put my foot in it whatever I do.' He laughed.

'Right in this moment,' she said with a cheeky grin, 'I wasn't thinking of your foot, Toby. I don't think you'll need your foot for this part. It's going to be a bit like playing *The Golden Shot*.'

For the next hour they tried different positions without much success. Either Toby wasn't comfortable, or Sue wasn't. They ended up rolling round in fits of laughter.

'Perhaps we should have consulted the Karma Sutra beforehand,' Toby suggested.

'Or write our own version.'

His hands couldn't wander so she shuffled up and thrust her boob into his mouth.

'These are my Toby jugs,' she said with a laugh.

She was suffocating him. They were so big. He pulled away then nuzzled her on the back of her neck. Suddenly the natural curvature of their bodies made it possible. With a last-minute adjustment, they finally found the right method and giggled and laughed.

Afterwards, he stroked her gently on the back with his foot, his heel pressing in, making circles on her skin.

'I can see I'm going to have to cut your toenails,' she muttered as she drifted to sleep.

'I never realised how strong your arms were until tonight,' he whispered.

As he slipped into slumber, his dreams were haunted by visions of a life not lived and paths not taken. In the midst of this turmoil, Lucy emerged from the shadows of his mind, her long, slender legs entwining around him. Her embrace felt suffocating, like a serpent coiling tightly around his neck, both alluring and constricting, blurring the lines between desire and danger.

21

Jasper arrived at the sleek new skyscraper. His newspaper had recently moved from Fleet Street to Wapping in East London. There had been a monumental political struggle including a protracted strike by print workers, thousands being effectively dismissed for resisting new technology, yet the Wapping operation launched without a hitch. It meant a longer journey for Jasper, but he didn't mind, most of the time he worked from home.

He took the lift, and strolled down the wide corridor with his heavy bag slung over his shoulder. The sunlight bounced off the glass panels that lined the corridor and separated the offices. The glass created a bright and welcoming ambience. He was still getting used to this modern way of working and didn't like the fact that open-plan offices didn't offer much privacy.

Through a glass door, he approached his desk by the window. A few colleagues glanced up, offering smiles and greetings. Meanwhile Stephanie, his secretary, hurried to the drinks machine to make him a coffee.

He stood at the window for a few moments gathering his thoughts, one hand clutching his polystyrene cup of coffee, the other jangling coins in his pocket. The view was breathtaking, and he would never tire of it. The Thames glimmered in the sunlight, and he watched the boats and barges going under a bridge. The iconic Tower Bridge stood majestically in the distance, its impressive architecture a striking contrast against the skyline. The sky opened up, painted in shades of blue, dotted with wispy clouds and below, the urban landscape unfolded before him, a tapestry of barren landscape, buildings waiting to be erected.

His thoughts were interrupted by Sam's booming voice, and when he twirled round the editor was standing in the doorway smoking a cigar. They hadn't seen each other since Toby's wedding over a week ago, leaving much to discuss. Sam had been preoccupied with thoughts of his friend Adam, who was gravely ill in hospital, and he didn't know if he'd pull through.

'Morning, boss,' Jasper called as he grabbed a pen and notepad from his desk. It wasn't until he got closer that he realised Sam didn't look himself at all.

He followed Sam through to his office, pulling out a chair and resting his coffee cup on the desk. Sam sank down wearily in the chair opposite him, his exhaustion evident in his features. He didn't just look tired, he looked ill. His face was puffy and waxy like a candle and there was a tinge of yellow in his cheeks. Even the whites of his eyes had a hint of yellow. Sweat was beading on his forehead and his hair was damp.

'Are you all right, mate? You look out of sorts today.'

Sam gave a heavy sigh. 'Adam passed away last night. I stayed at the hospital with him.'

'Oh, mate, I'm so sorry, that must be really hard for you.'

Jasper had known Sam for years and knew what Adam meant to him. He'd left Toby's wedding early to be back at the hospital.

Sam looked defeated, the shadows under his eyes deep and pronounced, and an aura of despair clung to him. Taking a sip of his now cold coffee, Jasper felt a knot in his stomach thinking about how isolated Sam must feel. He knew it wasn't something that he'd be able to share easily with others. With the increasing fear surrounding the disease, and the terrible stigma, AIDS was a spectre that lurked in the shadows of society and there so much not known about it.

Jasper was just thankful he wasn't single, he'd be paranoid every time he slept with someone. People were warned to take precautions like wearing condoms.

Just the other day, while discussing the disease with Sandy, she suggested that it was wise to keep washing your hands in case it spread in public places. She even mentioned that she wouldn't be sipping Holy Communion wine anymore out of fear of catching it.

'Are they any nearer to finding a cure?' Jasper asked.

'Just about every drug is being tested. I've even heard a whisper from within the medical community that they might be using thalidomide to treat it.'

'Really?'

'I thought you were supposed to be the fount of all knowledge when it comes to thalidomide. You're slipping.'

Jasper was embarrassed. He should have known this. He'd read about the drug being used to treat leprosy, but not AIDS. 'That drug, it's both an angel and a devil.'

'Pretty much. There's a tremendous amount of luck in science, it's like an Easter egg hunt.'

Jasper smiled at the analogy.

'Such a potent weapon shouldn't be kept from AIDS sufferers because of a tragedy that happened thirty years ago before science knew better.'

Jasper winced. Sam had no understanding of the daily struggles faced by thalidomide victims. There was a certain irony about a drug that could save lives and be a miracle cure, but on the other hand could cause so much devastation.

Sam shifted in his chair and mopped his brow. 'They're fairly hopeful this latest drug, AZT, will successfully pass clinical trials. Progress is too slow though, and in the meantime, more people will die. One shocking fact I read, more were diagnosed with AIDS last year than in all earlier years combined.'

'The government need to do something.'

Sam shrugged. 'What can they do? The drug companies need to find a cure. Lots of money is being ploughed into the project.'

'There's so much misinformation going round. Can we catch it from a toilet seat or shaking hands, or a cup? Can we catch it from sitting in the same room? I wouldn't know.' Jasper threw up his hands in despair.

AIDS seemed like something that affected other people, those he didn't know, especially celebrities. He remembered the shock he felt when Rock Hudson passed away the year before. 'I dunno, mate. There needs to be a government campaign, maybe a TV advert or leaflets through every letterbox in the country warning people to be vigilant.'

Sam let out a mirthless laugh. 'Not sure what good that would do.'

'Is it something we all need to worry about? It seems to be spreading, and if we're all at risk, yes, the government should be planning a campaign of awareness, they can't just ignore it and hope it will go away.'

'The government *have* set up a campaign. It's chaired by Willie Whitelaw.'

Jasper nodded slowly. That sounded very hopeful. Willie Whitelaw was a good politician with an impressive track record. If anyone could deliver results, he could.

'I'll get Phil to interview Norman Fowler, find out what progress the campaign is making.' Phil was the newspaper's political editor.

'The government should have acted faster. It could have saved Adam.'

'A few years ago, people wouldn't have paid any attention. But maybe they will now. A campaign needs to match public interest. Timing is everything for the message to resonate.'

'I can't imagine Thatcher the milk snatcher diving into an AIDS campaign. It's not really her bag.' He gave a cynical laugh.

Sam swivelled his chair round and gazed out of the window, twisting his moustache between his fingers looking like an old Hollywood villain from the twenties. He was a thousand miles away. *He shouldn't be here*, thought Jasper, but he was the editor, he didn't like taking time off, even for bereavement and even though his sub-editor was more than capable of stepping into his shoes.

Suddenly he twirled round, facing Jasper with a serious expression. 'You have a nose for a good story. Find out what the government are planning on doing, do some digging, interview a few patients, find out what drugs are being used. Liaise with Phil, he's in the know.' He picked up a biro and started tapping it on the table like a determined woodpecker in a forest. 'Let's write an exposé.' His face broke into a smile. 'I owe this to Adam, we could write it in his memory, but tone down the sensationalism, there's been enough of that with this illness.'

'That's a rather large remit.' Jasper chuckled, unsure where to begin.

'Once you embark on the journey, start delving, the story will unfold with its own magic and write itself.'

22

It was an obscenely beautiful day as Bill and Patsy strolled hand in hand along Eastbourne Pier. Laughter echoed around them, punctuated by the cry of gulls soaring overhead. They dived into the amusement arcade and fed pennies into slot machines. Patsy squealed every time coins clattered into the tray, rushing to scoop them up. Bill grinned, absolutely loving how happy she was, like a kid on a treasure hunt.

God, how he loved being with this woman.

Leaving the dark arcade, they squinted against the dazzling sunlight, momentarily blinded by the brightness.

An enticing smell of fish and chips wafted from a nearby stall, but they'd only just eaten a delicious Welsh rarebit and Battenberg cake at Favoloso Café on Carlisle Road. Patsy was a dainty woman with a small frame, but he'd observed she had a healthy appetite. Her waist, her feet and her hands were all so tiny especially next to his timber-like frame, and he wondered how she managed to eat so much and where she put it all. Sometimes her appetite was bigger than his. Maybe it was driven by nervous energy. The woman was a whirlwind, even the air around her seemed to crackle, and he envied her spontaneity. At times it was as if she were a coiled spring ready to unleash. He'd never been able to act on impulse. He was indecisive, something that Rona had found frustrating and she'd often chided him about. He was the complete opposite to Patsy. He was a plodder. Everything happened in his own time. Everything from tidying up the house to making Toby a new gadget.

On this occasion, he was spontaneous. The weekend had been booked as a surprise, on a whim and for once he'd known his mind. And since Toby and Sue were still on their honeymoon, they weren't around to ask awkward questions.

Bill chuckled to himself. He still hadn't announced to them that he and Patsy were a couple but it wouldn't take much to guess what was going on. He'd wanted to enjoy his relationship without any pressure and negative comments, and he also wanted to be sure how he really felt about Patsy.

Now he knew, and he was going to do something about it.

He was going to pop the question and planned to do it right here on the pier. Eastbourne was a perfect place, both refined and romantic with its beautiful carpet gardens, Victorian and Regency hotels, and views across to the Downs leading up to Beachy Head. Best of all, neither had history here, it was a new experience for both of them, and they were creating fresh memories untainted by the past.

Leaving the amusement arcade behind, they stood at the railing gazing across the beach watching the waves curl and slap the pebbles. Families dotted the shoreline enjoying picnics laid out on colourful blankets. A few swimmers were slicing through the briny water while small children ran in and out of the sea ducking the waves and shrieking. The Allchorn pleasure boat was just leaving the beach on its round trip to Beachy Head lighthouse. They chatted animatedly about everything in sight and pondered whether the tide was coming in or going out.

They wandered on, the wooden boards creaking beneath their weight, as if the pier itself was joining in on their conversation. As they reached the end, a group of fishermen were gathered, right at the spot where Bill had intended to propose. His heart plummeted. As he and Patsy approached, he noticed several bright red buckets sitting by their feet. He peered inside, watching the writhing maggots squirming. Instantly, Patsy's face twisted in disgust.

'Yuck,' she exclaimed, pulling back with a shudder. Bill couldn't help but chuckle at her reaction.

But the moment was lost. This wasn't the right time. He needed a plan B, but it wasn't going to happen today, the timing didn't feel right.

They strolled back towards the promenade, relaxing on the beach for a couple of hours before Patsy suggested a quick wander round the shops before closing time. Bill knew there would be nothing quick about Patsy browsing clothes racks, any more than if he had suggested he drop into the boozer for a swift half. Unlike Rona, Patsy did love her clothes shopping. She took great pride in how she dressed, as she had today, wearing a pale blue dress with a pearl necklace and a simple cream jacket. He liked a woman who took care over her appearance.

Heading up Terminus Road, they passed his favourite ice cream bar, Macari's, then gazed at the display of candy pebbles and sticks of rock in an old-time sweet shop before strolling across the road past the Greek restaurant where they were booked to dine later on. There hadn't been much on at the theatre, nothing he'd fancied anyway, so it would be a meal and drinks instead. He felt a twinge of uncertainty about his decision to book a table at a Greek restaurant. The allure of sophistication had swayed him. He thought a Mediterranean atmosphere would create the perfect romantic setting.

As they passed a dingy café called Notarianni's, a 1930s time capsule, he thought *thank goodness I didn't book a table here.*

Bill sat outside the Debenhams' ladies' changing rooms twiddling his thumbs and wishing he'd slipped into the pub for a pint. Patsy emerged with a parade of dresses, each time asking for his opinion as if he were a fashion critic. He hadn't a clue, they were all nice, but maybe he preferred the dresses that grazed the knee as they showed off her lovely legs. She was beautiful for her age, and hadn't let herself go like a lot of women.

But where does she get all her money? Is she expecting me to buy her a new dress? If I'm buying a ring, I can't afford a dress too!

She selected a couple of outfits while he hung back from the till, not wanting to give her the impression he would foot the bill. He hated appearing stingy, but he'd already paid for the hotel and all the meals for the weekend. He didn't want to set a precedent, she'd expect it and take advantage.

Money doesn't grow on trees.

When it came to the engagement ring though, he planned to splurge—within reason, of course—it was a very special purchase and he wanted her to have exactly what she wanted and show it off.

Carrying the shopping bags, they headed back to the Haddon Hall Hotel to change for dinner. Trotting up the steps, they noticed the reception area was buzzing with activity. As they walked through the door, they were hit by lively conversation and raucous laughter. They went straight to the bar to buy drinks and managed to find a couple of chairs in the crowded room, plonking themselves down among the large group of guests.

It was hard to hear themselves speak as it was so noisy. 'We'll go up in a minute, shall we?' he suggested to Patsy.

Bill wasn't always the most observant, but suddenly he noticed they were all men dressed as women in outrageous and flamboyant dresses. He looked at Patsy and she raised her eyebrows and smirked.

'Wow, what have we stumbled into?'

She winked at him. 'I think you'll need to watch your back, Bill,' she said, laughing.

A man wearing a long red dress, curlers in his hair and bright fuchsia lipstick caught Bill's eye and smiled over at them. 'Sorry about all the noise, I bet you thought you'd come away for a quiet weekend.' His voice was effeminate, and he laughed.

'Are you actors, what pantomime are you in?'

Hearing Bill's question, several turned around and laughed.

Patsy tapped Bill's knee and addressed the fellas. 'Oh, bless his heart. My partner here hasn't twigged.' She winked at the man in the red dress before letting out a laugh that sounded like a hyena. Bill felt suddenly small and diminished, but the penny had finally dropped.

Trust me to be slow on the uptake. Jeez, we're in a hotel full of cross-dressers.

Patsy continued to tease him, but he couldn't see anything remotely funny about men dressing as women unless they were performing on stage. It just wasn't right. A fella should be a fella. They looked ridiculous in dresses. Lovely on women, but awful with hairy legs, massive feet, and pints of beer in hand. The look was completely wrong.

Maybe he was just an old-fashioned sod, but he couldn't get his head around any of it. *Why would they want to do this?*

'Maybe you should have come in your sequinned dress, darling. Isn't it time you embraced your inner diva?' one of them said to Bill.

He huffed. He couldn't bring himself to laugh. 'You wouldn't get me in a pair of stilettos.'

Then she turned to the fellas. 'So, what's the occasion then? There are some lovely outfits among you.' She laughed and told them she'd just been out clothes shopping and could match them in elegance. Bill wanted the floor to swallow him up.

'We leave our wives behind and come to Eastbourne once a year to be women.'

Bill and Patsy exchanged a look, then Patsy continued to question them between splutters of laughter. 'Do your wives know what you get up to?'

'They haven't a clue,' a man in a green silky dress said. 'It's our little secret.'

Laughter rose around them. They reminded Bill of little children misbehaving behind their parents' backs.

Bill shook his head and muttered, 'I thought I had my secrets, but this is something else.'

'What secrets have you got then, Bill?' she asked as she turned to look at him in alarm.

'Only a secret stash of pork scratchings in my shed.' He laughed.

The guys laughed and tossed him over a bag.

'I don't have secrets,' he lied as he thought about Toby. What on earth would she think if she found that one out, but if they were going to get married, maybe she should be told. 'At least nothing that would compare to this kind of secret. It's a pretty big whopper to keep from the missus,' he added.

'What would they say if your wives ever found out?'

'They aren't likely to. We've travelled all the way down from the Midlands. We don't want to risk bumping into anyone we know.'

'Sod's law you will, mate,' Bill interjected. Secrets always had a way of surfacing.

Bill wanted to get away, these men and the conversation were making him feel very uncomfortable, but Patsy was chatting and looked as if she was enjoying herself. He excused himself and nipped to the gents, hoping by the time he returned she'd be ready to head upstairs to get changed for the evening. He couldn't wait to leave the hotel. Then a sudden thought struck. He'd have to face this lot over breakfast. He was already starting to feel queasy at the prospect.

Bill was just finishing in the gents and about to zip his trousers when someone pinched his bottom. 'Keep your filthy grubby mitts to yourself,' he shouted but didn't see the culprit, just a flash of pink, and by the time he'd turned round, they were gone.

He managed to coax Patsy away and they headed upstairs in the lift. She was in a giggly mood, all merry as if she'd been drinking, but he was still incensed by what had happened in the loo. 'They're a bunch of bum bandits,' he said, all annoyed.

'Don't be silly, Bill, you can be so old-fashioned at times, it's just a bit of harmless fun.' The comment stung, he'd never considered himself old-fashioned.

'You wouldn't be saying that if you'd seen what happened in the men's loo. One of them touched me up. I had my bum pinched.'

Patsy roared with laughter. 'Sorry, I shouldn't laugh.' Tears were pouring down her face.

'At least someone finds it funny. It still stings,' he said, huffily rubbing his bum.

As he trailed after her down the corridor to their room, she was still making jokes and taking the mickey.

It hadn't been a great start to the evening, and for the first time that day, he wondered if he should leave the proposal to another time. But this was what the weekend was about. That's what he'd planned to do. And so with that thought, he vowed to make an extra special effort. He'd brought a jacket and tie with him and a smart pair of trousers.

'You look rather dapper tonight,' Patsy said as they emerged back into the corridor after a shower and change. 'Is it a special occasion I don't know about?' she asked with a cheeky grin.

'No, no, I like to make the effort and your new frock looks nice, love.' He linked arms and they set off, managing to sneak out without being drawn into another conversation with the cross-dressers.

Athens was quiet for a Friday evening, and they were shown to a table near the window. A Greek family were gathered around a large table in the centre, filling the air with laughter and chatter. They'd even brought their little children, not a good sign, Bill thought as he spied a toddler in a highchair. The waiter appeared to know the family as he was chatting to them in what Bill assumed was Greek.

They looked at the menu, ordering wine before deciding on lamb kleftiko and beef stifado.

'Will that make you stifado?' Patsy asked Bill with a cheeky glint in her eye, reaching under the table and giving his knee a quick rub. This wasn't the Patsy he'd known years ago when she was married to Arty. When had she developed this naughty streak?

He'd been considering the best time to pop the question: before the meal or during? But her cheeky comment had taken his mind in a different direction and as with the appearance of maggots on the pier, the moment was again lost.

'We get on well, don't we?' he asked halfway through the meal, gathering courage, suitably oiled with wine and fuel in his belly.

'It's been such a lovely day, thank you for my surprise weekend away.' She reached for his hands, winding her fingers through his like a network of vines. Her eyes sparkled under the dim lighting, and he felt a dart of desire shoot through him.

'I wanted to do something special, you deserve it, Patsy. You've made me a very happy man this past year and I hope I have you.'

'You certainly have, Bill. When I think of the dark place I was in that day we met at the cemetery. I've come a long way since then. I never imagined I'd meet someone after my Arty passed. The thought of being on my own for the rest of my life was a daunting prospect. You've put the spring back in my step.' A smile lifted the corners of her mouth.

'I'm not just a passing fancy then?' he teased.

'Are you heck.' She forked her lamb. She was dainty in every sense—how she ate, her figure, and the way she moved. He saw her on stage as a ballerina in *Nutcracker*.

'That's a relief.' He smiled and made a dramatic sweep of his forehead with his arm.

In that moment, something seemed to shimmer and stretch between them. He felt his skin prickle.

This was the moment he'd been waiting for, but the stage wasn't set. God, he was nervous.

At the exact moment he was about to open his mouth and utter those four words, the baby in the highchair sitting at the central table decided to throw a tantrum. And as if things couldn't get any worse, the restaurant's speaker on the wall above them crackled and emitted a piercing high-pitched noise just before the music abruptly switched.

They looked at each other. 'Wonder what that was all about?' Patsy said with a frown.

'Maybe an alien was trying to speak to us through the PA system.' He laughed but thought what a bad omen it was.

'Bill.' She looked at him with a serious expression tinged with sadness. There was a distinct shift in her mood, as if she'd been brooding.

'Do you mind if we eat up and go? I like it in here, but all these pictures of Greece are reminding me of a holiday I had with Arty. He loved the Greek Islands. We both did.' She pushed her chair back; she'd not even finished her meal. It was such a change of heart from a few minutes earlier.

Her words, taking him by surprise, felt raw, a private confession he'd rather she'd kept to herself because this evening was supposed to be about them, not her past. He realised then that he could never measure up to the connection she'd had with Arty; their marriage had spanned many years. They had children together and shared countless experiences, creating a wealth of memories. He couldn't match that, not at this time in his life.

'Of course, love,' he said softly. 'Let's go somewhere else where we can feel more comfortable.' He hoped a change of scene would restore her spirits.

'Why don't we take a stroll? We've done enough sitting

this evening.' Her statement carried a touch of criticism, but he chose to overlook it.

Outside, they wandered down Terminus Road, turning right along the fairy-lit seafront and pausing to enjoy the music from a tribute band performing at the magnificent landmark along the front, the Art Deco bandstand. They were playing all the greats and the audience were interacting well. It was a tremendous atmosphere, and suddenly Bill realised he should have booked tickets. It was a perfect evening for sitting outside, being so lovely and warm. They could even have taken a blanket in case it got chilly. And there was room for a dance on the lower tier.

It was dark and they continued their walk up the steep incline towards the district of Meads, the cliffs looming ahead like ancient giants watching over the shore, the inky sea to their left. The sea was still, eerily so. A vast millpond that merged with the darkening sky. They picked up a bit of speed as if they both needed to work off energy. Stopping near a green, they considered walking down the narrow pathway through the bushes that was part of an intricate network that led down to the shore.

Bill gasped and squeezed Patsy's hand, suddenly noticing the full moon in all its glory, a bright orb in the sky, high tonight, edging the tops of the waves with silver and making a glowing pathway across the sea that danced with every ripple. It was a beautiful sight and perfectly framed between two tamarisk trees.

This was the moment he'd been waiting for.

He looked up at her, the moonlight shimmering across her face. There were marks of wear and tear on her face, a faint hollowing of the cheeks that once were blooming and firm, and despite the passing years, she glowed with a natural beauty. They were so close now, he could see the soft beating in her neck, the gleam of her teeth between her parted lips.

He took her hands. 'Marry me, Patsy.'

There was a moment's hesitation, too long, and he knew the answer before she went to speak. His timing as usual was wrong, her comment in the restaurant had told him that Arty was on her mind. He was shocked suddenly by his own insensitivity.

'You've taken me by surprise, Bill, I never thought about marrying again. I don't know what to say.' The breeze was picking up and lifted strands of her hair.

'Maybe best not to say anything. I'm sorry, I shouldn't have asked,' he said flatly.

He looked away embarrassed, but she grabbed his arm and forced him to look at her. 'I'm flattered, Bill, I really am, it's not a yes or a no, I just need time to think, to consider.'

'That's all right then.' Her words lifted him. 'I'm sorry if I shocked you, I've been thinking about asking you for a while. We could be so happy, Patsy, I just know we could, don't we deserve some happiness?'

Instinctively they turned to head back down the hill.

'Wouldn't this be a nice place to live, Patsy?' he asked.

She stopped and looked at him with a puzzled expression. 'Is that why you brought me down here, because you want us to live here?'

He shrugged. 'I could think of worse places. There's nothing holding us back. There are trains to London, it's lovely here and we'd be by the sea.'

'What's wrong with Blackpool? It's by the sea too. The beach is much nicer. All that sand, it goes out for miles. And the donkeys, I'd miss the donkeys. I don't like pebbles.'

'You've got to admit, Blackpool's a dump now compared to what it used to be. The seafront is very bland and flat, not like here with its lovely views and magical cliffs. I can imagine us walking along the front every morning. How relaxing it would be.'

'You're a snob, Bill.' She laughed. 'What's happened to your northern roots? You're not a southerner, you don't belong down here, you should move back to Blackpool and pick up where you left off. We'd have a grand life.'

'But somewhere like this would be a fresh start, untainted by memories, we can make our own life.'

'It's okay here,' she said, not sounding at all convinced. 'But too big an upheaval. My kids are up north and all my friends. You can't replace good friends.'

'Your kids drive.' If her love for him was deep enough, would she make the move? But it worked both ways. Did he love her enough to return to the north? Or was their decision weighted more by life's practicalities than by love itself?

'Would they bother though? I doubt it. And you're forgetting, I'm a grandma now.'

'You can still see them.'

'They grow up too fast, I'd miss out on big milestones, and I'd miss them terribly.'

The conversation felt suddenly futile. Would they ever agree where to live, or were they fated to travel the motorway for the rest of their lives?

23

Bill lay awake, unable to sleep. Usually he slept like the proverbial log, but tonight he lay awake chewing the cud. So many questions and dilemmas were crashing through his mind. Was he wrong to expect her to move down south, up sticks and leave behind everything she'd ever known? He'd casually suggested moving to Eastbourne, because it felt right. It was lovely here and he could see them building a life together, settling into retirement when the time came, making new friends, exploring new hobbies like bowling, or even sailing, though maybe that was a bit ambitious.

Deep down, he realised he wasn't being fair. He'd dismissed everything that was important to her and since he was the one proposing a future with her, it was his call to move up north. She was right, he could just pick up his old life again.

He drifted to sleep and in the morning the rain woke him, pattering against the sash windows, and he could hear the rhythmic swoosh of passing cars splashing in puddles outside.

The rain had broken the spell of Eastbourne, a reminder that while the sun painted a picture of perfect living, the reality was less inviting.

He hauled himself out of bed, and while waiting for the kettle to boil to make them tea, he peered at himself in the mirror. His pyjamas were rumpled from the creases of sleep, his belly was so big he looked as if he was about to give birth, and his chin and chops had sprouted their morning whiskers.

The state of me. No wonder she's turned me down.

She stirred, muttering a sleepy good morning as she propped herself up on her elbow, and beckoned him back to bed with a flirty glance.

I can't be that bad if she's inviting me back to bed!

'You're not getting up already,' she said. 'I want a cuddle first.'

They lay for a while in a warm embrace before she kissed him on his forehead and pulled away. 'I've been thinking about last night, our conversation. In fact, I've thought of nothing else all night.'

He sat up, positioning a pillow behind his head. 'I'm sorry, I shouldn't have put you on the spot like that. I don't know what I was thinking, expecting you to move down here. Your life's up there.'

'And I wasn't appreciating how much your life has moved on. You're settled down here and you've got Toby and Sue to think of now. I admire that in you, Bill, I know you want to be around for them. You're a good dad. And to be fair, they will need you to be close by.'

'I've spent the best part of my life worrying about that boy, it's time to enjoy ourselves in the time we have left.'

'He's *your* son, and he may be an adult now, but he'll always need you, no matter what.'

Her words were stark and seemed to shout at him, making him prickle, and without thinking he blurted, 'Sandy and Jasper, they can help out too.'

She looked at him, baffled.

He coughed and spluttered. He'd have to be careful what he said.

'I'm sure they're helpful, but at the end of the day, they're just friends.'

'Yeah, but they're younger, they can cope better than me.'

'Bill, you can't put the responsibility of Toby onto friends, that isn't right at all. They've got little Angela to think of.'

'They're happy to help.' How had the conversation taken this path?

'I'm sure they are, they're just do-gooders,' she said, rattling on. 'I've come across that type before, it makes them feel better to help those less fortunate than themselves.' She let out a mirthless laugh. 'It paves their way through the Pearly Gates when the time comes,' she added with a wink.

Her thoughts were rankling with him, but he managed to restrain himself from saying something he'd later regret. 'They care about Toby,' he said simply.

'I can see that,' she trilled. 'Maybe too much.'

He shrugged. 'You can never care too much. Everyone deserves love.'

'I can see how doting Sandy is on Toby, I saw it in her eyes at the wedding. She looked very proud of him and Jasper's wonderful to him. He got that job because Jasper pulled a few strings. But you mustn't rely on them and take advantage, that's all I'm saying.'

If she knew the truth, she wouldn't be saying all this.

Sometimes the secret was too oppressive to bear. Why

were they still living a life shrouded in secrecy after all this time?

If he was going to marry Patsy, there must be no skeletons in the closet, he knew that she deserved to know the truth. If he kept this from her and it came out, it could destroy their relationship. Besides, Toby's life had moved on significantly, it wasn't as if it would make any difference now but could potentially impact on Toby and Sue's future.

And then it occurred to him--returning to Blackpool, where Toby was born might not be the wisest decision. There were still people he knew up there from back then and they might start asking probing questions.

24

As Claudia and Heidi touched down in Germany, a whirlwind of thoughts raced through Claudia's mind. Jasper's offer to share the story of Heidi's birth loomed large, but the timing felt all wrong. She also worried about the potential fallout that might result. The last thing she wanted was to jeopardise Heidi's chances of reuniting with her parents. Keeping away from the press felt safer and simpler, not just for Heidi, but for herself too. And for Heidi's parents. If the Stasi were to find out, there might be implications for them also. Yet she was curious as to how Jasper might write their story, and a flicker of hope sparked––perhaps the publicity could help find her parents. She just didn't know, but was she prepared to take that risk?

That evening as she got ready for bed, she took out her diary from her bedside cabinet and began to read.

10TH SEPTEMBER 1961
I'm running late for work today, dashing through the hospital corridors with my heart pounding in my chest. Baby Heidi is

leaving—she's being sent to an orphanage. It's been arranged and there's nothing I can do to stop it happening. It's just dreadful and heart-breaking.

I've read stories and heard rumours about Verschickungskinder *and the emotional impact on children of being separated from their families. I'm extremely worried, I've been awake all night, I don't want Heidi to be sent to Möwennest. She's not sick, she doesn't need treatment. Please, God, find her parents before it's too late.*

As I step into the ward, the oppressive heat envelops me. I glance around to find the doctor in a flap, barking orders at the ambulance crew. There's a sense of urgency hanging thick in the air, and I know they have come to collect Heidi.

He stops talking and looks at me as if I've come to rescue him from a crisis. 'There you are. The crew are overbooked today, you're going to have to take Heidi to Möwennest, they're expecting her this morning.'

The next minutes disappear in a whirl as I prepare Heidi for the journey by bus across the city. I don't even notice the humming strip light winking overhead, where the bulbs need replacing. Or the other babies crying for milk and attention. My focus is solely on Heidi. Poor mite, this scrap of a baby whose future is so uncertain, now alone in the world. I lift her from her cot. She's tiny, innocent, just a featherless bundle. I wrap a blue blanket around her.

The journey by bus takes me an hour and in this brief time, as I look at her soft skin, pink cheeks, and downy head, she ignites the flame of maternal love. My eyes fill with tears. I don't want to part from this small and helpless child. She needs me. I need her.

I glance out of the dirty windows and watch Berlin dissolve into a succession of warehouses and bland suburbs melting into green fields that stretch out in every direction.

I get off the bus and walk along the main road of the small village, past houses adorned with climbing roses that are starting to wilt, their leaves crisping in the heat. A cat regards me lazily and a friendly dog wanders up a path to greet me.

Further along, I catch my first glimpse of Möwennest and stop in my tracks. It's an imposing building and dominates the landscape. An unsettling chill runs down my spine. An oppressive heaviness hangs in the air filling me with dread, and I slow my pace feeling an overwhelming urge to protect Heidi, fearing the very shadows of this grim place could swallow her whole.

As I walk past the final house before the village gives way to open fields, I hear someone cough and glance over a wall to see an elderly man struggling to his feet, his knees cracking like twigs. He has a trowel in one hand and a muddy bulb in the other.

'Guten morgen, meine Dame,' he says as he raises his cap.

I pause to talk to this stranger because right in this moment I'll do anything to postpone the inevitable. As I've passed the village, he's curious to know where I'm heading, warning me there's no pavement further along the road.

We glance towards Möwennest and he shakes his head. 'It's no place for a baby.' His expression darkens and there's a nervous tic around his jaw.

If I felt uneasy before, I'm even more so now. Instinctively I hold the baby tight to my chest. 'Why do you say that?'

'My late wife worked there as a cleaner. She saw the most shocking things. Those doctors, they were never meant to walk free.' His voice lowers to a whisper, but I catch his words. 'A monster, he should be locked up and the key thrown away.'

A nervous sensation travels across the back of my neck like the whisper of a ghost. 'What sort of things?' I'm not sure I want to know, but I have to ask.

His demeanour softens. 'Would you like to come in for a few minutes? It would be nice to have company. The house gets lonely. Would you like coffee? I rarely get visitors these days, you'll have to take me as you find me.'

I nod and take a deep breath. 'Thank you, that would be nice.'

He turns and heads towards the door, kicking off his boots. I follow him into his tiny front room where he takes off his gardening gloves and goes into the kitchen at the back. As I wait for him to make coffee, my mind is in turmoil. If the orphanage is as bad as he says, how can I leave Heidi there?

He sets the cups down on the table before perching on a wooden chair. After taking a sip of his coffee, he wastes no time as he begins to warn me about what the orphanage is really like.

He leans forward and his chair squeaks. 'When it opened in the 1930s it was a holiday home for handicapped children, a place where they were sent to give their parents respite. Except that many of them didn't end up going home. And many more were rounded up, hunted down and brought to places like Möwennest.' He rubs the grey scruff around his jawline and pauses.

'The thing I remember the most were the dark clouds, the sweet cloying smell that caught in my breath. You couldn't go outside on days like that.'

In the room's silence, one word hangs heavy, unspoken between us.

Aktion T4.

He looks at me, his brows knitting. 'After the war, the place was shut down. I'm sure you know what they did to handicapped children, but it wasn't long before that place was up and running again, as a children's home, for kiddies whose parents had died in the war.'

'The war seems a long time ago now, the country's changed,' I say brightly, trying to be optimistic.

He raises his eyes and gloom stares back at me. 'The regime was forcibly overthrown, but its ethos and ideas have endured.' He stands and looks out of the side window over the fields and towards Möwennest. 'People don't change, not in rural places like this. Old ways persist.' He gives me a long hard stare. His chin trembles. 'Even after all this time.'

His words unsettle me.

He points a bony finger towards Möwennest. 'That place practises extreme discipline and corporal punishment. Don't send the child there. I'm warning you.'

'What did your wife see?'

'All sorts of things. It wasn't very long ago either. Children are separated from their siblings, they get punished for just talking, tied to their beds, thrown into solitary confinement, forced to eat their own vomit. I could go on but it's too horrific.'

'I'm sorry, I've brought it all back to you.'

Heidi stirs and feeling warm in my arms, I remove the blanket. Until now he doesn't know she is disabled. When he sees her impairment, he gasps and recoils in shock.

'You didn't say the child was deformed. You mustn't leave her there. I beg of you.' He reaches out in desperation, his bony fingers clawing my hand.

I blink and turn away. I must put on my professional hat and keep my emotions under wrap. 'I have to see it for myself, she's not my baby. I'm just following instructions.' I hastily get up and thank him for the coffee.

He watches me from his window as I continue along the path until it ends abruptly, leaving me to walk along the roadside, my arm brushing against the straggly hedgerow for the rest of my journey.

Drawing closer, I notice the windows of Möwennest have bars and the walls are covered in black mould patches and lots of moss. I have the sense that the shadows of our ugly past are spilling out through the walls of the house.

The garden has been overtaken by plants, weeds mostly. Nature is encroaching and reclaiming the territory. The place looks like a kind of prison, built sometime in the last century, of Gothic appearance with ugly turrets and scary gargoyles, not somewhere where children could play freely and be happy. By the time I arrive at the rusty metal gate, it feels as if I'm about to step into one of those old horror movies. I imagine Max Schreck coming out to greet me and I shudder at the thought. As I walk up the path towards the front door, I suddenly notice a row of children, identically dressed in shabby white gowns, standing at the window of one of the downstairs rooms. I stop in my tracks. I wave but nobody waves back. They look malnourished and devoid of happiness, there's not a hint of a smile on their faces.

I should turn back. I can't leave Heidi in this place. But she isn't my responsibility. I was asked to bring her here. I'm just doing my job.

I don't have to leave her, not if it's unsuitable. I'll meet the staff. My gut will guide me.

Ivy scrambles up around the arch of the front door and I head up the stone steps and give the large rusty knocker a hard rap. There's no answer on my first knock, but I can hear shouting coming from inside. Leaning towards the door, I strain to listen. There's a shriek. More shouting. Silence. I knock again. This time it's answered.

When I lock eyes with the man standing before me, my breath catches in my throat and for a moment I cannot speak.

I'm staring into the face of a killer.

Out of uniform, dressed in sweater and slacks, I might not have recognised him—but there's no hiding who this odious man is. He's someone I'll never forget. He might look different with his hair no longer black and slicked back, but it's him.

'I hoped I'd never see you again.' I'm all breathless. 'You're running a children's home.' I'm so shocked my mind goes blank.

'I'm sorry, have we met before?' His voice cuts right through me like a knife. It's so familiar, it's jarring and conjures up every memory I have of those terrible times.

How could he have survived those years unscathed? He shouldn't be free. Was he tried and his case dropped?

People kept their mouths shut because there was no other way, and immediately yesterday became history. Some disappeared, others were caught, and a few made their return, undetected.

A chilling certainty floods through me. I can't leave Heidi here. I turn and flee, desperate to escape as fast as my legs can carry me.

The old man was right, he really is a monster.

The memory of being forced to work with that man will haunt with me forever.

25

Toby and Sue arrived back from Florida in a taxi. They got out and the driver helped them in, carrying their luggage and opening the doors for them.

Toby had agreed to move into Sue's flat in Pinewood Court until they were able to find a bigger place. He knew what he was in for, and had mentally prepared himself, but as soon as they were inside, his heart sank as he glanced round, finding it hard to imagine living here. What had he been thinking when he'd agreed to this? Why had they rushed into getting married? There was hardly any room to swing a cat and where was he going to work? He spent half the week working from home, he needed his space. They were going to get in each other's way.

This isn't a great start to married life.

And to make matters worse, one side of the lounge was piled with unopened wedding presents that Bill had dropped off while they'd been away.

He was especially dreading the presence of creepy

Norman. He hoped they could move soon, but he knew how attached Sue was to her flat.

After she had graduated from Herewood College in Coventry, Sue moved into an apartment complex in Essex specially designed for individuals with disabilities, that aimed to prepare them for independent living. It was called Dolphin Court and was built and managed by John Groom Disabled Association and financed through donations and gifts. It was a stepping stone to her future, and she was very lucky to have been offered this rare opportunity. There were fifteen self-contained flats and a round-the-clock emergency call system. Personal care staff were available and lived on site. Some disabled residents lived there for years and others stayed for a short time to develop the skills and confidence needed to live in the community. Each resident underwent an assessment to determine their needs. It was a step on the road to independent living, a transition from residential care to living in the community. Dolphin Court helped her confidence and because much of the equipment in the flat had been designed for her, she found that she could do things quicker, like cooking and preparing food but some things still took longer and were a struggle.

When she took the job at St Bede's, Sue moved into her current flat in Pinewood Court. She was fortunate. Her flat was on the ground floor, but there was one poor disabled man who lived on the top floor. It was ridiculous that the council had allocated him a top-floor apartment when he used a wheelchair. Toby couldn't understand the logic, but apparently his previous flat was a dump and had a damp problem which had given him asthma. It wasn't at all practical to be on the top floor though and he had to be carried up and down the stairs like a sack of potatoes. He'd told Sue the whole ordeal was really getting him down and he was on yet another waiting list to be rehoused.

Sue's flat had wide access to each room. The kitchen worktops and sink were low as were all the lighting switches throughout the flat.

It was all very well staying the odd night, but Toby now realised the limitations. There was only one parking space. He'd left his car back at Bill's because it was easier.

He glanced round at the poky lounge. Where was he going to put all his stuff?

This isn't going to work.

'Where can I put my clothes?' he asked her as he headed into the bedroom. Bill had dropped off boxes containing his belongings while they'd been in Florida.

'I haven't thought about that.' She scratched her head. He couldn't believe she hadn't considered this, but they hadn't discussed it. 'There's a little bit of wardrobe you can have.'

He opened the wardrobe and peered inside. It was crammed full.

Bloody women and their clothes.

'It doesn't seem fair you want me to pay half the bills if I'm not even getting half the space.'

'I've still got to heat the place and you'll be using water. I assume you're going to want a bath and to eat off clean plates?' she said sarcastically.

'I suppose.' He felt mean and knew he'd take a different attitude if it was their home.

'What's in this other wardrobe?' He opened the doors of the cupboard on the other side of the room. 'Whose is all this?'

'Oh, that's Norman's stuff. He's got no space. It's his dad's, he's not had time to sort it.'

'That's ridiculous, it'll have to go. Sorry, but I need the space.'

'What will I say to Norman? He's been really good to me. He's still getting over his dad's death.'

'Sod Norman.'

'We've only been married five minutes and already we're bickering.'

He spun round to face her. 'You're putting him first, like you always do. I'm your husband now, I'm the most important person. I might as well go back home, the way you're treating me.'

He headed into the hallway. 'Can we reorganise your spare room? It's not as if it's being used for much. Maybe we could ask Dad if he can build some cupboards.'

'I don't want cupboards all over the place. I use that room for storing my spare wheelchairs.'

He peered into the room. There were three wheelchairs huddled together, like three weary travellers sharing a whispered conversation. And in a corner, several pairs of her prosthetic legs were haphazardly stacked.

'Why did the legs get sent to the corner?' He laughed, trying to make light of the frustrating situation he found himself in.

'Because they couldn't stand the drama anymore,' she quipped.

'You could form a dancing troupe with that lot. Do you really need three wheelchairs? It is a tad excessive, hon.'

'I'm just wheeling and dealing with extra back-up plans.' She laughed.

'Very funny, but seriously, I've never seen you use any of these. And all these legs. At the wedding, you were adamant it was the last time you'd wear them.'

'All the wheelchairs get used,' she snapped defensively.

'They're spares. One is for outdoors, the other indoors and the one by the window is years old but it still works.'

'You don't have three cars, so why three wheelchairs?'

'In case one breaks down.'

'What's likely to go wrong? You can get Dad to fix it.'

'It could take days to fix, in the meantime, what am I supposed to do? How would I get around?'

He went into the kitchen to make coffee, stopping in his tracks as he glanced round, immediately reminded of the low worktops and sink fitted specifically for her needs. He'd been too hasty, agreeing to move in. But he'd been in love, and when you're in love, he realised, it was all too easy to agree to anything.

The place was adapted for her needs, and he had no idea how he was going to cope. He felt a growing sense of despair as he contemplated the hurdles that lay ahead. He couldn't help but wonder if married life was this daunting for everyone as he grappled with all of these challenges.

'I've looked in the fridge, we need milk and bread, I'll nip out then.'

He opened the door to be confronted by Norman standing there holding a bag. 'Hi, Tobes, I thought you might need a few bits. To save you going out, I've popped into the Co-op. Did you have a nice holiday?'

Sue came up behind him. 'Hi, Norman, come in.' Then she turned to Toby, saying, 'come on, out the way, let him in.'

Bloody hell, we've only been back five minutes and that man is here. That seals it, we've got to move.

26

It was now October and Jasper was facing significant challenges while trying to cover the AIDS epidemic, largely due to the fear and stigma surrounding the disease. It was not just a health crisis, it was shrouded in taboo, and he faced immense obstacles in his efforts to shed light on the crisis. It weighed heavily on him, knowing how much it mattered to Sam, but he was determined not to let him down. So much depended on this piece, and Jasper was anxious about writing anything that might upset Sam.

When Sam asked him what he'd managed to dig up and how he was getting on, he had to admit that he was finding it difficult.

'It's not been easy,' he said. 'You can't get close to patients. The hospitals have strict protocols to stop the spread of the virus and protect the patients' privacy. I spoke to one poor chap, but it didn't feel very personal, I had to communicate through a porthole. It's like Fort Knox. It makes genuine, heartfelt storytelling almost impossible.'

Sam sighed and puffed at his cigar.

'I'm struggling, mate.' He swept his fingers through his

thinning hair. 'And it doesn't help knowing how important this is to you. I'm having to navigate a landscape rife with prejudice and bigotry. I've come across some awful attitudes. "They deserve it, they're gay, they're getting their comeuppance," and "it's not fair, all this money to support people with AIDS, they're a drain, what about heart disease and cancer, where's the money for those illnesses?" You'd think we were dealing with the plague. We need to tread carefully. We're trying to bring attention to a pressing public health issue, all the while grappling with society's fears. There's word the government are going to roll out an awareness campaign so they must be taking it seriously. Numbers seemed to be going through the roof, which is rather concerning.'

'It's no problem, Jasper, I can get another journo to cover it.' He twiddled his moustache and looked thoughtful. 'There's something happening up in Manchester and I know you used to work up there, you know the area. It's not a big story, I doubt it will make the headlines, there are too many other things going on, but it's something that might interest you—and the lad. Some disabled people are protesting outside Manchester Town Hall because the only access is up a set of steps.'

Jasper sat up, all ears. *How interesting.*

There had been protests by disabled groups in America in recent years, but over here, it was more unusual for the disabled to protest, although around the country there were isolated incidences of people linking up and sharing ideas. His mind was firing with a flurry of thoughts. This could be a recurring theme in the coming years; it was clear that Thatcher's government were failing millions of disabled people.

How much more can people take?

This modest protest could very well be a catalyst for broader action nationwide, potentially igniting real change for disabled individuals. It suddenly felt essential they cover the story.

The following morning, Jasper and Toby set out on their journey to Manchester, catching the fast train from London Euston. The train sped along the tracks and as they listened to the rhythmic clatter of the wheels on metal hurtling through the countryside, they relaxed back in their seats and took the opportunity to catch up. They hadn't seen much of each other since the honeymoon.

''Ere, lad, do you realise this is the first time we've managed to get some time for ourselves, a boys' day out. So, how are you finding the struggles of married life? Is it everything you thought it would be?' Jasper asked after the conductor had checked their tickets.

'No, Dad, you could have told me I'd be under the thumb from day one with no time to myself and it's definitely no picnic in the park.'

Jasper stared at him with a grin.

'What is it?'

'Toby lad, do you realise, that's the first time you've called me Dad.'

'Blimey, I must be slipping.' He sniggered.

He uncrossed his legs and leaned forward. 'What are you finding so challenging?'

Toby paused as if reflecting before responding. 'Living on my own as a disabled person was one thing, but living together with someone who is also disabled is very hard.' This was the first time he'd confessed this to anyone, and it felt like a burden lifted off his shoulders. He sighed. 'You literally have no idea how difficult it all is. Everything's in the wrong place. The flat's been adapted for her, not me.

Back at home, Bill set up my space to suit me and I didn't really appreciate it till I moved out. She snores, keeps me awake, flings her arms all over the place. Those arms, they're so strong. And she accuses me of flinging my legs around. I feel like a slave. "Toby can you get this, do that". I didn't know I'd signed up for this. I get told off for waking her up when I get home after working late and when it's the time of month, she's almost impossible to live with. And the worst bit, I can't bugger off home when I've had enough.' He let out a mirthless laugh. 'Was it like this for you?'

'We did have a fractious start to our relationship but when you love each other you get through. I've become very deaf over the period I've been married. They're good at nagging and shopping. Let them get on with it.'

'We just need to move. We need a place built for us.' Now that he had started, he was on a roll. 'I'm fed up with the carer. She treats the place like it's her own. She's always sitting around talking long after her shift ends and there are the little irritating things she does, like not drawing the curtains properly or not wiping the draining board and she's always putting things back in the wrong place. I'm used to order, it's the only way I can cope. I'm sure she does it just to make my life more difficult.'

Toby stared out of the window at the fields and hamlets rushing by and remembered how difficult it had been without a carer in America. He wouldn't want to face that situation again, yet having a carer day-to-day also presented its challenges. It was like a double-edged sword.

He turned back to Jasper. 'And then there's that creep next door, Norman. I call him Stormy Normy, the way he steams in, always sticking his nose in. "Do you need anything, Sue?" I want to bop him on the nose but he's good for running errands.' He sighed. 'I shouldn't be too ungrateful, we need him. Trouble is, every time we need him, he comes running. The other day I dropped something in the kitchen, and he's there. He probably hears us having nookie. Surprised he doesn't crash through into the bedroom when he hears Sue in the height of pleasure.'

'Toby.' Jasper winced. 'Spare me the details, lad. How's Sue coping? What does she think?'

'She's always moaning. Maybe we should have lived together first. She's always telling me to put the toilet seat down, and says I leave things on the floor, and they get in the way of her wheelchair.' He sighed. 'I shouldn't say this, but sometimes it's frustrating being married to a wheelchair user. We can't just be spontaneous. Everything has to be planned. Take today, we wouldn't be sitting in this carriage. We can't have a day out in London––not easily anyway. We'd be in the cold, noisy guard's van like parcels. And we have to map our life around the carer because she comes at precise times. And sometimes we tell Gill not to come and I help Sue instead, but I struggle, and I can never do anything right. "My pillows aren't right", "No, not like this, like that". "Don't you ever listen to me? You're in your own world". Jasper, I can't do a thing right. I should look forward to coming home in the evenings, she always used to be so chatty and bubbly, but all she wants to do is watch soaps. *Coronation Street* one night, *EastEnders* the next. And even *Crossroads*, for God's sake. I never knew she was such a telly addict. We always used to talk about the books we'd read, but I can't remember the last time she read a book.' The more he ranted, the more aware he was of how unhappy he'd become. Marrying her wasn't supposed to be like this.

'The honeymoon period is definitely over then?' Jasper laughed.

Toby raised his eyebrows. 'Thank God for work. If I was

at home all day, she'd drive me mad. She's forever whinging about her job. I keep telling her to stop complaining and do something about it.'

'That's not so easy though, finding a new job, especially in her circumstances.'

'I know, tell me about it. When you're disabled there aren't so many choices.'

Jasper pulled a tenner from his pocket and handed it to Toby. 'Here, son, treat yourselves. Take her out for a nice meal. Sounds as if you both need a night out. Time to focus on each other again.'

'You sure? That's really nice of you.'

With so much to chat about, the journey passed quickly. The train thundered through tunnels and carved its way through countryside. They caught glimpses of farms and gardens, fields of cattle and sheep, canals, and rivers. Narrowboats pootling along. And then slowly the cityscape came into view. As they approached Manchester Piccadilly, there was a grinding of metal on metal as the train slowed.

It was a sixteen-minute walk from Manchester Piccadilly to the town hall. As they rounded the corner, the iconic Victorian gothic building with its impressive clock came into view. Its grand façade featured intricate stone carvings and arched windows. It had a magnificent entrance, but it was the stone steps leading up to it that the protestors were unhappy about. The sight of the building always took Jasper's breath away, for he appreciated grand architecture, but today he was focused on the commotion around it—the traffic was stalled, a few police officers were present, and there was a lot of shouting. A group of around twenty disabled people had gathered around the foot of the steps with placards and they were chanting slogans. Jasper quickly took in the scene from a distance before crossing the busy road. A few skinheads were jeering at the police officers, and he wondered if they were local youth, complaining about being on the dole.

'What's all this about? I thought it was a disabled protest,' Toby said.

'Looks like the usual culprits of these events are here. I'm not sure if their presence is a hindrance or a help.' He observed the far-left brandishing signs with slogans such as 'Tories Out' and 'The system is broken, fight for revolution,' and there were others holding anti-apartheid placards.

Jasper headed across the road with determination, eager to engage with the protesters.

'Come on, lad, we need to find out what's going on.'

The anti-apartheid group quickly realised they were journalists and bounded over, eager to share their views and have their voices heard. Toby got swept up in the crowd, and stood listening to their passionate outburst, while Jasper remained focused and made a beeline for the disabled group.

'I'm Jasper, a London journalist. Can I ask you about your reasons for being here today. Why are you demonstrating?'

'Of course, we need all the media coverage we can get,' a woman on crutches said, beaming at him. 'Unfortunately, I've got a hospital appointment in a bit so I can't stay, but Mick and Jan here will fill you in.'

Jasper looked down at Mick and Jan, both in wheelchairs. 'We want better access. It's frustrating, this is such an important building, but there's no way we can enter it. We need level access. Every entrance has steps and inside there's a tiny lift, no accessible toilets, no hearing aid induction loops, no Braille signage.'

'We want full access to the corridors of power,' a protester behind him shouted.

'And what have you been told by Manchester City Council? How are they responding?'

'They say it's not possible because it's a listed building.'

'It's a shit response,' said a lady in a wheelchair nearby in an angry voice. 'It means we can't go to any public meetings.' She shouted out, 'Nothing about us without us.' Jasper had heard this slogan before, it was a rallying cry.

While Jasper talked with the protesters, people streamed past or entered the building. It was a busy part of the city with people going about their day.

He turned round in shock to hear a young man shouting at the protesters. 'You shouldn't be allowed out, you lot belong in an institution.'

'You can see what we're up against,' Jan said to Jasper as she glared angrily at the young man. 'The bigotry and rudeness is unbelievable.'

Jasper was now joined by Toby but while they chatted with the protesters, they continued to be interrupted by comments from people walking by. One old lady came over and took her purse out, handing Jan a tenpence piece. 'Here we are, lovey.'

Another woman wandered over beaming. 'You're incredible, all of you. God bless you.'

A group of teenage girls wandered past, and Jasper overheard them giggling as they said, 'Oh look, day out for the spazzers, there's a few Joeys here.'

A middle-aged man in a suit trotted up the steps clutching a briefcase and as he passed them, he looked all arrogant and remarked, 'Get out the way, you're blocking the entrance. If they put in ramps for you, that will be our rates going up.'

An old man wearing a flat cap came trotting by and called over, 'They should have put you lot down at birth.'

'Too right,' an old lady joined in. 'You're a drain on our health system, you don't contribute anything, you're a bunch of social spongers.'

Jasper was horrified by all the throwaway remarks people were making, and was impressed that the protesters refused to react. It showed a certain toughness. They appeared battle-worn, which made Jasper realise this was a struggle they had grown used to.

Suddenly, the old lady let out a shrill scream, and Jasper spun round to see her drenched in egg, the yolk dripping down her face and clothes. The protesters erupted with cheers, their spirits lifted by the unexpected support. Meanwhile the far-left group roared with anger, chanting fiercely in protest at the old lady's cruel words. 'We're all oppressed by the capitalist machine.'

Toby, who'd been talking to one chap in a wheelchair, went to join Jasper with an excited look on his face. 'When we're finished here, we need to get over to Anson Road.'

'What's over there then, Tobes?'

'The GM something or other.' Toby was so excited he was all flustered. He glanced down at a woman wearing a pink bobble hat who'd just parked her wheelchair beside him.

She laughed. 'It's where the GMCDP offices are. Sorry, it's a bit of a mouthful. Stands for The Greater Manchester Council of Disabled People. They'd really welcome the publicity, especially a visit from two London journalists from a national newspaper. They've just opened their first offices, it's only a Portacabin in a car park, but the work they're doing––they're a campaign group for the disabled–– it's amazing,' she gushed. 'They produce an information bulletin called *Coalition News*. It's all about linking disabled people, sharing knowledge, experience, pressuring government for change and organising protests like this one.'

'Brilliant, we can just grab a taxi and get over there. If it's not convenient, we might be able to come back another time.'

Arriving at the Portacabin a short while later, they headed up the ramp and found the door propped open. Just inside there was a woman on crutches clutching a mug of coffee, and she beamed and welcomed them in as if they were long-lost friends.

'This must be the only building in the whole country with a ramp,' Toby quipped.

'Simple changes can make all the difference, but petty-minded councils prevent it from happening.' She tutted and raised her eyebrows. 'You must be Jasper and Toby. I'm Wendy and welcome to my Wendy house.' She smiled and shook Jasper's hand and warmly took Toby's, oblivious to his disability and with none of the awkwardness that Jasper had often witnessed. 'I had a phone call to say you were on your way.'

'That was very efficient.' He pondered the logistics of the lady in the bobble hat making a call from a phone box and concluded that someone must have helped her.

'It's great you had time to pop over, we don't have any bigwigs here today like Ken Lumb or Viv Finkelstein, but this is our humble crew.' She introduced the team, pointing to each person with her stick. They looked up and greeted them with a cheerful "hello".

'It's so important for us to have space to promote ourselves.'

'You're a campaign pressure group?' Jasper asked.

'I guess we're a bit of everything. *Coalition News* is a

bulletin that answers questions on transport, access, benefits, and other issues affecting disabled people.' She reached over for the kettle and offered them tea before pointing to a couple of chairs.

After they'd sat down, she looked directly at them. 'Society makes people disabled. That's our ethos. It's society that puts barriers in place. We want those barriers removed because only then can we be an equal and valued. We have different needs. That's what this organisation is trying to achieve, in a nutshell.' She turned to the others. 'Have I summed it up correctly?'

'Pretty much,' one of the team said, glancing up from his typewriter.

'Let me give you an example,' she continued, looking at Toby. 'You have an impairment. I'm not interested in the name of your medical condition, that's not important—it's about how *your* body works. It works differently to what we might consider to be normal. But a disability is the barriers and prejudice we face. It's not our bodies or mind which disable us, it's society.'

Jasper and Toby exchanged glances. Toby was frowning, he looked confused, thoughtful, and then as if a lightbulb had switched on in his mind, clarity and excitement washed over him.

'Oh my God.' He stared at Wendy and exclaimed, 'Those words are so powerful and profound. I'd never considered it that way before.' He paused and stared at Jasper. 'I've just realised what I need to do, how I can make a difference.'

27

By the time they got back, it was very late. Jasper opened the door for Toby after dropping him back and whispered his goodbye before slipping away. He crept in, mindful of not waking Sue. From the hallway, he could hear her snoring and knew that terrible racket would prevent him from sleeping. Besides, his mind was racing with ideas. The visit to Anson Road had sparked a wave of inspiration. This social model of disability was a brilliant approach to the challenges he and thousands of others faced. He was eager to share the excitement of his day, but she wouldn't thank him for it. He would have to wait until the morning. Instead, he sank into the sofa, throwing a blanket over himself before pulling out the copy of *Coalition News*. He skimmed through it but didn't get very far. The words were swimming in front of his eyes and soon he drifted to sleep. When morning came, he was roused by the sounds of Gill bustling about in the kitchen.

Damn that woman. Back again, as always. This routine felt relentless. It was Saturday morning, neither of them had to rush to get up, yet a lie-in was impossible. He just wanted to slip into bed and kiss his wife gently awake and snuggle into the comfort of their bed. Life revolved around that bloody woman. And knowing her she'd stay a while, lingering in their space. Frustration bubbled inside as he flung out his legs dramatically, and then an uneasy thought struck him—what if she saw him sprawled out on the sofa and assumed they'd had a row? That was the last thing he wanted. He sprang up and made a poor attempt at draping the blanket around his shoulders as he made a dive into the bedroom to get his clothes for the day. Sue was sitting up in bed holding a cup of tea and it sounded as if Gill was in the kitchen washing up.

'What time did you get in?' She spoke with the tone of a mother, instantly making him feel like a guilty child.

He was fumbling around for his clothes, but the light was poor, and he was trying to hurry before Gill came back in. Already he felt stressed. 'It was late, and I didn't want to wake you.'

'Gill's asked why you slept in the lounge, God knows what she thinks.' She tutted.

'I don't care, Sue, it's my home, I can do what I like.' The truth was it didn't feel like his home, and he couldn't do what he liked.

'How was Manchester?'

'I'll tell you later after she's gone.' He nodded towards the closed door and pulled a disgruntled face. 'I'm going to nip out for a bit.' *Until she's gone*, he wanted to add. He felt deflated, the excitement had gone. He'd been so eager to share everything, but now that moment had passed.

After his walk into town, he felt better. With Gill gone, a day to themselves lay ahead—at least until she returned to help with the night-time routine. As he burst through the door, he heard laughter coming from the kitchen. His heart sank. Norman was here. What was he doing here so early? Would they ever get some time to themselves?

Sue called out and he joined them in the kitchen. The cupboard door under the sink was open, and Norman's head was inside, a spanner in hand. Toby realised he'd dropped by to fix the dripping tap, even though Norman knew that Bill could do it. Irritation settled in; the less Norman visited, the better. He loathed the man, he was like a weasel, always searching for a reason to insert himself into their lives and always making a mountain out of every molehill as well as singing his own praises like he was right now.

'What would you two do without your stormy Normy around?' he said as he fiddled with the pipes under the sink.

He straightened up and wiped his hands on a rag. He cast a patronising glance at Toby and Sue. 'I'm your lifeline, just think of all the disasters I've saved you from and I don't charge a penny.' He finished with a self-satisfied chuckle, clearly revelling in his own heroics, unable to help himself with that last little dig. Toby knew his game—trying to make them feel eternally grateful.

This could have been avoided if he'd asked his dad to come sooner, but these days Bill was busy racing up and down the M1, doing chores for Patsy and spending time with her. It was clear something was brewing between them, though Bill hadn't said.

'That should fix it now, but if the drip starts again, put a bowl under the tap to collect the water. Water's in short supply you know.' He droned on. 'I did tell that woman, whatever her name is, to bottle it and use it for the kettle, but those carers, they don't listen. You're paying her, Sue, you've got to start being a bit more assertive. Look how she's left this draining board and dishcloth.'

Jeez, anyone would think it was his flat.

'Thanks for popping over, Norm.' Toby left the kitchen and went to open the front door hoping Norman would follow him. After a couple of minutes, he realised he wasn't going to leave in a hurry, and he let the door swing shut. Norman hadn't finished his rant and now he was rooting through food cupboards.

'Shall I fetch some hot chocolate from Sainsbury's for you?' he was saying. 'And looks like you're nearly out of coffee. You don't want to get low on coffee with all the visitors that pass through this flat.' He chuckled as he held out the coffee jar, estimating how many teaspoons were left.

'It's okay,' Toby said. 'We're going to the supermarket soon to do the weekly shop.' The shop didn't have a specific scheme to help the disabled but if they weren't busy, there was usually a member of staff that was happy to assist them: picking items from the shelves, putting them onto the conveyor belt and loading up the car.

Norman looked horrified. 'How on earth are you going to manage? How do you push the trolley? That's what you've got me for. I can fetch in bits and pieces as and when. Tell me what you want for dinner, and I'll get the ingredients.'

'We're going out for dinner,' Toby stated.

'Really?' He watched Sue's eyes light up then fade. 'Where though?' she asked flatly. 'There aren't many places with disabled access or accessible toilets. There's that new restaurant, but the tables are crammed in so tight, it would be awkward manoeuvring my chair round.'

'How about the Duck and Bucket? That inglenook fireplace makes it so cosy, and they serve a great pint of beer.'

'You've got to be joking, have you not noticed the steps? The entrance is really narrow and there are several stone steps leading down to the bar area.' Toby cursed himself, realising how unobservant he was, but it had never been relevant until now.

'Isn't there a back entrance?'

'There is but it leads straight into the kitchen and there's a narrow corridor leading from there to the bar. It's totally impractical and don't even ask me about the toilet because I wouldn't know.'

'All right, well how about Puglia? You like a pizza.'

She looked at him, incredulous. 'How am I supposed to sit in one of those booths? And where would I put my wheelchair?'

At first Toby thought she was being deliberately defeatist. If she'd wanted, she could have slid into a booth. Maybe she was embarrassed to. Or perhaps she just didn't like eating out locally. They talked about every pub and restaurant in town, and each had obstacles that made it hard for disabled people. Was this how it was going to be? Their lives severely restricted every time they wanted to go out?

The excitement of a night out had vanished, leaving him feeling totally deflated. A headache was starting to form on his forehead as he figured out what to do. He didn't want to just shove Jasper's money in his pocket and waste it on something meaningless.

They'd just have to order a takeaway instead, but it was disappointing. He'd never really considered just how difficult it was to go out for a meal with someone in a wheelchair. Crazy really, considering he'd been around Sue for a number of years. He realised they'd never gone out to a restaurant. It was so unfair in this day and age when they could put a man on the moon but not a wheelchair into a restaurant.

This situation needed to change.

Perhaps I should get in touch with NASA. Maybe they can come up with something.

His mind took off like a rocket.

28

They headed into town to do the food shopping. Inside the supermarket they made their way over to the customer desk to ask if an assistant could help them shop. Some stores were more helpful than others and would assist in picking items off the shelves, packing bags and taking the shopping to the car but it wasn't a service they advertised or officially offered.

'We're quite busy at the moment, why don't you have a coffee in our café, and someone will be available very soon.'

'How long is that likely to be?' Toby asked. He hated having to wait around and waste half the day. It was an annoyance but couldn't be avoided. He sighed, resigned. At least the store was good enough to provide assistance. Not all stores did.

They grabbed coffees and Sue carefully balanced the tray on her lap as they went to the table. The discussion about tonight's outing had been all about her limitations, but right now it focused on his. He couldn't carry the tray.

As far as tonight was concerned, if they couldn't go out, they could order a takeaway and enjoy a night in. He knew it wouldn't be the same and he felt disappointed. There'd also be dishes to wash afterwards, and mess to clear up, but what was the alternative? He had to face facts––they simply didn't have the choices that able-bodied people enjoyed.

'Now you realise why it's so much easier for Norman to pick things up,' she said in a stroppy tone. 'You hate shopping as much as I do. People getting in the way, trolleys bashing into you, people being rude, kids running round and everything we want being on the highest shelf and always having to ask for help.'

'I don't want that prat doing our shopping.'

'Sometimes, Toby, you can be so pig-headed. You let pride get the better of you.'

'It feels like I'm married to you, him and the carer. I didn't realise I was taking on a big extended family. At least your mum and dad keep out of our way. I couldn't cope with them fussing round too.'

'If it wasn't for Norman and Gill, where would I be now?'

'I'm here now, I should be looking after you.'

'To be honest, you're no use without any arms, that's why we have a helper.'

He looked away out to the store where shoppers were busy pushing trolleys, feeling the cruel comment like a sting. Moments like this, he really felt inadequate. He never expected this from her, and in that moment despised her. He hated these diggy little arguments, they were becoming more frequent. How he missed his old life. When Bill was annoying, he'd retreat to his room, but he couldn't just do that, he was married and no longer a teenager.

Toby watched as Sue poured milk into their cups. 'I've been thinking.' A sudden thought had fired.

'Don't do that, it's dangerous,' she joked as she pushed the mug towards him to make it easier for him to pick up.

'Yesterday was inspiring, I wish you'd been there. And our talk about inaccessible pubs and restaurants has sparked so many thoughts.'

She took a sip of her coffee. 'I think you're starting to realise what you've taken on with me.' She laughed.

'I knew I was marrying a crazy woman.' He laughed and leaned over to kiss her. 'People assume that disabilities impose restrictions and yes, we do have to face restrictions––all sorts—but the restrictions aren't imposed by our disabilities, they're imposed by a society which discriminates against us and creates the restrictions. We get fed this idea that we have to somehow overcome our disability as if it's a personal misfortune.'

'We do have some benefits. I'm your arms, you're my legs, but I was basically telling you all this ages back. It's the social model of disability. Do you listen to a word I say?'

All his excitement vanished in an instant. He felt like a lead balloon sinking in disappointment. He'd thought this was a new theory––maybe it wasn't––but the team at Anson Road had been so inspiring in what they'd said, they made it sound as if it was.

'Maybe we've discussed it before, I can't remember.'

'Tobes, if I could put a pound on every time you say that, I'd be a millionaire. I'm sure you live in your own world half the time.'

Not wanting his spirits dampened, he ignored her and ploughed on. He had plans and they formed part of his career. 'There isn't much that doesn't affect us. Anything with steps, which is nearly everything, swing doors which are too heavy to open, public transport, London Underground. It all affects us. Just think how much easier our lives would be with better design and construction. Society is not ready for our disabilities. Can't you see, society's disabled us.

It's perfectly possible to provide ramps as well as stairs, fit doors which open easily, build underground stations with lifts, build buses with steps low enough for a person in a wheelchair. We're differently able. That's how I've always seen myself.'

The more he ranted, the more passionate he became, and he reflected again on the idea he had while returning from Manchester.

I love public speaking. I wonder if I can turn my passion into income. I could inspire government and industry and spark meaningful conversation, but how do I start?

'There's not much we can do about it. Your head is full of ideas. It's nonsense. We've just got to put up with the way things are. You can write to the council or a restaurant or wherever, they aren't going to listen. We're in the minority, we don't count, there's no point in having lofty ideas, Toby, you're just wasting your time if you think you'll get anywhere and even if you do, there won't be consistency. A dropped kerb here, a dropped kerb there. It isn't going to help, every pavement needs to have a dropped kerb. Think of the cost. The council would say, "sorry, we'd love to help, but we don't have the budget". And it's no good if one telephone kiosk is updated, if others with the narrow, heavy doors remain.' She paused. He could see the cogs in her brain turning. 'Wheelchair accessible toilets at the bottom of a flight of stairs, what's all that about?' She laughed. 'Don't get me started, T-Bone.' This was her latest nickname for him. 'The whole thing drives me mad.' Her face was starting to turn a shade of pink. He was making her think. He could see her on a protest. She could be a feisty soul when she got going but she had become cynical.

'We've got to build contacts, raise awareness, campaign. That's what the Manchester group was all about. We should start somewhere, we're a team now, Sue-Bear. Two's better than one.'

When they got back to the flat with their shopping, Norman rushed out to help.

'I told you we need him,' Sue said, waving to Norman as he sprinted across the car park.

'I'm surprised you don't invite him into our bed, maybe he can perform better than I can,' Toby said with bitterness.

'Now you're being childish.'

In that instant, Toby felt deflated and utterly inadequate.

Ideas were brewing in his mind though, but he didn't know where to start. There were so many battles to be fought but the starting point was to create awareness and trying to educate people in the needs of others. He didn't realise then that something ordinary, trivial, and everyday would be a catalyst for change.

29

It was Monday morning and Toby was working from home writing a piece about the Manchester protest. *It's ridiculous in this day and age that people still face difficulties in assessing facilities in their local community. A demonstration outside a town hall hopes to raise awareness of the physical challenges some people face. How can we be so oblivious to the needs of others? The forgotten people have found their voice and surely this can snowball into a national campaign. It does make one wonder why it's taken this long for it to happen.*

His thoughts were broken when Sue brought him a cup of coffee, and he stopped typing. She worked part-time in the office at St Bede's and was spending today typing up her CV and looking for a new job. It wasn't that she was desperately unhappy in her job. It was easy work, convenient and suited her, and they were her friends as well as work colleagues, some she'd grown up with at St Bede's. She needed a change as she felt stale, frustrated, and that she had so much more to offer. She also felt shut off and isolated from the wider community, as if she was trapped in a disabled bubble, and that wasn't a healthy situation to be in.

As she put the cup down beside him, she asked if he could nip down to the bank at lunchtime to withdraw some cash for her, as her benefits had just come through.

Her question pulled him from his thoughts, and he stopped typing and looked at her.

'What's up?' she asked, frowning. 'You always go to the bank for me, I can't get in there.'

He pushed back his chair to give her his undivided attention. 'Yes, and I'm more than happy to. But I shouldn't have to.'

'Fine, I'll ask Gill instead.' She looked huffy and turned to go.

'No, that's not what I meant. It should be possible for you to go in the bank on your own.'

She sighed. 'Not that old chestnut again, Tobe. It's an old building, it's got steps and a narrow doorway.'

'How many of your friends bank with them?'

'Everyone at work does. It's the only bank in town.'

He grinned. 'All the more reason for them to make some alterations then.'

'How?'

'If they don't want to lose your custom and if they don't want the negative publicity, they'll do it. I'll ask Dad, he can come up with a solution, he's a builder. Think about it, Sookie. All they have to do is build a ramp going up to the entrance.'

She looked blankly at him. 'What are you suggesting?'

'We need a plan. I'll ask them why they don't have disabled access. I'll have a chat with the manager, he seems an affable chap, I'm sure I could talk some sense into him. Obviously, we know what they'll say, but it's about going through the motions. Then we'll ring their head office and beyond that, we can write to the council, the local MP, and if nobody listens to us, we'll gather a group to stage a protest outside. We can get interviews with the local press and radio. If we never raise it, nothing will ever change. It's no good us sitting back and accepting it.' He stopped talking.

'You look very tired.'

'That's because you woke me at four. You kicked me.'

'No, I didn't.'

'I don't think you realise how strong your legs are.'

'I could say the same about your arms.'

He hated all this pointless bickering. Sometimes they would be in a mood with each other for hours and all because of something so trivial. She'd thrown him off-track, and finding it hard to return to his article, he decided to get the bank over with. Hopefully she'd be in a better mood when he returned.

At the bank, the cashier led him to the manager's office. The manager only had five minutes to spare between appointments, so Toby jumped right into the reason for his visit.

'I can't help, I'm afraid,' the manager said. 'It's a head office decision, it's out of my control.'

'How many of your customers are disabled?'

He scratched his head, looking embarrassed as it was clear he had no idea. 'There aren't many in wheelchairs, at least not enough to justify making expensive changes. Then there's the planning laws. It's an old building, Grade II listed, and a ramp would take up pavement space.

'My dad's a builder, he could build one.' It was a silly suggestion, and showed how he was floundering. It seemed an impossible feat, taking on a mighty organisation with offices worldwide.

Back at home he wrote to the bank's London head office. A week later he received a rebuff, a short and off-hand reply with an apology simply stating that it wasn't practical and there weren't enough disabled customers and mums with prams to justify the cost.

'Oh my God,' he said to Sue. 'This is great ammunition for my newspaper article. This is goldmine stuff.' It highlighted the attitude of corporate organisations. They had the power to make change happen but couldn't be bothered.

'I can't stand this kind of attitude,' Sue said, grabbing the letter from Toby. 'It's everywhere. No wonder I struggle to get on trains or use telephone kiosks with people like them in charge. Do these people even have a heart? Compassion seems to be lost in a world ruled by indifference.'

'It's about changing people's attitudes. It's not going to happen overnight. As far as these managers are concerned, why would they bother making changes for the sake of the 1%? We're the minority and minorities go unheard. Our voices are drowned out by the majority.'

Toby wasn't going to let it drop. The following morning, he typed a letter to the local councillor and trotted off to the town to post it. The sun pressed warm on his back and shoulders as he strolled down the road. He glanced in at people's windows; sometimes they were empty, and sometimes people were staring right back at him, and he felt conscious of his arms and rushed on. It was always like this, people staring. He'd grown used to it, but it didn't mean he wasn't bothered by it.

After passing a few shops on his way to the post office, he spotted Henry, Lucy's burly dad, across the road. He was carrying a rolled-up newspaper under his arm. Henry saw him, waved, and strode across the road to join Toby. He had put on yet more weight and Toby imagined him rolling down the hill like a barrel of beer.

'How's married life, boy, is she treating you well?' he asked wheezily in his thick Irish accent.

Toby was about to respond when it suddenly struck him that Henry was on the council.

It's not what you know, it's who you know was a phrase that sprang to mind.

'All good, thanks, how's Lucy doing? I've not heard from her in a while.'

He gave a curious smile and there was a glint in his eye. 'I think she's keeping her distance now that you're married. She doesn't want to stir things.'

Toby bristled. He didn't want to be restricted and feel stifled just because he was married. His female friends were important to him, he wanted to be able to still see them.

'Everyone noticed how upset Sue was when you slow-danced with Lucy at the wedding,' Henry added.

Toby felt awkward. Had he been more insensitive than he realised? No wonder Lucy was giving him a wide berth, and if Henry noticed that Sue was upset, it was likely most of the guests did as well.

He quickly changed the subject and told Henry about his visit to Manchester and the chat with the bank manager. He held up the letter he was about to post, before asking if he could put in a good word for him at the council.

'They'll be debating and voting on next year's proposed budget on Wednesday. We always welcome the public's feedback on budget priorities. It's a good idea you writing to your local councillor about the issue with the bank, but what about giving a short speech to the chamber?'

Toby was so excited, his brain had frozen. 'A speech?'

'Yeah, why not? I've heard you speak, you're very eloquent. If you can't shake up some of those crusty old fellas at the council, I don't know who will.' He laughed. 'Leave it with me, boy, I'll be in touch.'

Toby said goodbye, then posted his letter and walked home with a spring in his step, thrilled by the prospect of doing what he loved.

He was going to give a speech.

This was a speech on a subject he was passionate about. He needed to make sure the message hit home.

30

Toby stood at the centre of the room, his heart racing as he nervously glanced round the council chamber, its walls echoing with the weight of countless decisions made within. The room smelled of wood and dusty velvet drapes. The faces of the councillors turned towards him as they waited for him to begin, expectant and scrutinising. He glanced round looking to see if anyone was disabled, but he was aware that some disabilities were hidden so it was often hard to tell. A few coughs broke the tension, but then a thick silence enveloped the room. Toby took a deep breath, his lungs filling with air, his head buzzing as he prepared to share words he hoped would change minds.

He very briefly introduced himself with a few opening words before launching in.

'How many of you here today know a wheelchair user?'

He paused and glanced around. Nobody raised their hand. 'Have you ever stopped to ask how they get on, how they manage steps into shops, restaurants, the cinema? How they cope when they can't get into a toilet because the doors aren't wide enough or there are steps? Or do you simply look the other way with pity, grateful you don't have their problems? These are the everyday concerns of the disabled, things that you all take for granted. Why should we be treated differently?'

His voice echoed across the chamber.

He paused for effect.

'Why should we be excluded from all the activities you're able to enjoy? It's okay for you. You can go where you like, do what you like, but for us, we have to plan meticulously. All we're asking for is a few moderate changes instead of being boxed in and excluded from society. We've spent our lives in institutions shut away and excluded. It's time we were included, respected, treated as citizens. I know things can't change overnight, but you could make a start by thinking of our needs when you consider your next planning application. Buildings should be accessible, ramps incorporated. It might not be possible with old buildings, but new ones can be accessible.' He paused, glanced round again. 'As counsellors you have the power to make a difference. Think of the legacy you could all leave.' He recognised a few faces from the local press and various events he'd been to. 'You, Mr Burrell sir, you could be the first in the country to make these changes. You, Mrs Buckle, could go down in history. Providing a toilet for the disabled is surely much better than cutting grass in the local park. Let it grow, it's better for the wildlife.'

He gave his closing words to rapturous applause, and afterwards as people mingled over tea and biscuits, Henry came over, slapped him on the back and congratulated him on a brilliant speech before introducing him to Mr Copeland, the councillor for Ash Vale ward.

'Young man, you're a fine speaker.' Mr Copeland was a

short balding man with a collar of dandruff on his tweed jacket. He stood there jangling his coins in his pockets as he spoke. 'I'm involved in a small business networking group, and we hold regular meetings and run events that help small businesses grow and sustain their operations. I'd like to invite you along as guest speaker, you're very inspiring and of course we'd be able to pay you. Your title could be *I'm no different, so why treat me like I am?*'

Toby felt a jolt of excitement. Was this really happening? The idea of being paid for something he genuinely enjoyed doing, it was amazing, such an achievement and who knew where it might lead?

31

It was a busy day for Sue at work. She'd spent most of the morning using the microfiche to answer invoice queries, then she'd typed a few letters. Invariably there would be a few mistakes and she'd need to Tippex them, and sometimes it was infuriating when someone hadn't screwed the top on properly and it was all flaky and dry. Now it was the afternoon, and she was pulling folders from metal filing cabinets and adding documents she'd photocopied on the Xerox machine. All these jobs made her back and neck ache. They involved leaning down, straining as she twisted and stretched to reach things, but Sue had worked in an office since leaving college, she was used to the aches and pains and wasn't one to grumble. She was just grateful to be in work. Lots of disabled people she knew were struggling to find work, some had never even worked, while others sent job application after job application to no avail.

'Everyone ready for a cuppa?' It was Sheena the supervisor's birthday, and she'd brought in a tray of delicious-looking cream cakes she was now offering round. It always seemed to be somebody's birthday and while Sue was rather partial to a cake, she was conscious of gaining weight because being confined to a wheelchair it was so much harder for her to exercise and stay trim.

Sue was glad of the break and sat up in her chair, jigging from side to side, stretching her arms to release the aches. At a recent Thalidomide Society conference, a psychotherapist had demonstrated a series of exercises they could do which had been very helpful. One exercise Toby was gladly helping her with because it involved sit-ups on the bed. They'd collapse afterwards in a fit of giggles and usually end up making love.

They gathered round the supervisor who was handing round the tray of cakes, and everyone wished Sheena a happy birthday and asked what her plans were.

'I'll probably go out on Saturday evening, but I'll be busy during the day.' She beamed over at Sue. Sue liked Sheena, she was always cheerful and fun to be around, just the type of person they were glad to have on Saturday's protest outside the bank. She was quite feisty and wasn't afraid to get her message heard.

Sheena suffered with spina bifida, and despite her disability and all the operations she'd endured, she made the very best of life. She had career ambitions and talked often of her passion, sailing on tall ships, and it was her dream to sail round the world on one. She'd previously worked for the bank Coutts, and on her way to work one morning, coming through Charing Cross station, she fell over in the crowd of commuters in the busy concourse. Nobody came to her assistance. She lost her crutches. She was trampled on. It took what felt like ages before a few people helped. The experience had really shaken her up to the extent that she changed her job to avoid public transport and crowds.

'You're going to the protest?' one of the women asked.

'I'll be there. I'm bringing along some friends. I don't think they're bothered about disabled access, doesn't affect them but they keep banging on about the bank profiting from apartheid in South Africa. They've been to a few protests aimed at forcing the bank to withdraw from South Africa. My friends have also picketed Shell garages asking motorists to boycott them.'

'I don't really care about South Africa,' the receptionist said before tucking into a choux bun. 'I just wish people would protest more about things happening on their own doorstep.'

'Well, Sue, you have at least six people coming on Saturday.'

'And I'll bring a couple of mothers with their prams. They can't use the bank either,' another said.

'I hope you've all got your banners and placards ready,' Sue said.

'Make sure you're there early, they won't be open for long, with it being a Saturday.'

Saturday came round quickly, and Toby and Sue arrived early. Jasper dropped them off and helped them set up a trestle table for leaflets they'd made after phoning the GMCDP for ideas. Sue had bought stencils from WH Smith, and St Bede's were happy to photocopy the finished leaflet which highlighted the shocking facts about the lack of disabled access into banks and building societies across the country.

They'd only been there a short while when Sue noticed a group of Japanese heading across the road towards them to find out what was going on. 'When does the performance start? Is this a carnival?' one of them asked excitedly.

Toby frowned. 'No, we're here to protest. The bank doesn't have access for wheelchairs and prams.'

The Japanese turned away and scuttled off looking disappointed.

The bank was about to open soon, and the staff, including the manager, were arriving. They looked surprised when they saw the placards and trestle table, they hadn't been informed about the protest.

'Sorry, guys, but you can't just pitch up here, you're blocking the pavement.'

Just then Henry bounded round the corner as if on cue. 'I'm on the council, and I say they can.' He smiled at the manager. 'Come on, Fred, isn't it about time your bank made this place more accessible?'

'It's not up to me, mate, and you don't make the law either. This is a public highway. If they want to walk up and down with their placards they can, but they can't block the pavement and they'll have to take this trestle table down.'

'Huh, it's a shame you don't show more concern for your disabled customers and mothers with prams. They are all customers too and just as important. Without customers, you wouldn't have a bank.'

Anger swept over Sue. She hated the way the manager was ignoring them, speaking about them not to them, as if they were invisible or mentally incapable of holding a conversation. Their voices went all too often unheard, and this was typical of the way the disabled were treated in general.

'You can see they're disabled,' Henry said with a scoff. 'They can't just walk up and down.' He glanced at Sheena, who was leaning on her crutches.

'Customers will be arriving soon, they'll be in the way.' He waved his hand as if they were pests and his face flushed crimson with fury as he stormed off up the steps.

Sue turned and saw Jasper capturing the manager's furious expression on camera. He always got brilliant candid shots, he was a clever man, a real asset to their cause.

Noticing Jasper taking his picture, the manager shouted, 'You can't just take photos. Clear off.'

'Sorry, mate,' Jasper replied. 'It's a free world, I can take photos anywhere and I will.'

'Don't just open doors,' Sheena shouted. 'Open access.'

The manager disappeared into the building, and a few moments later the doors opened, the lights went on and they were open for business.

A cheer went up among the crowd of protesters. Sue glanced round and counted twenty-one of them. It was a good turnout.

They started chanting. 'No more steps, we need ramps.' 'We deserve to be heard.' Play the fair game, we're all the same.' 'A ramp is all we need.' 'People before profits.' 'Society tried to silence us, but our voices will echo loud.'

The shopping street was getting busy, and people were coming over to see what all the fuss was about and were happy to sign their petition.

Norman and Lucy came to join them, and with more people queuing to sign the petition, the pavement became crowded. Everyone was glad of the support and there was a lot of hugging and general camaraderie. Lucy handed round a bag of sweets and the manager of the bakery came over with buns. It was a protest, a demo, yet this felt like a day out with friends. Being in a group of like-minded people, having a laugh and a joke, Sue hadn't experienced this much fun in ages. She felt energised, as if at last there was a purpose to her life. She glanced over at Toby, and knew he was feeling the same.

Busy watching more people sign the petition, Sue didn't notice a police officer wander over until she saw the black shadow in the corner of her eye. She looked up to see him staring down at her.

'So, you're the cause of this trouble, young lady.'

The conversation was interrupted by Norman bounding over. 'Dad, I thought you weren't on duty today? Thought you were playing golf.'

'I've been drafted in today as an extra because of this lot. What you doing here, you're not involved with them, are you?'

'I've come to support my friend Sue, I see you've just met her.'

'Oh, this is the girl, the Sue that lives in your block of flats. The one you're always chasing round looking after.'

'Yes, that's the one.' Norman introduced him to Sue.

'Nice to meet you at last, my Norman's very fond of you, young lady.'

Toby spun round with a waspish look on his face looking like a spare part, and glared before stalking off to join Lucy. How childish he was, Sue thought. Anything to do with Norman always sparked petulance. In some ways she did understand and felt embarrassed for him. Toby hated rudeness, to be ignored as if he didn't exist, and he often stropped off till he'd calmed down, or on this occasion playing tit-for-tat, joining Lucy, trying to make her jealous. He knew the right buttons to press to get his own back just as she did.

'You can have a peaceful protest, but sorry, you can't block the pavement,' Norman's dad told Sue.

Just then the manager looked out of the window and

raised his hand at Norman's dad with a look of relief on his face. He burst through the door but as he descended the steps, an egg hit him right in the face and splattered down his jacket. A tomato followed and dribbled down his white shirt. The crowd burst out laughing and cheered.

The manager raised his arms to shield his face as more eggs were pelted. As Sue looked round at the scene unfolding, she noticed the guy from the local press was here and busy taking pictures.

'Who's got egg on his face now?' someone shouted.

'You're not so clever now,' another protester called.

'Clear off, the lot of you,' the manager shouted back.

It was getting busier as more shoppers gathered to watch the spectacle as if drawn to a carnival.

As the crowd grew, Norman's dad tried to jostle people along and Sue heard him radioing for support. A few moments later a police car arrived to manage the crowd and, in the chaos, Sheena lost her balance and was knocked to the ground, her crutches flying off in two directions.

Sue stared in horror as people stepped over Sheena. Nobody made any attempt to help her up until Toby shouted at them. Sue wished she could wade in to help. Through a gap in the crowd, she caught a glimpse of Sheena and gasped when she saw the terrified look on her face.

Another police officer shouted for everyone to clear some space, and moments later an ambulance arrived. Two medics bent to talk to Sheena, who told them she was in agony. Sue felt awful.

I've caused this. I'm responsible. If she hadn't invited Sheena along, this would never have happened. *What's this protest going to achieve anyway? The manager isn't listening.*

'This is what happens, it's disgusting,' a protester shouted. Sue didn't recognise him, it wasn't anyone she knew but she saw the placard the man had been holding, which was now propped against the wall of the bank. He was a member of the Socialist Workers and his placard read, 'Bring on the revolution.' He reminded her of Citizen Smith. He was even wearing a beret and Afghan coat like Che Guevara.

Sue glanced around. She was worried for Sheena but she was also amazed that so many people had come to support them, they'd never expected this in their wildest dreams, though whether it was going to make a difference was anyone's guess. And now things had turned ugly, she just wanted it to end. She watched as the medics lifted Sheena on a stretcher onto the ambulance. She was too far away to zip over and comfort her. Then she cast her eyes back to the commotion with the manager. Two people in wheelchairs were being questioned by a police officer.

'What's happening?' she shouted over to Toby. She was staying put, there was no way she was going to attempt to get through the crowd, especially not after seeing what had happened to poor Sheena.

Toby bustled through the crowd towards her. 'Things are getting out of hand. They're interviewing the ones who threw the eggs. They say it's common assault.'

'That sounds serious, but they can't arrest them, how would they take them in for questioning? They're in wheelchairs.'

'If they're determined, they'll find a way.'

Minutes later, a van arrived, and two officers got out and went to the back, opened the doors, and let down a ramp. They wasted no time in pushing the egg throwers up the ramp and into the van.

'How ironic, the pigs have ramps for their vans but the

bank with all its money can't afford one,' Sue's friend Sally shouted.

The police dispersed the crowd and told everyone to go home. Jasper and Norman helped tidy up while Toby and Sue counted the signatures on the petition. They were staggered to find there were over two thousand. Despite everything bad that had happened over the course of the day, it had been a small success. If this could be replicated across the country, Sue thought, so much more could be achieved.

32

The following day, Toby wasted no time in sending the petition to the CEO of the bank with a covering letter, while Sue rang Sheena to find out how she was. The hospital had checked her over and she was a bit bruised but okay.

A few days later they were invited to London to meet with the CEO.

'He's obviously read the papers.' Several papers had covered the story, and Toby had written one of them. 'I bet he wants to quell this as soon as he can. It's not good for the bank's publicity.'

'How does he expect us to get to London? I can't use the tube and it's humiliating sitting in the guard's compartment on the train. Cattle class, that's what I call it. We're supposed to be a civilised society, how can we continue to tolerate being treated like third-class citizens?'

'That's tomorrow's battle, my love, all in the fullness of time. This is brilliant news, the CEO is taking notice.' He beamed at her and did a little jig around the room looking all excited. 'He should come down here. I'll ring up and ask his secretary if he'd be able to. We could meet him at the bank, and he can see the issues for himself.' There seemed no point in going up to the head office when it was about the local bank.

They arranged the meeting, but poor Sue had to wait outside on the pavement.

Toby headed inside and was immediately confronted by the manager, who had a triumphant look on his face. 'Your friends were charged for throwing eggs at me. It was childish of them. They deserve all they get.'

'Bring it on,' Toby quickly retorted with a big smile. 'There's no such thing as bad publicity. The more publicity the better.'

Just then, a tall and impeccably dressed man with an air of authority came out of a side office. He had to be the CEO, and a quick glance at his name badge confirmed this.

'Right, Mr Murphy,' the CEO said as he stood aside and gestured for Toby to enter the office. They sat down. 'I've been made aware that you held a demonstration on the 15th November to protest about the bank's investment in South Africa. Well,' he said with a smile. 'I'm pleased to be able to tell you that we are pulling out of the South African market. Your little demo was one of many going right back to the sixties. So hopefully this announcement will satisfy your demonstrators and the signatories on your petition and put an end to the matter.'

Toby stared at him, confused. 'The demonstration had nothing to do with your involvement in South Africa. A few people supported that cause, yes, but the demo was primarily about disabled access to the bank. You obviously haven't read our petition very carefully. Sod South Africa, that doesn't affect access to the bank. As you are aware my wife is disabled and uses a wheelchair and she's unable to join us in here as she can't access the building. She's stuck outside. This highlights the whole crux of the matter. Perhaps we should adjourn the meeting to the pavement where she can join in.' He was starting to feel hot around the collar.

'Don't be ridiculous.'

'If we join my wife outside, I can show you the issues she faces, you can see exactly the problems and then we can discuss what you are going to do about it. We're forgotten members of society. You say you care about your customers and their needs. It would be nice to see it put into practice. Are you aware of how many of your customers have a disability, and how many mothers with prams there are that require access to your bank? You're more than happy to make profits from us. It's time you gave a little back.'

'This is a bank, not the NHS. I couldn't possibly say. Why would we need medical records on everyone?'

When they got outside, Toby was delighted to see a photographer was on the pavement taking photographs and chatting to Sue.

'What the hell are you doing?' the CEO asked. 'No photographs please, no press.' He gave a wave of his hand. 'I didn't know you were bringing them along, Mr Murphy.'

'I was just passing and recognised Sue from the demonstration. But I can see I'm ruffling a few feathers.'

'I'm more than happy to have my photo taken,' Toby said. 'Aren't you?'

Toby showed him the steps and the difficulties some people faced.

Just at that moment, two mothers with prams arrived. 'You go in,' one of them said to the other. 'I'll look after the kids.'

'It's not just us, mums with prams can't get in either. I'm

sure you know, I have access to the national press, and I can use it if I want,' Toby said.

They then headed back into the office and the CEO launched into what sounded like a well-rehearsed speech giving all the reasons why they couldn't make the building accessible.

'If we put in an application, the council would refuse it on the grounds that it's a historic building and the highway's agency would refuse too because a ramp would block too much of the pavement. And a portable ramp would be refused by the company because it contravenes our policy. We can't provide a ramp up three steps, only two steps. There are recommended gradients. Beside, we don't have the staff to keep putting one up, just for a few customers. We cater for the many not the few. The number of people with disabilities is very few. I'm sorry, I know this is not what you want to hear, and it might seem simple to you, but it cannot be done. You can always take your business elsewhere, there are other banks. But I'm afraid if you keep causing a nuisance, we'll have to close your account. And that wouldn't look good if you're trying to obtain a mortgage. We can make arrangements for you to bank at another of our branches. Our Guildford branch doesn't have steps.'

'I'm sure that will make a great story.' He chuckled. 'Bank closes account of disabled customer. How heartless that would sound. It's all right for you. You have all your faculties. You can walk in and out of anywhere you want. For us it has to be a well-planned military operation. You people haven't got a clue, you're not interested. All you banks are interested in is making money and you don't care about anything else. That's been proved by how long it took you to withdraw from South Africa.' Toby stood up. 'I can see our cause means nothing to you and I'm just wasting my time.

Our fight will go on regardless of what you think. We need to be treated with respect like everyone else.'

'I'm sorry you feel like that.'

He stormed out. 'Come on, Sue, let's get you in the warm, you must be freezing out here. I have a story to write, to go out next week in the newspaper.'

As they walked away, the enormity of the challenge hit him. This was a national issue, like all the other challenges they faced such as public transport, employment and benefits. National action was needed. He was at a loss to understand how it had all gone on for so long without anything being done. This was a start though, and even though they hadn't achieved what they'd set out to, they had created awareness and proved to themselves they could organise a protest and garner support.

33

A few weeks after the protest, Toby decided to show Sue his culinary skills. He'd been planning it for a couple of days and knew he had all the ingredients ready. This was the first proper meal he was going to put together and it had taken him a while because he wasn't used to Sue's kitchen. It was a challenge and designed around her needs, not his. Tins were stacked in cupboards in a certain way. Items frequently used had been put out of his reach and her utensils were piled on top of his specially designed ones. For all these reasons, he'd left her to do all the cooking.

He opened a few cupboards but couldn't find what he was looking for, and with mounting frustration he went into the lounge and asked Sue, 'Do you know where all the bits are that I bought on Saturday?'

'No, I didn't put them away, Norman did. If you can't find them, go and ask him. If you don't like it, next time put them away yourself.'

'Jesus Christ, whose flat is this, ours or Norman's? We don't even know where our own food is.' He was incredulous. 'I'm fed up with this, Sue, we need to get our own place that's designed for us around both our needs and away from bloody Norman. The further the away the better. How about the Outer Hebrides? But that wouldn't be far enough from that prat.'

'Don't be ridiculous, he's only trying to help.'

'Seriously, Sue, we need to get a bigger place. Everything is a challenge for me. We need a bungalow specially designed for us.'

'Don't be silly, they don't build bungalows for people like us.'

'We could buy one and have it adapted. We need to get onto the Thalidomide Trust. Our needs have changed now we're living together.'

'Okay, you get in touch with the Trust, see what they say, I wouldn't hold out hope though.'

'We know it's possible. Why don't you speak to some of your friends, see how they went about applying for help.'

'It would need parking spaces, wide doors, a special bathroom.'

'What about a garden, could we manage one, if we had a gardener? Imagine summer evenings on a patio with a bottle of vino.'

'No, we'd probably have to get it paved, easy maintenance, neither of us are up to mowing or weeding and we can't expect others to help.'

'I'm sure Norman would help.' He let out a mirthless laugh.

'You're obsessed with Norman.' She raised her eyebrows and tutted. 'Actually, Norman loves gardening, he'd take care of it, and he wouldn't ask for a penny.' She gave him a cheeky grin.

'No.' He raised his eyes, not bothering to hide his exasperation.

'You can be such a stubborn mule, Tobe, we've got to take all the help on offer.'

'The answer's still no. Dad would be more than happy to help.'

'We can't keep relying on your dad. He's got Patsy to think of now. He spends so much of his free time going back and forth to Blackpool, where would he find the time?'

She stopped talking and gazed out of the window before turning to him, a thought lighting her eyes. 'Do you know, Tobe, wouldn't surprise me in the slightest if he doesn't move up there to be with her.'

Toby was so shocked at the suggestion that his dad might up sticks, it felt like a punch to the gut, and all he could do was stare at her in disbelief. 'No way, he wouldn't do that to us.'

'It's his life, he must be thinking about retiring soon and anyway, why can't he find happiness? We did.'

'We need him.' As soon as he said it, he felt annoyed with himself for being pathetic and selfish. He was a grown man, he'd have to cope.

'No, we don't. I've never needed my parents. And Bill won't always be around.'

He felt bad, how rough it was to be denied supportive parents. His heart quietly broke for her. 'I'm sorry. I was just very lucky.'

He hated the feeling of being dependent on his dad, of needing him, but it was hard to underestimate everything Bill had done for him over the years, how he'd supported him and made his life easier. She was right, it was Bill's life, he'd spent long enough alone, he deserved happiness. He knew all of that, but it didn't stop him feeling sad. It was hard to get his head around the thought of his dad moving away.

While he was deep in thought, she was rattling on about the garden again. 'It would be such a shame not to have a proper garden.' He was only half listening, but her next sentence coming so unexpectedly had his full attention. 'What if we have kids? They would need somewhere to play.'

'Bloody hell, Sookie, next it will be a dog and a cat. We can't even look after ourselves yet. Besides we haven't got the room.' The thought of the kitchen and lounge turning into a baby's dumping ground filled him with horror. He pictured himself stepping on rogue toy bricks like they were landmines, tiptoeing through a maze of rattles and dummies like it was an Olympic obstacle course, and a kitchen overrun with gadgets he couldn't operate, cupboards full of tinned milk and jars of pureed food. He half-expected to hear the sound of a toy siren signalling the arrival of the Baby Apocalypse.

'Actually, seriously, Toby Jug, do you think it would be possible for us to have a family?'

'I don't see why not, some of our friends have had children. But don't get any ideas, we've only just got married, don't come off the pill.' He laughed.

'It's something we've never talked about before. As we've both got impairments, how would we cope?'

He was thoughtful for a few moments. He'd never considered children either, not until now. Oddly, when he'd proposed, starting a family hadn't crossed his mind—just being with her was enough and building his career was his priority. 'Between us we could manage, and we've got Gill, I'm sure she'd love to help.'

'And Norman would be delighted.'

'No, absolutely not,' Toby said with a laugh.

'I could probably just about manage to change a nappy, but it would be hard for you.' She laughed. 'That's something you wouldn't be able to do with your mouth. Imagine it.'

'Yuk, I'd get poo all over my nose, how horrible.' He pulled a face. 'But maybe I could use my feet. I'd just have to practise. I've mastered most other things, but changing a nappy, I think that would have to be the greatest challenge of all, far greater than learning to drive.' He was imagining the baby wriggling and kicking and the logistics of it all. 'Nah,' he said, 'I think that would probably be one task I'd be happy to pass over to Gill.'

'I thought you liked a challenge, Tobe Le Rone. What's wrong with you?'

They laughed and the conversation led on to a discussion about other baby-related tasks. As with everything in their lives, from driving to getting married to planning a honeymoon, starting a family would also be a meticulously project-managed affair.

'There's plenty of time for all that, we're still young but we should look into getting somewhere bigger.'

34

After jumping through a few hoops with the Thalidomide Trust, Toby and Sue were able to buy a property and the Trust agreed that Bill could carry out the modifications. They also arranged for a home assessment by an occupational therapist who would provide support and guidance.

It took weeks of looking round, trying to identify a suitable location near the town, their friends, and the train station for Toby to get to London. He only went to London when Jasper was going too though, because if the train was packed and there was nowhere to sit, he couldn't hold on to anything unless he was able to stand against a seat or the side of the train to stop him from falling over.

It was now the spring of 1987, just weeks away from the general election, when they found their dream bungalow. It was purpose-built for its previous owner—a disabled man who was keen on gadgetry and the latest technology. He was a young paraplegic following a nasty accident on his bicycle, and because of the compensation he'd been awarded he'd been able to invest in aids. He was moving to a new area to be with his girlfriend.

The internal doors were wide and were fitted with special lever handles which were easier to grip. The living area was open plan and accessible with plenty of room for manoeuvring a wheelchair.

The bungalow was in a quiet cul-de-sac with a neat brick drive spacious enough for up to three cars. A tidy row of daffodils, crocuses and tulips giving a burst of colour lined one side of the driveway. The front door was to the side of the building. It had a threshold ramp, and the door was power-operated, assisted by motion sensors and a keypad. The estate agent said they were very lucky to find modern access, as these doors were rare in homes and more common in public buildings.

The bathroom had a wet area with a shower and bench. The shower attachment was low down. There was a loofah on the tiled wall in the shower area for Toby to rub up against to scrub his back and a heater was fitted, turned on with a long cord, so that he could dry himself. Bill fitted a bidet shower––a hand-held triggered nozzle which was attached to the wall close to the toilet. These were common in some other countries, particularly the Muslim world, but they were useful for people with Toby's impairment and one reason why he preferred to work from home. He'd also long since been circumcised to assist with his personal hygiene.

The bath was fitted with a hoist and Sue was able to shuffle from her wheelchair onto a bath chair and rotate it across the bath, descending into the water using a corded controller. It was all amazingly easy and modern and she really appreciated the extra space. They both realised how fortunate they were to have the Trust's financial support.

Most disabled people didn't have mod cons in their homes and as a result their lives were much more of a struggle.

Electrical alterations had been made to the bungalow so that light switches and sockets were at an easier height. When he was young Toby had got into the habit of using his tongue to flick light switches, and Bill was forever telling him it was dangerous.

They had the bungalow extended and a patio door was operated by a button on the wall opening onto a small garden. The work was nearly complete and one afternoon a couple of weeks before they planned move in, they popped round to see Bill. They needed to discuss the garden to ask if he could help with mowing and weeding. If they couldn't get help, it would be paved. Bill had said over the phone, 'I've been meaning to have a chat with you both.'

As they pulled up outside the cottage, Toby had a sinking feeling. He wasn't looking forward to the conversation and hoped it wasn't about his dad's future with Patsy. For reasons he couldn't quite understand, she simply wasn't right for Bill. As they got out of the car and approached the door, it hit him––seeing his dad with another woman felt wrong.

Who is this Patsy to come waltzing in and try to replace Mum?

He was already feeling uneasy, and his discomfort deepened when Patsy opened the door acting as if she owned the place. She greeted them with an over-the-top welcome, almost as if she was on a mission to win him over, while Bill hung back, as if he were an irrelevance in his own home.

Since getting married, Toby felt a strange sense of disconnect when returning to his dad's cottage. It didn't feel like home anymore and it was difficult to conjure memories of his early family life. Patsy had completely transformed the cottage. The once chaotic place now felt overly neat and orderly. The furniture had been rearranged, and the sitting room felt different. He couldn't help wondering if she was trying to change Bill, turn him into someone he wasn't, and although her influence had to be good—after all, messiness was never a great trait—he worried that she was too controlling.

He couldn't see them living together. God knows, he knew how tough it was to live with someone, but maybe all it took was time to adjust. He'd fallen into a pattern with Sue and at the start, their marriage was like a comedy show, the type of show you regretted buying tickets for. But a few months in and they'd established a routine and roles. She cooked, he washed up—despite ending up very wet every time because of his lack of arms. He took the bins out, she made the bed. There was a synchronicity between them, a dance, and they were the choreographers.

Toby studied the settee before plonking himself down. 'Bloody hell, Dad, this is clean.'

'Yes, Patsy got someone in to give it a professional clean. Looks as good as new, doesn't it?'

'I didn't recognise it,' Sue said, laughing.

Patsy busied herself making tea, then carried the tray to the coffee table and began pouring milk into cups.

Bill immediately jumped in with the announcement Toby had feared. 'Patsy and I have some news.'

Sue was all excited, hardly able to contain herself, but Toby stood there cringing and feeling very uncomfortable.

'We're getting married.' Bill proudly pulled Patsy's left arm towards them to show off an enormous diamond ring. Sue squealed and Toby raised his eyebrows and tried to contain himself. *What a waste of money*, he thought to himself. *If it all goes tits up, she's done all right.*

'I've decided to semi-retire and move back to Blackpool to be with Patsy. Makes sense. I spend my life on that M6.'

'Congratulations.' Sue was still whooping. 'I don't blame you. I've been hoping this would happen. If you make each other happy, then why not? Besides, you need a woman to keep you on track,' she said, laughing at Bill.

'There's still life in the old dog yet,' Bill said with a smile before turning to Toby and slapping him on the back. 'You beat me to it, son, only just though.' When Toby didn't smile or react, Bill frowned and said, 'You okay, son, you look a bit pale?'

'You've got to let him get on with his life, Toby, it's his turn to flee the nest,' Sue said.

'Isn't this all a bit rushed? Don't get me wrong, I'm happy for you both. How's this gone on without us noticing? You're a dark horse, Dad.' Toby's tone of voice was flatter than he'd intended. 'I know it sounds selfish, but we were hoping you'd be able to redesign our garden.'

'Toby,' Sue scolded.

'I'm sure he can still do it,' Patsy answered for Bill. 'But it's time you retired, love, and slowed down, you've done your bit.' She smiled into his eyes adoringly and gave his hand an affectionate squeeze.

Toby bristled. It made him feel really strange. He'd never thought about Bill with another woman that wasn't his mum, and he was finding it hard to get used to it.

'I won't be moving yet, not till next year, so there's plenty of time to get the bungalow finished. What have you decided to do with the garden?'

'We've got a bit of a dilemma,' Sue explained. 'If we decide to have a family, it would be better to turf it, but a patio would be simpler, easier to look after, especially now you've said you're moving, we won't have anyone to mow and weed.'

Bill and Patsy looked at each other with surprise on their faces and there was a stunned silence before Toby quickly jumped in. 'Obviously that wouldn't be for a few years.'

'Oh yes,' Patsy said as if she couldn't agree fast enough. 'Children are a big responsibility. You've got enough on your plate for now.'

'God, I've never thought about you having children. Would you be able to? How would you cope? Children are difficult enough, never mind the additional challenges you both have,' Bill said. 'Get settled into your new bungalow first, there's plenty of time for all that.'

Patsy glared at him. 'Bill, don't be so insensitive, they've got dreams too.'

Toby sucked back on his teeth with a sharp intake of breath. He didn't want to have this conversation.

After they chatted more about the garden, they left. On the way home in the car, Sue tore into Toby, criticising him for his reaction to Bill and Patsy's marriage plans. 'Couldn't you be a bit more positive?'

'I'm just not sure about her. She's taking over his life.'

'Rubbish. She's lovely, she's just the sort of woman he needs. Don't be so negative. You should be happy for them.'

Toby sighed. 'I hope he isn't rushing into things and being pressured by her to move. He's never shown any interest in going back up there, if anything he complains about how rundown Blackpool is these days. Just seems bizarre. I know my dad and I think he'd want to be around for us especially if we end up having children.'

'When you love someone, it doesn't matter where you live. I'd have gone to the ends of the earth for you, Tobe, I love you that much.'

The comment made him feel suddenly shy. 'She's got grandchildren, and I think they live locally to her. I reckon that's why she won't move down here. But if we have children one day, what about us? He's going to miss out and he won't be around when we need help.'

'For God's sake, Toby. He can't put his life on hold for you indefinitely. He deserves some happiness. He's been on his own long enough. Everybody needs a little love and there's no point in worrying about what might or might not happen. I don't even know if I can have kids. Look at me,' she said, laughing, 'It's probably not possible and how do we know the child wouldn't inherit our impairments? That would be my greatest fear, I wouldn't want a child to go through what we've been through.'

'The only way we're going to find out is by asking. Why don't you book a doctor's appointment? We could both go along, wouldn't do any harm, would it? At least it would settle our minds.'

A selfish and completely ridiculous thought was running through his head. Just supposing Sue got pregnant soon, would it scupper his dad's plans? He was sure Bill was only going along with this move to keep Patsy happy. It couldn't be what he wanted. Feeling guilty for these cynical thoughts, he quickly brushed them away. There was no way he wanted children yet and he wasn't about to have a family to ruin his dad's plans or his own. He wanted to establish his career first.

35

A fortnight later, Toby and Sue headed into their doctor's surgery in Haslemere. After checking in at reception, they went through to the busy waiting area where Sue anxiously glanced round hoping nobody would recognise them. The last thing she wanted was to explain to a friend why they were here. Her gaze dropped to the floor as she desperately tried to avoid the stares of the little children and their parents.

She wondered what thoughts went through people's minds as they sat and stared. Some people saw them as freaks, and if they knew what they'd come to see the doctor about, what would they say? Would they be horrified?

I'm not like these people. I belong somewhere else. I'm not really part of this world.

I'm just as worthy. Our children will be forged from the same place as all these able-bodied people—love.

As they waited, her stomach was performing somersaults. It was one thing to talk about this with Toby privately and casually, but they were about to discuss their hopes and fears with the medical profession. It felt strange, and suddenly she had the urge to spin round and make a dash out of the surgery. What were they doing? They were just fooling themselves believing they could be parents. They didn't have to go through with this, just to be humiliated. She felt like a fraud, a fake, it was like having imposter syndrome.

When their names were finally called, Sue was glad to leave the waiting area. The doctor's consulting room was small, and Sue's wheelchair took up most of the space between the couch and his table.

'How can I help you?' The doctor swivelled round in his chair, his hands on his lap. He was much older than their usual GP and looked as if he was close to retirement.

Knowing Toby would be too shy to talk about personal matters, Sue said, 'We're thinking of having children at some point in the future and we've got no idea if it's possible.'

The doctor smiled. 'If you're making love and you're not taking contraception, well yes, it's possible to get pregnant.'

Toby and Sue glanced at each other. 'No, that's not what I mean. As you can see, we're both disabled, our mothers took thalidomide. You can see how the drug has damaged us, but we don't know how it might have affected our reproductive organs if at all, and is there a chance a baby could inherit our impairments especially as both of us were damaged by the drug?'

'Well let me tell you this. I'm a crusty old GP who's been around a while and seen a fair few things including actually prescribing the drug. I was involved in the court case, I swore an affidavit. It was a terrible time for all of us, perhaps the darkest period of my entire career.'

'You know all about it then,' Toby said.

'I think at this early stage, you can assume all your bits are working as they should. If after a year of trying, nothing happens, then come back and we can run some tests. And regarding inheriting your impairments, they can't be passed on because they aren't caused by genetics. Let me put it this way, if an able-bodied woman fell over and broke her arm while she was pregnant, it wouldn't mean her baby would be born with a broken arm.'

After the appointment, they drove over to Wisley Gardens. They both had the day off and Sue was glad of this time, she wasn't in the mood for work. They needed to reflect on what the doctor had said. Although they'd agreed to wait before starting a family and knew that pregnancy wasn't guaranteed, this still felt like a pivotal moment in their lives.

Toby sat on a bench and Sue pulled up beside him.

'What's on your mind?' she asked. 'You look pensive.' He was staring into the flowerbed. The garden was a riot of colour and looked beautiful.

'I just feel a bit bewildered, it's a lot to take in. Recently married, new house, career taking off, which means I'm going to be away from home sometimes, and now we're talking about starting a family. I'm not sure I'm ready yet and on top of that, Dad potentially moving away. My emotions are all over the place, Sookie. And to be honest, I'm not sure I'm cut out to be a parent, I can't even look after myself.' He laughed.

'I know, I know, I wasn't thinking of starting a family right away, I just thought we needed to know so we can plan. I'm still getting used to you, Tobes, I couldn't cope with two kids in the house,' she said, teasing.

He'd been watching a butterfly on a nearby flower. 'Charming,' he said with a grin. 'Women are a complete mystery. It'll take me a lifetime to fathom you out.' Then he looked serious. 'It worries me, what would it be like for our kids growing up in a world that questions and doubts us, their parents, the people who love them the most, and how would our lives impact theirs?' His words contained so much passion that for a fleeting moment she imagined him as a champion for disabled parents, giving talks on the subject, a sort of leading authority.

'Children just need love.'

'Sometimes that's not enough. They need parents who can figure out life's problems.'

She stared at him. 'We can do that and if we can't then we get support, we work it out, that's what we've always done and we're good at it.'

'I'm sure most couples just decide to have kids and get on with it, but I can't be like that,' he said, frowning. 'It's such a huge life-changer.'

She reached out and touched his shoulder. 'I know, but like you say, it's not something we should rush into. I vote we get more practice in.' She laughed cheekily but Toby was just staring off into the sunlight.

'Sorry, it was that look of horror on Dad and Patsy's faces when we told them we were thinking about having kids, it's really got to me. He's always supported me in everything I've ever done, never once doubting my capabilities, and doing everything he possibly can to help me. Okay, he didn't want me to go to university but that was because he's not academic himself and doesn't see the value of a degree. He might not be the brightest bloke, but he's got a practical and wise head on him.' Toby paused. 'But on this, he doesn't believe I can be a parent, I just know it. I could see that doubt in his eyes.' Toby's face was etched with disappointment. 'I wonder what Jasper and Sandy would think. Would they be just as horrified?'

'Who cares what other people think?'

'We care, we might deny it.'

'Maybe he's just worried for us, how we'll cope and whether we can provide a safe environment for a child. Think about it, Tobes, neither of us could run after a child and pick it up. What if it ran into the road, what then?'

'We'd have to think very carefully about safety.'

'That goes without saying.'

He looked directly at her. 'No one's making us have kids, it's not compulsory, maybe it's not the best idea. We're happy enough, just the two of us, aren't we?'

He reached over and kissed her, and in that moment as he looked into her eyes, she knew he was trying to reassure her that he loved her no matter what, but now that the idea of having a family had planted itself in her mind, it was there to stay. She knew that deep down, without the family she'd long craved, she'd be unfulfilled.

The more she thought about it, it meant everything to her, and she realised why that was. Growing up in an institution, she'd been denied the love of a happy family and had been virtually estranged from them. She'd missed out on so much, her parents had been self-absorbed, thoughtless, and detached. They'd come and gone out of her life as if she didn't matter and her feelings didn't count. How different her own family would be if she was given the chance. She'd make sure of it, and she'd shower her children with so much love and attention and give them everything she'd been denied herself.

It was the purest form of love between a mother and her

child, she'd give it an open heart and open ear and be all the things her parents weren't.

The thought slapped her in the face. She realised she didn't want to miss out. She didn't tell him that. She didn't want to put pressure on him. He had his career to think of, and like he said, it was early days.

36

That whole spring and early summer, they were like ships passing in the night. Sue barely saw Toby because he was focused on the forthcoming general election, writing articles with Jasper on various issues that affected the electorate from the economy to the environment. He was still a member of the Young Conservatives and in the lead-up to June 11th, every evening in a small group which included his mate Dave, he trawled the streets campaigning. Sue was interested in politics––up to a point––but wasn't particularly interested in the election. Toby on the other hand was passionate and determined for the Tories to win a third term. He was always bleating on about Thatcher's achievements. Sue wasn't so convinced. Benefits were being cut, unemployment was on the rise as well as hospital waiting lists and people seemed to be getting poorer. She couldn't tell Toby this though, it would end in an argument, it wasn't worth the effort, he was blinkered and worshipped Thatcher. She had to admire him though, he had balls. She could just imagine him on the doorstep ramming home the message, blagging his way, trotting out statistics, a master of lies and deceit like every other politician. He'd developed the skin of a rhino which gave him immunity to having doors slammed in his face usually with a few choice words like, 'Bog off, I'm in the middle of watching *Coronation Street*,' to send him away with a flea in his ear.

One such evening when Sue was on her own, Sally popped round after work to keep her company. Sally had a mobile hairdressing and beauty business and was doing very well. Sue had to smile, every time she saw Sally she told her how much she'd earned in tips. It seemed that she earned a lot more in tips than other hairdressers and was convinced it was because of her impairment. Sue had lost count of the number of times her clients told her she was amazing and incredible, but to Sally her feet were her hands. Lately she'd made even more tips, the clients giving her extra because she was having a baby. She was in the first trimester and most mornings felt very sick. How she managed to work, Sue had no idea.

'I don't know how you do it, Sal, can't you stop working?' Sally had just arrived and as Sue reached for the bag of take-away curry she was holding between her teeth, she wondered how on earth the poor girl was going to be able to eat spicy food. But apparently Sally had an intense craving for Indian food which she found bizarre.

'I love work, I'd miss all my clients if I was stuck at home all day, I'll be working till I drop.'

'No, don't do that,' Sue laughed. 'You don't want your waters to break and flood a client's carpet.'

Sue led the way into the kitchen where she had plates and cutlery ready. Taking the lids off the containers she spooned chicken korma onto Sally's plate and prawn biryani onto her own. She adored prawns in every guise: in a Marie

Rose dressing, fried in garlic and butter and tossed with a few salad leaves for a tasty starter, and mixed into tagliatelle for a main.

Sue was very hungry and wolfed her food down, but Sally picked at hers, barely eating.

Sally wiped her brow. 'I don't know why I ordered this, I think I've gone off curry. The smell is making me feel queasy.' Her face looked all pasty.

'I'm not surprised. I don't think many pregnant women would be eating curry.' Sue laughed. 'But you're eating for two now, you need something. Have a poppadum.'

She sat back and rubbed her belly. 'I feel stuffed, but I've barely eaten.'

'Imagine craving coal, I wonder what that's all about.'

'Have you thought any more about starting a family?' Sally asked.

'We've talked about it, but we're going to wait, we haven't been married long.'

'Neither had we, don't let that stop you.'

'I'm happy to wait, there's no rush.'

The following morning, Sue woke with terrible stomach cramps and a band of pain across her forehead. She reached over and took her contraceptive pill along with a couple of paracetamols and a glug of water, then saw that Toby was already up. She could hear the rhythmic sound of him tapping on his typewriter. She was desperate for the bathroom and as he was working, she didn't want to call out for help. When she heard the key in the lock and saw Gill's face appear at her bedroom door, she was relieved.

'Gill, thank God, can you help me to the loo? I'm about to throw up, had a dodgy curry last night.' Luckily Gill was quick to grab a bowl from the kitchen because she could feel the bile rising in her throat.

'That'll teach you to eat prawn curry,' Toby said later that day after she'd thrown up several times. 'You won't ever see me eating shellfish. I avoid all foods likely to give me the heebie-jeebies, it's way too tricky for me to deal with. You should be grateful you've got arms,' he said with a laugh.

A few weeks later, Sue met Sally for coffee in the park. Sally flopped onto the bench complaining of swollen ankles and the need to pee frequently. 'I'll be glad when this little blighter decides to make an appearance. I've still weeks to go.'

Sue took the rim of the mug to her lips, but as the hot liquid touched her tongue, she grimaced and smacked her lips. It tasted burnt and too strong and made her feel a bit queasy. Normally she loved coffee, describing herself as an addict. This wasn't the first time she'd felt repulsed by coffee and in the last few days she'd taken to drinking Earl Grey tea instead.

'I don't know what's wrong with my taste buds lately, I've gone off coffee.'

Sally's eyebrows shot up and she looked at her quizzically.

She smacked her lips again and ran her tongue around her mouth, tasting her saliva. 'I've had this horrible taste in my mouth the last couple of days, a sort of metallic taste.'

'Oh yeah?' There was a strange thoughtful look playing on Sally's face as if she knew something that Sue didn't. 'Is your period late by any chance?'

Sue whipped round and stared at her in horror. 'Why?'

'You could be pregnant. That's one of the first symptoms, that and achy boobs.' She smiled.

'No chance, I'm on the pill.'

'Miracles happen.' Then her eyes lit up with a sudden realisation. 'Oh dear, please tell me you've been using another form of contraception since the dodgy prawn curry event.'

Sue froze. 'Ah, erm.' Her period was late, and although she hadn't given much thought to it, the idea was now lodged in her mind.

'Come on, chuck the coffee away, we're taking you down the chemist, via your flat. You'll need to pee into a pot.'

'Lovely.' Sue laughed. 'I can't do that, Toby's at home and the only pot I've got is a jam jar.'

'Maybe not the best plan then, you don't want to have to explain to Toby what you're up to. The chemist will give you a sample pot and we can nip round the corner into the disabled loo. The chemist is very good, they'll do the test in twenty minutes. It'll be peace of mind, girl.' She rose from the bench and beckoned Sue to follow.

Sue was so stunned she couldn't speak when the chemist delivered the news from behind a counter stacked high with throat lozenges, indigestion tablets, and hay fever remedies, while a gaggle of people waited for their prescriptions beside her. A couple of older ladies looked down at her in surprise and a young woman turned her head and stared. Sharing such personal news in a crowded shop felt completely inappropriate, especially before she'd had the chance to tell her husband. She couldn't wait to get out into the fresh air.

Outside, Sally leaned down, gave her a big kiss on the cheek and squealed with excitement. 'Wow, I knew you were up the duff. I can't believe we're both going to have a baby. They can be friends, it's going to be amazing.'

'The test might be wrong.'

'Course it won't be. Book a doctor's appointment, he'll confirm it.'

'Am I ready for this? Is Toby ready?' It was such a shock,

she felt disorientated as if she was inhabiting a world she didn't belong in.

They went for a walk and chatted about pregnancy and babies, but Sue's mind was all over the place, she felt disconnected from the conversation as if she was observing herself from a distance. As she headed home, she worried about how Toby would react. All she could think was how unexpected this was; he'd made it clear he didn't want a family yet and even hinted at not having one at all. This was all her fault; she should have remembered the warning on the leaflet that clearly stated the pill might not be absorbed into the bloodstream after a bout of vomiting and diarrhoea.

What an idiot I've been. This could have been avoided.

There was an overwhelming feeling of fear and apprehension bubbling inside her. This whole pregnancy thing, it was unknown territory, and added to that, she was scared to tell Toby and just hoped that once he'd got over the shock, it would be what he wanted. As she approached the block of flats, she stopped. Her heart was racing, but through the myriad emotions, she couldn't help but feel excited.

A baby. I'm going to have a baby.

37

Toby was engrossed in writing an article when Sue arrived back. He didn't want her to break his train of thought, so he called out, 'Give me five minutes, love, I'm nearly finished.' He expected her to head for the kitchen and leave him to it, but she burst into the room, her wheels squeaking on the laminate. He carried on typing, desperate to hold on to the words in his mind, but there was something that unsettled him, she was too quiet and then she sniffed loudly. He took his eyes from the sheet of paper and turning to look round, saw she was crying.

'Whatever's the matter, popsicle?'

'I'm pregnant,' she blurted.

'Are you serious?' His eyes went straight to her belly.

She nodded, her eyes bright with tears. 'I know it's not what we planned...'

He was struggling to process the news. 'But we talked about waiting. I thought we agreed.'

She started crying and he went over and leant to hug her. 'I know, I know,' she said in a choked-up voice. 'But it's happened. It must have been when I had that upset tummy.

The dates tally. I should have thought about the pill not absorbing, I've been really stupid, I'm so sorry.'

He pulled away from her, wishing he could take her face in his hands but that was something he couldn't do without arms. 'It's okay, it's just a lot to take in. I can't believe it, Sookie.' He beamed at her. 'I love you, Mrs Murphy, we'll work it out, I promise.' He could feel tears prick his eyes and a sudden welling of emotion. 'I'm going to be a daddy.'

'How do you feel about it?'

He gulped. 'Honestly, I'm terrified, but excited too. But what about you? Do you feel okay? You don't have any aches and pains?'

'No, Tobe, I'm not ill, I'm just pregnant.' She was blushing now and smiling at him.

'I would tell you to sit down and put your feet up but...'

'Hey, I may not have legs, but I've still got arms to clout you with.'

'When can we tell people? I want to ring Bill and Jasper and Sandy, and Dave, bloody hell what will he say? He's still busy playing the field, our news will really freak him out.'

'Slow down,' she said, laughing. 'We've only just found out. It's early days. We should wait. I need to book a doctor's appointment, get it all confirmed first.'

A FEW DAYS later Sue sat in the surgery's waiting area trying not to let the stares of the little children and their mothers get to her. She realised this was just the first appointment. There would be many more, here and up at the hospital, and this was going to be the worst part of the process. To other people she was a freak of nature, but how were those same people going to look at her now, a disabled mum-to-be? Would the other pregnant mums exclude her from their conversations, look on in pity and assume she'd never make it to full-term? How she longed in that moment to be just an ordinary able-bodied mum, like her own mother was twenty-seven years ago.

When she was called in to see the doctor, it was a different man, much younger than the previous. After telling him she'd taken a pregnancy test and it was positive, he looked at her and asked bluntly, 'Is that a good thing?'

'It was planned, if that's what you mean,' she lied, feeling shocked and small. Would he have asked an able-bodied woman the same question?

'Okay, I won't need to do a further test as those chemist ones are very reliable, so I'll go ahead and book you a midwife's appointment for a week's time.' He looked at her with concern. 'We're going to have to monitor you carefully.'

She felt quite indignant. 'I've got all the right bits to grow a baby, just no legs.'

'Yes, but you might not have a normal pelvis. The midwife might want you referred to the consultant for an X-ray and to have your pelvis measured. We'll assess the situation at a later date, but it's possible you might need a caesarean. I'd be a little worried about you giving birth normally. You might find it a struggle.'

Suddenly overwhelmed, Sue didn't know what to think. A C-section meant a longer recovery time and possible complications. How on earth would she cope with caring for a newborn?

She didn't want to be in his stuffy room any longer. She needed fresh air and to be alone with her thoughts. She'd talk to the midwife instead, it felt too personal a subject to discuss with a man even though he was a doctor. What did he really understand about a woman's body?

Outside, she scooted down the path and back to her car,

desperate to get away from the surgery. It was a beautiful August day, and the sky was the colour of denim, one of those hot and humid summer days where it felt as if the whole world was starting to melt and the pavement tarmac was sticky on her wheelchair tyres. It was a challenge getting into her car, folding her wheelchair after shuffling onto the driver's seat, hauling it over her shoulder and into the back, and even though it was never easy, she was used to it and had developed strong arms.

She sat at the wheel just staring ahead as tears started to prick at the corner of her eyes, turning her vision misty. She'd been so caught up in the frenzy of excitement, the wonder of a new life growing inside her, that she'd barely thought about how her disability would affect the pregnancy and birth. But now alarm bells were ringing, and for the first time she felt frightened and alone. What if there were complications and she couldn't bring a baby to full-term, or it didn't survive the birth? A sense of panic rose inside her. She didn't know anybody else in her situation, there was no one to share the experience with or reassure her it was going to be okay.

We were born into a world that didn't expect us to thrive. They claimed we wouldn't survive past childhood. We were labelled defective, but we've turned that stigma into a badge of honour.

And now, here we are getting married and having children of our own.

Even though Sally was also impacted by thalidomide, that was pretty much where their similarities ended. They had different limb damage. Sally had no arms whereas Sue had no legs.

She leaned forward and slumped her head on the steering wheel while she cried and tried to pull herself together. She felt frightened and really needed to talk to someone. She wished she had that sort of relationship with her mum but the last thing she wanted was her mother ridiculing her. She didn't want Toby to see her like this, he'd only worry, and this was supposed to be a happy time for them.

As she started the engine and pulled away from the kerb, the memory of her wedding day flashed through her mind. Sandy had taken her aside, reassuring her that she was always there to listen if Sue ever faced any difficulties or needed someone to confide in. At the time, the kind offer had taken her by surprise, but she'd not given it much thought until now. She'd always liked Sandy, she was a together sort of woman, confident and self-assured, and when Sandy had worked at St Bede's, Sue had the impression a few of her friends might have gone to her to chat over problems. She would be a good person to talk to if she wasn't busy with the B&B. She glanced at her watch, realising Sandy had probably long finished making beds and clearing away. It was an ideal time.

Sue liked the fact that Sandy wasn't family, she was a friend of the family, one step removed, a bit distanced, which made it easier to talk to her.

She sniffed, blew her nose, and dabbed her eyes. A sadness curled around her as she thought about how cold her mother was. It hit her then, she was the one person she should be able to turn to but couldn't. She'd never been there for her and that wasn't about to change despite her pregnancy.

On a whim, she found herself indicating left at the bottom of the road and heading up the hill towards Sandy and Jasper's house.

38

Sandy glanced up from filling the kettle just as Sue pulled up on the driveway. This was a surprise. She'd not seen Sue in weeks and presumed she was busy working and settling into married life. It had been a busy morning of breakfasts and making beds, but it was all done now. Sue had come at just the right moment before she'd had the chance to think of more chores that needed doing. There was never a dull or a quiet moment in this house, but then again, it was August, their busiest time of year.

She hurried outside and went round to the driver's side as Sue wound the window down. She'd been crying, her mascara was all smudged and her eyes were red. Her heart leapt; surely they'd not come to blows already. They'd barely been married five minutes, they were still in the honeymoon period.

'Everything okay?' she asked.

'Are you busy, have you got time for coffee?' Coffee now made her queasy but she'd force herself to drink it.

'Come on in,' she beckoned. 'I've finished my chores.'

She went to the back of the car and took the wheelchair out, and unfolded it beside the driver's door for Sue to get into. Sue was unusually quiet. As they went inside, she glanced round and asked if Jasper was working from home.

'He's in London today.'

'That's good.' Her face seemed to relax, and Sandy wondered what she was going to tell her that she didn't want Jasper to hear. It was a bit odd her coming round here like this.

They made small talk while she brewed and poured the coffee, pulling out a chair beside Sue as she looked directly at her. 'I can see that something's bothering you, what's on your mind, pet?'

Maybe it was the warmth in her voice or her gentle touch, but Sue broke down in tears. 'I'm pregnant.'

This, she wasn't expecting. She stared at her, eyes wide and mouth agape.

'Shit, I shouldn't have told you, our parents don't even know yet.'

Sandy bristled. *Jasper and I are Toby's parents.* She could hardly believe it. For a brief moment, it was as if the oxygen had been sucked from the air, and she could barely breathe as she tried to process everything and the implications.

The child I thought had died is now going to be a dad. And oh, my goodness, I'm going to be a grandma.

'Promise you won't breathe a word, it's just I needed to tell someone,' she pleaded. 'And you used to work at St Bede's, you were always so kind if anyone had a problem.'

'It's okay, your secret's safe with me,' she reassured, rubbing her arm, and keeping up a pretence through gritted teeth. She was supposed to feel honoured the girl had come to her, confided in her, but all she felt was pain. Sue hadn't a clue, nobody, not even Toby, her husband, had sat her down and told her the truth.

Somebody needs to tell her. I can't watch from the side-lines, pretending to be a family friend as Bill and Patsy play grandparents. But it's not my place to tell Sue. Toby needs to do it. The sooner the better. She's not going to be happy. Their marriage is built on lies and half-truths.

Every emotion she'd ever felt wanted to explode out of her body right then, but she had to keep a lid on them and focus on poor Sue. She wasn't sure how to word her next question without upsetting the girl, so went for the direct approach.

'Was it planned?'

'Not exactly, we were going to wait. I've just been to the doctor. My head's all over the place, Sandy, I just feel scared. They said I'll need to be monitored carefully and I might need a caesarean. What if my body can't cope with pregnancy?'

Taking both Sue's hands, she looked into her frightened brown eyes. 'Now you listen to me, pet. You're going to be okay, if I can do it, so can you.' She smiled as she tried to reassure her.

'But you're not disabled.'

'When I had Angela, the doctors at Guildford were amazing. They'll look after you.'

At least she wouldn't be giving birth in a mother and baby home. The memory of Toby's birth, and a vision of the doctor lying to her about her baby's death just hours later, shimmied into view and she found herself shivering despite the August heat. Over the years she tried to forget, but sometimes, in low moments, the memories would return to haunt her. A strange and unhinged feeling came to her now—the realisation that she was going to live it all again through Sue.

Sue took a sip of coffee and looked out of the window. 'I'm dreading telling my mum and dad, especially Mum.'

'Why? They'll be so excited, their first grandchild.' A fist of pain squeezed her insides. They didn't deserve to be grandparents, not after how they'd treated Sue over the years. It was despicable. She'd observed it all from a distance, their lack of visits to St Bede's, the excuses they made, the indifference, even on the poor girl's wedding day. The only reason they'd paid for the wedding was to save face and maintain the illusion of being good parents, not wanting to appear mean. They were horrible people and Sandy had done her best to avoid them that day. She couldn't stand false people who had no compassion. It was obvious they only cared about themselves, and it was all about keeping up appearances. Others could fall for the illusion, but it didn't wash with her. It felt terribly sad and unfair too, knowing she and Jasper would make wonderful grandparents.

Sue raised her eyes to the ceiling, not bothering to hide her exasperation with her parents. 'They won't be pleased about it. My mum's always been critical of everything I've ever done. I'd be a spinster locked away in a Leonard Cheshire home if she'd had anything to do with it.'

'Oh dear, yes she's a funny old stick.'

'That's one description.'

'She might surprise you. People go all mushy when they see a baby. She'll probably knit a matinee jacket and matching booties, and it will be hard to keep her away.'

Sue looked incredulous and a laugh escaped her mouth. 'Are you sure we're talking about the same woman?'

They both laughed and it helped to ease the situation.

Sandy glanced at her watch and shot up. 'Oh gosh, is it that time already? I'm so sorry, I'll have to dash, I'm seeing the accountant shortly.'

She followed Sue to her car and helped her in.

'You won't tell anyone, will you?' Sue asked.

'Of course not. That's for you to announce when you're ready and further along. Everyone's going to be really pleased for you both, you'll see.'

Waving goodbye, she hurried back inside to gather her books, stuffing them into her handbag. After her conversation with Sue and all the emotions still welling inside her, Sandy knew it was going to be hard putting her business hat back on.

There was so much to consider but she was clear about one thing, Sue needed to know who Toby's real parents were. Toby should have told her before the wedding.

In a healthy marriage, the only secrets should be surprise parties and gifts, never hidden truths. How would Sue react to the news, given all the time she'd known Toby? Would it cause a rift between them?

Then she realised something else.

Patsy would have to know too. She was about to marry Bill. Surely, he didn't want to walk into his marriage in a cloud of secrets that could one day end up a problem. It was far better to be transparent. His situation was much more serious. Bill had been involved in the abduction of a baby and there was no telling how Patsy would react.

The words 'kidnap' and 'abduction' sent a chill down her spine.

Sandy had never been happy about keeping this secret, but they'd made her go along with it because Jasper had convinced her it was the right thing to do to protect Bill.

It suddenly felt as if everything was about to implode.

39

Sandy dashed off to the accountant, but she couldn't get the conversation with Sue out of her mind. There was so much the poor girl didn't know. She wondered how she might react when she found out the truth. Would she feel betrayed, would it drive her and Toby apart or bring them closer together? Sue and Toby had been friends for years. How would she feel knowing he didn't trust her enough to confide in her?

There would be a backlash, tears and hurt, but she needed to know. Toby would be hurt because he was protecting, shielding her and she would be hurt because he should have shared everything with her. *So much hurt.*

She waited until the next time Toby popped round. He was often at the house because he and Jasper were always holed up in the office discussing work projects. It was quite nice because it meant she got to see him a lot. She knew Sue wouldn't be coming too because this was her swimming day. She went to a class for the disabled in the hydro pool at St Bede's. There was a special slide to assist in getting in, and afterwards she was hoisted out of the water. Sandy had accompanied her on one occasion, amazed at the facilities and therapy. All sorts of people were receiving treatment, from people paralysed in road traffic accidents, those recovering from surgery, and children with developmental delays to individuals with neurological conditions. Because Sue was wheelchair bound, she needed regular exercise and therapy to maintain her muscle strength, for weight management, circulation and to help maintain the flexibility of her joints, all of which helped the quality of her life.

Midway through the morning Sandy took coffee and biscuits in and bit the bullet.

'Guys, it might not be the best time, but I really need to talk to you about something that's been on my mind for several days.'

They both looked up with worried faces.

'This sounds ominous, love, what's wrong?' Jasper said. He frowned and Toby looked pensive.

'Sue popped round to see me and during the conversation it suddenly dawned on me that there's so much she doesn't know about you, Toby.'

'What do you mean? She knows everything.'

'Ah, but she doesn't know you're our son. And I believe it's a secret that we should no longer keep. I remember the shock of discovering you were still alive, but she's your wife, Toby, you should tell her. If she finds out by accident like I did, she'll be equally devastated.'

She glanced at Jasper. His demeanour had changed, and he was all stiff and tight-lipped. She knew she had hit a nerve reminding him how she'd felt. She'd never quite forgiven him for keeping that corker of a secret and they'd nearly come to blows over it.

'The longer you leave it,' she continued, 'the harder it will be, and the more damage will be done to your relationship, and then there's the danger one day we'll trip ourselves up. Or my bloody mother will go and say something. I've never forgiven her for the way she revealed the information or for keeping my own background from me as if it didn't matter. Keeping secrets turns your whole world upside down. The truth will always out. Secrets have a way of revealing themselves.'

While she spoke, Jasper said nothing, but he was turning pale and the atmosphere was charged with emotion. They were each grieving in their own way, it was the elephant in the room.

If the elephant isn't confronted, it will tear this family apart.

'But if I tell her, what then? She might tell someone outside the family.'

'We take that risk. I could tell her if you wanted me to because you men can be a bit blunt.'

'Oh, all right, and how's that going to look? What am I supposed to say to her? What words am I going to use?'

'Better dealt with by a woman, whatever we say gets twisted and taken the wrong way, we'd end up making a complete balls-up of it, and you'd have to pick up the pieces anyway,' Jasper said with a sniff.

'Don't throw it back at me,' she said indignantly.

'We've been over this many times,' Jasper said, rubbing his forehead with that look of despair he often had. 'We had no choice, we kept it a secret to protect Bill.'

'Okay, guys, the problem's now mine. I'll talk to her. But...' Toby paused and looked from Sandy to Jasper. 'I'd rather leave it for now.' He stared and wiggled the fingers of his left hand. He always seemed to do this when he felt awkward, which made Sandy realise maybe he was about to spill the beans and announce the pregnancy. She'd have to look surprised. Toby would be mortified if he knew Sue had already told her.

'I can't tell her now, look there's something I need to tell you, and you'll have to pretend you don't know because we agreed not to announce it yet. Sue's pregnant. You're going to be grandparents.'

Sandy's expression quickly shifted, and she widened her eyes in mock surprise, her mouth forming an exaggerated "O" as if the news was a complete shock. She fiddled with her hair, a nervous habit as she pondered how Sue would react to the secret, but she was genuinely pleased for them both. 'That's amazing news, Toby, how exciting. A baby.' Then she glanced at Jasper, her face beaming. 'I guess that means we're going to be grandparents.'

Jasper thumped Toby on the back. 'Well, you're brave, lad, I take my hat off to you, it will be a challenge, but you always did love a challenge. You never told us you were planning a family.'

'We weren't. We've seen the doctor and got their advice, it's just we never planned to have one this soon.'

'God, I feel suddenly old. A granddad, bloody hell.'

Sandy suddenly realised that to the outside world Bill and Patsy would be the grandparents, not her and Jasper. It didn't seem fair to be denied this joy. She wanted to be involved, she knew that. She'd have to re-plan her life, do less bed and breakfast so that she could help. The more she thought about it, the more she wanted this. She wasn't there for Toby, but she could be for her grandchild.

I'm sick of this remaining a secret. I want to be the proud doting grandma.

She imagined a host of scenarios involving Bill and Patsy. An unexpected pang of jealousy stabbed at her. Then another thought hit. 'Patsy's going to have to know too.'

Toby and Jasper looked at each other in horror.

'She's marrying Bill, she'll have to be told,' Sandy said bluntly. 'God knows what she's going to think though.' She looked at Toby for his opinion, but he just shrugged and looked overwhelmed. 'Hopefully she'll be understanding, after all, it did happen a long time ago, but she may not be, Bill needs to be prepared for that conversation. I don't know her that well.'

Toby sighed. 'I'm still getting to know her myself. She's all right, she's a bit controlling though. I hope Dad isn't moving back to Blackpool just to please her, he's got to do what's right for himself.'

Sandy left them to crack on and as she washed the mugs, she wondered how it would all unfold. She felt happier now they'd discussed it. Toby would be chatting to Bill first, then Sue, when he felt the time was right. Her biggest worry though was Toby leaving it until after the baby's birth. It was cowardly and bound to backfire on them all.

40

Bill was in the pub by himself enjoying a contemplative pint. He was sitting in the corner nursing a banging headache brought on by a rather stressful conversation with Toby. Toby was right of course. He did need to tell Patsy. She'd agreed to marry him, and he'd decided to give his notice at Christmas with a view to packing up and heading up there in the spring. That would give him a few months to plan the move. It would be strange moving into the house where Patsy and Arthur had lived their whole married life and where they'd raised their children. All the memories that were contained in those four walls. He wished he could persuade her to start afresh in a new house with him, in a different part of Blackpool, creating new memories and putting the past behind them, but she wasn't having any of it. She always made the excuse that her children wouldn't like it. But they were adults, they'd moved away and had their own lives. It seemed as if they were all tied to the past to the point of suffocation, as if none of them could move on.

He was happy to be getting together with Patsy, she was

a lovely woman, and he didn't want to miss this opportunity now he'd found love again. He hated the thought of growing old alone. But there was a niggling ache in his heart. She wasn't his dear Rona who would have done anything to keep him happy, from ironing his shirts to filling his belly with all his favourite foods. Patsy, on the other hand, never compromised and that gave him cause for concern. Everything seemed to be on her terms. He also felt sad to be moving away from Toby and Sue, not being around for them when they needed him, but at least they wouldn't be having children. He'd have hated to miss out on his grandchildren growing up.

The conversation with Toby had disturbed him. He'd come this far with Patsy, how was it going to look when he told her the truth about Toby? He wasn't good with conversations of a personal nature and struggled with probing questions. He could understand Toby's dilemma though. It wasn't great to be starting married life with such a big secret hanging over them, but why now? He could have told Sue months ago before they'd married.

It was a few weeks later when Bill finally plucked up the courage to tell Patsy. They were out walking on Thursley Common. The sun was shining brightly and there was a stunning variety of clouds in the sky set against the heathland. The scene reminded him of an old oil painting. Bill had always found it easier to have difficult conversations while walking. There was something about the motion, the rhythm of putting one foot in front of the other, not having to face the other person, just looking forward and fixing his gaze on the view. He recalled several conversations across his lifetime and the struggle to find the right words and put his point across. The hardest moment of his entire life was trying to convince Rona to return baby Toby to the hospital.

He'd seen her desperation for a child, the anguish in her eyes, that heart-wrenching yearning. There were moments when he'd considered doing it himself, it would have been the right thing to do, but all he wanted was her happiness and so he'd backed down and agreed to raise the baby.

He also remembered the tough discussions with her family about planning her funeral. At times, throughout the years, he felt as though he was always putting others and their wishes first, sacrificing his own needs and feelings and never having his voice heard. That was why he liked Jasper. Jasper had quickly recognised the danger of others knowing the secret and discreetly kept it from his own wife, even though, as Toby's mother, Sandy deserved to know.

They left the bright sunlight of the open heathland and headed into a shadowy tunnel of pines, the ground springy with tree needles underfoot. Bill looked up to see a Dartford warbler singing from a branch and they both stopped to watch it before it flew off. They turned and smiled at each other, and in that moment he felt comforted, knowing they shared that same joy of the countryside. It was something in their favour. He suddenly felt at ease and ready to tell her.

'Patsy, there's a big secret I've been keeping from you.'

'What is it?' The alarm that swept across her face made his chest tighten and he was forced to glance away. He suddenly felt sick to the core, knowing this should have come out months ago. As she cast him a doubtful look, the distance between them suddenly felt so immense he wondered if they'd find their way back, and for a brief moment, he feared he might already have lost her.

He took a deep breath before diving into the entire story of Toby's birth and Rona's kidnapping of him from the hospital, recounting the detail that now flooded back as he spoke. She listened and didn't once interrupt. They carried on through the wood and back out into the bright sunshine, passing a peat bog, barely noticing the dragonflies hovering over the stagnant water. When he finished speaking, the heavy weight he'd carried for years felt finally lifted from his shoulders, and her reaction suddenly didn't seem to matter. It was just a relief to finally share the burden with someone else.

'My God, Bill, you should have told me, did you think I'd walk away?' He hadn't expected this. They stopped walking and as they faced each other, he took her hands in his.

He could see the hurt in her face. 'You've had to carry that all these years.' She glanced away, staring into the distance, as if absorbing his story.

She turned back and looked into his eyes.

'Wow, you're far more a man than I thought you were. That's just incredible and completely selfless. God only knows what would have happened to Toby.' Her face was expressive and full of alarm. 'That must have taken Rona real guts, she could have lost her job, but if she hadn't done what she did, he wouldn't be here now. You both quite literally saved his life.' She shuddered. 'He would have died on that cold windowsill. That much is obvious. I can't believe the cruelty of those doctors, the sheer callousness, because he was handicapped, his life didn't matter.' She was spitting venom now and all those same raw feelings he'd had back then were returning.

'Yes,' he said sadly, staring off into the distance, his gaze fixed on a man with binoculars watching something in a tree.

Her eyes were filling with tears and her top lip quivered. 'How did you cope?'

He shrugged. 'Same as any other parent, we just got on

with it. You know what it's like, you've brought up two children. I can't imagine how hard that must have been.'

'But you make it seem so simple, Bill.' She laughed. 'Not only were you raising a child that wasn't yours, but he was handicapped. You're amazing.'

'We'd longed for a child of our own, but it wasn't happening. I can't pretend, I was never keen on adopting like Rona was. If I couldn't have one of my own, I didn't want one. But then I wasn't given a choice, she brought Toby home after her shift one night, a baby, just like that.' He let out a laugh at how ridiculous it sounded, and shook his head. 'Sounds bizarre, doesn't it? The whole thing was crazy as well as nerve-wracking.'

He looked away briefly, feeling his face burn as he remembered the darkest depths of his despair, the night he'd considered smothering Toby. She didn't need to know about that. He felt a profound sense of shame, but his mental state had been all over the place. All these years later it was hard to believe he'd reached such a low.

'I loved Rona so much. I was never comfortable with what she'd done but a repeated lie blurs the lines between illusion and reality.'

'Why can't you tell anyone?'

He stared at her. Wasn't it obvious? 'I was an accomplice to kidnapping. She was desperate for a child. We would have ended up being charged and may even have been sent to prison. When I realised that Jasper and Sandy were his real parents––and that only happened through a chance meeting with Jasper when he was interviewing the parents of thalidomide children––I had to tell them. They could have gone to the police, they could have kicked up a real stink, but they didn't. Patsy, look, I've spent my life running away from this issue, hiding behind a curtain, I'm tired.'

'It all makes sense now. Sandy dotes on Toby, I could see it at the wedding, I thought it was unusual for friends of the family to be so close, but it never crossed my mind, but I suppose, why would it?' He watched her face as another thought came to her. 'And that's why you and Rona moved away so quickly. We were shocked you'd moved as you loved it up there.'

'We had to get away, it was safer.'

'I feel honoured that you've told me. It shows you trust me.'

'I should hope I do, I am marrying you.' He laughed.

'What about Sue? Does she know?'

'Not yet, but Toby's going to tell her. He said he's choosing the right moment, so it might be a while before he does.'

'He shouldn't leave it. It'll be worse if he does. I'm not sure I would have been happy if you'd waited until after we were married. It's never a good thing to enter marriage with secrets. Those secrets are like shadows, secrets that appear innocent but only grow darker with time because honesty is the foundation love needs to thrive.'

She was right, and now he was worried for Toby.

41

Sue and Toby waited until she was seventeen weeks pregnant before they announced their news. By then, Sue had registered with the midwife and been to the hospital for a scan. She didn't enjoy these hospital appointments, the stares from the other mothers and their little children, and the surprised look when people realised she was pregnant.

The midwife was lovely though. She did her best to put her at ease, reassuring her they would be looking after her and monitoring her every step of the way. She'd sat with her pen poised as she asked all sorts of questions. How long were her monthly cycles, when was her last period, did she smoke, drink? Then there were questions about her lifestyle and her medical history as well as Toby's. When she'd put a cuff on her arm and taken her blood pressure, Sue found herself wondering how Sally's blood pressure was taken. Then she was lifted in a sling to be weighed. After that, the midwife wanted to test the protein in her urine. She gave her a pot to pee into, but she was so nervous she weed all over it. Sue thought it odd at that first appointment the midwife took her word for it that she was pregnant.

What if my body is playing tricks and I'm not?

One Saturday morning Sue was woken by Baby Prawn pressing a foot or an elbow into her bladder. Initially its movements felt like gentle flutters but as the pregnancy progressed, it was as if an alien was inside her, kicking, twisting, and rolling. Prawn was particularly active in the bath, and she loved watching the bumps and lumps as it pressed against her abdomen, and it kicked even more when she swished water on her belly. She'd call Toby in to watch, and he'd sit excitedly beside the bath waiting for the show to begin, but Prawn refused to perform to an audience.

She struggled out of the cosy cocoon of duvet, disentangling herself from Toby's long warm legs. She used to love a morning coffee but had given up and replaced it with warm milk as soon as she learned she was pregnant, not that a certain amount of caffeine was necessarily bad, but she'd spent too long praying her child would be healthy to do anything but turn her body into a temple. The fear of harming her baby weighed heavily on her mind and was difficult to shake off. For what felt like the umpteenth time, she wondered about her own mother's experience of carrying her to term, revisiting those nine months in her mind, examining every detail, and wondering if there had been signs that she was carrying a handicapped child.

I'd dearly love to ask her, but don't feel I can. We aren't close.

As it was still early, she hunkered back down and talked nonsense to Prawn. Going about her day, she usually gave Prawn a running commentary, telling the baby what she was doing and how she couldn't wait for his or her arrival.

Toby reached out and rubbed her belly with the heel of his foot and she turned and wrapped her arms around him.

'Do you think it's about time we told the family?'

'I suppose we should bite the bullet, get it over with. We could go round to Dad's today, I think he's around,' Toby replied.

'Sounds like a plan. I'm dreading telling Mum, I've had so much crap from her over the years, I don't think I can take any more. I just want to get it over with.'

'Will they be in today? Be good to kill two birds with one stone.'

'I'll give her a quick ring, tell her we're popping over.'

A couple of hours later, they were sitting in Bill's lounge sipping tea.

'So, lad, you said you had something you wanted to discuss. If it's about my moving to Blackpool, the subject's closed, it's not up for discussion.'

'No, but it might make you think twice about going.' Toby laughed mischievously. 'Or you'll be up there quicker than you can say Jack Robinson.'

'I'm pregnant,' Sue blurted.

Bill looked incredulous and for a moment he was speechless and then a smile broke out, so wide it took over his face. 'Oh, bloody hell, that, I wasn't expecting.' Then he laughed. 'You managed to get it to work okay then, boy, I am impressed, that's something I failed to do.'

Confused, Sue frowned and glanced at Toby waiting for him to explain, but he looked very embarrassed. His face was turning red, and he was staring at the carpet. What did Bill mean? She wasn't going to ask but flagged the comment, she'd find out from Toby later when they were alone.

'God, I suddenly feel old. A grandad, well I never.'

Sue could see that the news had really thrown him, but he looked so proud.

'When's it due? Are you keeping well, Sue? You look radiant, positively blooming, girl.'

'It's due in February, around my birthday,' Toby said.

'Oh, bloody hell, will be an expensive month then.' He winked at Sue. 'You can forget chocolates and roses on Valentine's.'

'If Toby forgot Valentine's, he'd be in the doghouse.' She nudged Toby and blew him a kiss.

Afterwards, in the car on the way over to North London where her parents lived, Sue remembered Bill's comment. 'What did he mean when he said he was impressed that you'd got me pregnant, something about failing himself? I didn't understand what that was all about.'

'Let me concentrate on driving, there's an arsehole up my backside.'

'Charming, lovely choice of words, Tobe.' She sniggered.

'We'll talk later.' He glanced in the mirror. 'Go on, Mr BMW, aren't you a clever boy, you can drive faster than me.'

'Pull into the slow lane then,' Sue said with a tut.

She shook her head, musing about how men loved to brag about their driving skills being far superior to women's, but she managed to drive and chat at the same time. It was hardly brain surgery.

As they pulled into her parents' driveway, a sense of dread crawled through Sue's veins when she spotted her mum at the window with an unreadable expression. There was no smile or welcoming wave.

She tried to shake her worries away, reminding herself she was an adult now, a married woman, expecting a child of her own. There wasn't going to be a repeat of her own childhood.

This child would be shown love and respect and the greatest gift of all—their time and attention.

All the money in the world couldn't replace those gifts.

42

Sue's dad bounded out of the house with his usual efficiency and gusto. She glanced at Toby, who gave her that knowing look. Her father was very particular about where they parked their car. He liked it tucked in beside the hedge. He never said why but they'd long guessed it was so the neighbours couldn't see it. Perhaps he was embarrassed by the size of their car and Sue's wheelchair. Sue always referred to her car as The Popemobile.

He was going to great pains now to direct them, standing in front of the car making his silly hand movements and with a serious expression on his face. This parking madness always seemed to dampen their visit. What did it matter where they parked? The drive was huge, but the way he acted, it was a supermarket carpark with a marked bay. One word came to Sue's mind.

Shame. He was ashamed of his own daughter. His own flesh and blood.

Sue kept a diary, and the entry she'd made the day before their wedding suddenly returned to her.

Shame is the thief of joy keeping our voices silent and our hearts heavy. It grows in the dark and whispers, we are not enough, but our love for each other will shatter that lie.

Family was supposed to be a safety net from prejudice, but prejudice cast a wide shadow across every aspect of their lives.

Her mum came into the hall, and leant down to give Sue a peck on the cheek while her dad launched into his usual interrogation about the journey. 'Which way d'you come? How was the traffic? Any road diversions?'

What did it matter? It felt like a boring game show. They could have taken a scenic detour through a dinosaur park, and he'd still ask about the traffic lights.

'It's a shame the twins aren't around today,' her mum said. Sue was relieved they weren't. She loved her sister, but she could be just as judgemental and hurtful as their mum, maybe more so, and had no filter when it came to harsh words.

'Don't stand on ceremony,' Pearl said to Toby, and with a flourish of her hand directed them into the lounge. 'I hope your wheels are clean,' she said in a stern voice. It was like being told off for wearing muddy boots.

Before Sue had the chance to answer, she'd bustled into the kitchen, returning with some old towels, and carefully laid them across the carpet.

All this fuss was starting to irritate her, so she chanced a mischievous dig. 'That's a nasty chip in the doorframe. Your DIY skills are slipping, Dad.'

He looked down at her, his eyes practically popping out. 'Your wheelchair did that, the last time you were here.'

Her heart sank and she wished she hadn't said anything. 'No, I didn't. I would have remembered.'

Her mum examined the chip. 'In fairness, we aren't sure how it happened, but you and your wheelchair.' She tutted and prised the door right back, stepping aside dramatically to let Sue in. 'Careful where you park it, don't knock into the coffee table.'

'What do you expect me to do? Hop through on my bum instead? You know how Dad hated me on artificial legs, perhaps I should just stay out in the garden.'

'No need for that, young lady, I was only asking you to be careful.'

What a performance it all was, they'd only just arrived, but already she was so looking forward to leaving.

'Lucky you caught us in,' Pearl said, sitting down on the sofa. It was a silly and pointless comment, surely they would have said if they'd planned on going out. Every comment was a dig. Sue couldn't bear it. And this was all before they'd even made their announcement.

'We wouldn't have come round if you weren't going to be in. We did ring.'

I just want to get this over with.

She glanced at Toby silently willing him to make the announcement.

When he didn't, she took a deep breath and braced herself. 'Mum, Dad, we've got some news.' She wanted to smile, but her nerves were giving her a pounding head and she knew what their reaction would be.

With a heavy heart, she watched their expressions cloud over, as if they were bracing for bad news. She wondered if they'd already figured it out. They eyed them warily.

'You're going to be grandparents,' Toby said.

Pearl's eyes popped in disbelief as she stared at her daughter. 'What?' she said, then looked to Jeremy. 'Is this a joke?'

Jeremy shrugged and said nothing. For a man who could

talk his socks off when it came to potholes and traffic diversions, he was speechless.

'What's up, Dad, has the cat got your tongue?'

'Don't be ridiculous, child, you can't be expecting.'

She reached for Toby's hand. 'I've had my first scan, Mum, I'm already seventeen weeks.'

Pearl gave a mocking snigger. 'I always knew it was a mistake for you to get married. How on earth are you going to cope with a baby?'

She leaned forward, a scowl planted on her face. Then she let out a disdainful laugh. 'I've never heard of anything so ridiculous.' Then her expression changed as a new thought seemed to dawn on her. 'I'm not going to help, I'll tell you that for nothing.' She glanced at Jeremy. 'We're done with raising children, aren't we, dear?' There was a martyred edge to her voice.

Jeremy sighed and looked flummoxed. 'I just hope you two know what you're letting yourselves in for,' he said in a gravelly voice. 'You don't know the first thing about babies. We're able-bodied and we couldn't cope, so how do you imagine you will?'

'They won't,' snapped Pearl. 'That's just it. They haven't thought any of this through. It's actually very selfish. Think of the child, growing up with disabled parents.'

She was speaking now as if they weren't in the room. 'The kiddie will be looking after them as soon as it's toddling, rather than them looking after it.' She let out a sarcastic laugh. 'You mark my word. And they'll be a drain on the state. That I definitely do not agree with. This government supports enough scroungers, without you two joining the queue. Why? You don't need to have a family.' As she spat her words, her face went red.

Sue couldn't bear it. Tears welled and she just wanted to

leave, but she noticed the towels were all rucked up and her passage out of the room wasn't straightforward and was bound to end in more criticism.

The conversation was broken by the phone ringing. It was on the windowsill behind Pearl and she went to grab it, answering it in a harsher tone than she probably intended. Her voice softened when she heard it was her other daughter, Wendy. 'Hello, love, Sue and Toby are here. Sue's pregnant.'

A hush fell over Jeremy, Sue and Toby. All eyes were fixed on Pearl. Sue glanced at Toby and strained to listen in on the conversation. 'Yes, I agree, I know, I know, that's exactly what I told them,' Pearl was saying haughtily between lots of huffing and puffing.

'What's she saying?' Sue asked.

Pearl covered the mouthpiece. 'She thinks it's risky. She's right, it is.' Her voice rang like a spoon against a glass.

Wendy raised her voice so they all heard. It was so loud, she could have been in the room. 'I'm not gonna lie, Mum, I think she's a complete idiot. I hope you told her she's a dumb fuckwit. Hang on a minute, how long have you known about this? Nobody bothers telling me anything.'

'All of five minutes. Your father and I are still getting over the shock.' She gave a sly laugh.

So taken aback by her sister's nastiness, Sue inhaled sharply. They were words that would stay with her. It was like a slap across the face.

What a bitch.

She glanced at Toby, and seeing the hurt in his eyes, knew that he too was struggling. He looked at the door, signalling to her they should make a move.

Pearl looked embarrassed. 'They're actually here now, I'll ring you later, pet.'

I bet you will, thought Sue, *to gossip about me.*

Pearl came off the phone.

'Sorry, Mum, Dad, I really can't stay any longer. Your comments are hurtful, and I heard what Wendy said.' Her voice felt completely detached from her body. She didn't like confrontation and rarely challenged their remarks.

'Don't take any notice of her,' Pearl said dismissively. 'You're far too sensitive. We're all just trying to help you both see the reality of your situation.' She was sitting all prim with hands on lap.

'Help? That's a joke. This is a big moment for us, but all you've done is put me down.'

'We're just concerned, we don't want you to make a big mistake,' her dad said. 'You do have choices.'

Toby stared at him. 'The biggest mistake was coming to tell you. You're more worried about the impact on you.'

Sue stared at her dad, incredulous. 'You think this was a mistake, don't you? You're implying I should have an abortion.' The thought horrified her. In that moment, she realised her mother would have gone down that path, if she'd had the choice.

The look that passed between her parents said it all.

'We just need your support,' Toby said.

'Not your negative thoughts,' Sue added, her voice cracking as she struggled not to cry.

Jeremy stood up and grabbed his newspaper, the *Daily Express*, tucking it under his arm. Sue knew he was off to the conservatory. It was where he always went "for a bit of peace and quiet".

'You two have very short memories. You're forgetting we paid for your wedding,' he said, lording it over them.

'What's that got to do with it?' Sue asked. 'I'm talking about your general support.'

He waved at her dismissively. 'Probably nothing, what do I know? I'm only your dad.' And with that he left the room, leaving them all to stare after him.

'Now look what you've done. You've put him in a bad mood, he'll be in that conservatory all day now, thanks for that, Sue.'

They made their excuses and promptly left. Her dad didn't even come out of the conservatory to say goodbye.

In the car on the way home, all the old emotions Sue had felt growing up came rushing back to her. 'You're not saying much, Tobe,' she said after a time.

'Sorry, I'm still in shock. My mind's all over the place. I was appalled.' He was quiet for a moment then he said, 'If I didn't know before what it was like for you growing up, I do now.'

After such a difficult day, she couldn't wait to get home and comfortable. Then she remembered Bill's earlier remark and how dismissive Toby had been about it. It was a strange comment, maybe there was more to it. Toby still hadn't told her about the nature of the remark. If he didn't bring it up, she would remind him later.

43

The car ate through the miles, the silence stretching between them until they reached home. It was only while sitting at the dining table that evening that they finally had a proper conversation. Their thoughts had been too painful to address earlier, and Toby knew they needed time to process the afternoon and the hurt.

He looked at her. 'How are you, pet, how are you really? I did feel your pain.'

She was pushing the food around on her plate.

'You need to eat.'

'I've got no appetite.' She pushed the plate aside. 'I'm okay, Tobe, it's just hard. But at least I have you.'

He couldn't reach out and stroke her, but he leaned towards her and flapped his hand. 'You'll always have me, I love you so much, and you're going to be a wonderful mum. We're in this together and whatever difficulties we have, we face together. Our child will be showered with so much love, it's going to have a completely different childhood to ours. This little one will never have to face loneliness and doubt.'

She frowned at him. 'You're making it sound as if we both had terrible childhoods. Yours was good, in the main. I know you were bullied, and your mum passing away must have been so sad.' She let out a mirthless laugh. 'The irony of it all, you had a lovely mother who just accepted you and loved you no matter what, but she's gone too soon, she can't see the amazing person you've become. She would have been a lovely grandma.'

Sue's eyes were filling with tears, and he had to look away. He couldn't go on like this, she had to know the truth.

'Sometimes, Tobe, and this is going to sound awful, I wish my mother had died rather than yours.'

'You mustn't think like that.'

'Mustn't I? Well, I do.' Her expression was hard. That was how she'd had to be over the years, hardened to the knocks, rhino-skinned.

'I think a lot of it with your mum is to do with guilt. She's lived with guilt all these years, she hasn't been able to let go of it, maybe nobody helped her come to terms with it. Think about it. She took the tablet, she buggered up your life.'

'Stop it.' She cradled her head with her hands.

'It's true. Every time she sees you, she's reminded of what she did.'

'But it wasn't her fault,' Sue screeched. 'Her doctor prescribed it.'

'Yes, we know that, everyone knows that, but it doesn't stop her feeling a huge sense of guilt,' he slammed back. 'People behave in peculiar ways. It's a sort of reverse psychology. She loves you, she's wracked with guilt, it's easier for her to push you away than face it, and so she gives you the opposite of what you need. And it's so deeply ingrained into her now that she can't change.'

'Well, if that was the case,' Sue shot back, 'why wasn't your mum like that too?'

'I guess everyone is different.'

Sue shrugged. 'Well that blows your theory out the water then.'

'Your mum isn't unusual, that's all I'm saying. My mate Steve, his mum dumped him in St Bede's too. Like some of the other parents, his were told by the doctor, forget this one, go and have another. Think about all the couples that broke up because they couldn't cope with the situation. Some even took their own lives. People react differently and besides, I don't think the twins had an easy upbringing either.'

'You were lucky, Toby, I don't think you realise that. I really wish I'd met your mum. It's strange, it feels like I've lost someone I never even knew. My mother-in-law. I often wonder what our relationship would have been like. Sometimes I daydream about it, I imagine us going round Debenhams and Dorothy Perkins together, her helping me choose clothes, choose my wedding dress. Grief isn't just about those we've lost, it's also what we've never had and the people we never got to meet.'

'I was fortunate, I had a happy childhood, but I have to tell you it's not all it seems.'

She stared at him, looking confused. 'Oh?'

'I've been keeping a secret all these years, the only people who know are close family.'

'I am close family, Toby. I'm your wife.' She looked affronted.

'Let me finish.'

'Sorry, go on.'

'Now that you're my wife, I feel I should share it, it's been a burden all this time.'

'Jeepers, what are you saying?' She looked all flustered.

'I've always said you can tell me anything.' Her expression turned to hurt.

'I wanted to tell you, but I was sworn to secrecy, it would have got people into trouble. In fact it still could.'

'Trouble, my God, what are you saying?' Her eyes were popping.

'This will come as a big shock, but Bill and Rona aren't my real parents.'

She looked completely confused as if the floor had just dropped from beneath her, leaving her gasping for a reality that no longer existed. 'What do you mean, they aren't your real parents? Are you one of those test tube babies? I remember the first one, Louise Brown.'

'No, nothing like that. As you know, back when we were born, we were rejected and many babies were left to die on hospital windowsills and in cold rooms. I was one of the abandoned babies. Rona was the midwife and the doctor told her to put me in the cold room and let nature take its course because there was nothing to be done for me, they thought I'd die anyway. But Rona saved me, she and Bill had been trying for a baby and couldn't have one. They wanted to give me a life. They had to live with the secret, even right up to this day.'

Sue's hands shot to her face in shock, her mouth hanging open in disbelief, and her eyes as wide as saucers. 'Oh my God, that's awful, so you don't know who your real parents are?'

'By a twist of fate, my parents came back into my life because of my real dad's interest in thalidomide.'

'So you know who your real parents are, do you see them or didn't they want to know?'

'You're not going to believe this, but my real mum is Sandy.'

'Bloody hell.' She stared off into the distance, lost in shock. 'I can't believe it. You've been hiding it all these years. Why didn't you tell me?' A flicker of hurt darted across her eyes.

'I couldn't. Bill was an accomplice to kidnap. He could have ended up in prison. He still could.'

'What was I likely to do, dob him in? Oh, Toby, credit me with something, please.'

'Well, now you know.' He got up and went to look out across the patio, gazing at the potted plants and hanging baskets.

'That explains so much, why you're all so close, I'd never figured it out, now I can see, you have so many of Jasper's traits and features, but I have to say, I'm really upset you didn't tell me. I don't think you would have bothered. It was only the horrible day we've had, my parents. Did you just feel sorry for me, is that it?'

He turned to face her and could see the doubts knocking about like a football in her head. She was still by the table. 'No, of course not, I've been trying to find the right time to tell you.'

'So you have two dads, must be so hard for both of them. One saw you grow up, the other didn't. They're so completely different in their personalities, everything about them, and yet they manage to be friends.'

Her eyes were welling up and as he reached her, she took him in her arms and they both broke down in tears. Their faces were so close, he could feel her shaky breath against his lips.

'Why is there so much hurt and complication in our lives?' he whispered, his tears wetting her hair and shoulders. He pulled away and she grabbed a tissue from the box on the table and dabbed his eyes.

'The hardest thing for me is calling Jasper, Jasper and Bill, Dad. Bill is still my dad, he's always been there, he's the one who's always worried about me over the years.'

'It must be strange, seeing them all together, and shit, Angela is your sister.'

'It's a horrible feeling, I'm often torn in my loyalties, especially when they discuss my best interests in front of me.'

'You saw how my parents deal with my best interests.' The look of hurt was back in her eyes.

'I've longed to tell you for so long and I know you're hurt but hopefully you don't think less of me.'

'It's a shock, I can't deny that, but it shows me you can keep a secret, that we're close enough to share it, I would never betray that trust.'

As they sat then in silence, she suddenly asked, 'So you're telling me, even Lucy doesn't know, you've not even shared this with her? Think carefully before you answer, I want the truth.'

He shook his head, his hackles rising. 'No, no of course not. You're the only one who knows apart from the family. I think Dad's going to tell Patsy though. And I'll tell Lucy.'

She reared up. 'Bloody Lucy, why tell her?'

'She's like family, but not.'

'We agreed when we'd tell people.'

He sniffed. 'I expect you've told Norman judging by all the baby clothes and stuff mounting in the spare room.'

'If you must know, he guessed.'

'He guessed,' he repeated in a sarcastic tone, feeling very deflated.

'Yes, I can't help it if someone guesses.'

'You kept that one quiet. I expect he sees himself as an uncle. He'll soon swoop in when I'm away on business. And how did he guess?'

'He's been to Boots and signed me up for a free baby pack.' She seemed evasive.

'Has he now? Did he think we were incapable of doing that ourselves?'

'Some people are just helpful, Toby, what is wrong with that?'

'I don't trust the geezer, where he's concerned there's an ulterior motive.'

'I bet you wish you were having Lucy's baby. And I bet she wishes she was having your baby.'

'Don't be so bloody ridiculous, God you're completely neurotic, woman. Lucy's nothing but a close friend.' He hated this, her jealousy, her obvious feeling of inadequacy.

And then he suddenly saw the truth of it.

Her struggle was likely rooted in the love her parents had failed to provide. In that moment, he grasped the profound truth of it all: the effects of thalidomide transcended the physical. It was like grabbing a stone, throwing it into water, watching the splash, and the spread of the ripples. Thalidomide was a rock hurled into their lives, annihilating and violating every aspect, its impact extending beyond them into the next generation. He realised then how futile it was to think they could simply pour love into their child's life and it would all work out.

Countless worries hit him at once. Would the child be embarrassed by them and avoid bringing friends home for tea and parties? Would it miss out on certain experiences, simple fun like going to the play park or the swimming pool?

Toby suddenly recalled the anguish of being bullied at

school. What if his child suffered the same fate because of him? And at home, was it inevitable he or she would end up taking on too many chores and responsibilities as well as the endless worry of having disabled parents? How could they avoid all this happening?

His heart plummeted. Were they being fair in going through with this pregnancy? Although her parents had been harsh and blunt in their remarks, maybe they were trying to warn them in a roundabout way of the challenges that lay ahead.

Over the next week, Toby became even more disheartened when they announced Sue's pregnancy news to friends. Not expecting their negative reactions, he was caught off guard. Lucy went very quiet and didn't say a lot. She struggled to say congratulations.

'It's a shock, Toby, I never thought of you and Sue having a child together.'

Dave's reaction was more natural. He thumped him on the back and said, 'bloody hell, mate, less time for the pub and enjoying yourself. You're a glutton for punishment. You really like a challenge, don't you? But good on you, mate, at least you've got lead in your pencil.'

A couple of friends including Mandy had the nerve to ask, 'will the baby be normal or handicapped like you?' And there were further comments like, 'You're taking a big risk.'

He remembered how he felt when Sue told him she was expecting. How could one moment be filled with such blissful happiness, only to be replaced by the weight of worry and uncertainty about becoming parents? The more he thought about it, the more daunting it looked.

44

It was getting harder for Sue as time went by, but Gill was a godsend and happy to do extra hours. It was early morning, and with her help, Sue hauled the cargo of her thirty-three-week pregnancy out of bed. It was nearly Christmas, and she was all puffed up like a space hopper. The pregnancy was progressing well, and she'd kept up her pelvic floor exercises and tried to stay mobile. She'd bought a large exercise ball and had a routine each morning that she religiously stuck to. She also had a set of weights which she raised above her head. Twenty of these exercises kept her stomach muscles tight and strengthened her arms.

The baby was due around Toby's birthday in early February. It was hard to believe that a human being was growing inside her but when it quivered and fluttered and brushed gently against the walls of her womb, it felt real and exciting. She was looking forward to holding it instead of only feeling it wriggling around her womb trying to play football or dance the tango, but she knew the peace of their lives would be shattered by its cries and demands, and she was mentally preparing herself.

They still had time to adjust to parenthood, but that wasn't the case for their friends Sally and Martin. Sue was eagerly awaiting an update; Sally's waters had broken the night before and they were expecting a phone call with news.

It was gone midday when the phone rang. Toby, at his desk typing, answered the call as Sue came dashing into the room.

'Hello, mate. Any news yet, how's Sal?'

'Yeah, she's fine.' He paused and Toby immediately picked up a flatness in his voice. He sounded fed up, with the weariness of a man who'd paced the hospital corridors all night and needed sleep. Toby's first thought was the labour was dragging on and the baby hadn't arrived yet.

'Has she had the baby?' he asked eagerly.

'Yes.'

He was having to drag the information out of him. 'Boy or girl?'

'A boy, but...'

Sue wheeled over, all excited. 'Girl or boy? What name did they go with in the end?'

'Hang on, Sue.' He shot her a look, motioning for her to be quiet. Martin was trying to speak.

What he heard next froze him in his tracks.

'There are complications.'

'How do you mean, what complications?'

'The baby's like Sally.'

'What?'

'He has the same deformity. No arms.'

A cold shiver ran down his spine. He stared across at Sue. He went to speak but the words caught in his throat and his mouth was suddenly dry.

'Are you still there?'

Toby stared beyond Sue to an undefined spot, barely registering her presence. 'I'm so sorry, I thought the doctors said this couldn't happen.' This was simply too awful to be true.

There was a pause. Martin didn't reply.

'Do you want us to come over?'

'We can talk another time. I must get on. I've still got lots of phone calls to make. Sally's going to be in hospital a while. She's in a side room. The baby's in the special care unit.'

'If we can do anything, anything at all, just give us a shout.'

When he came off the phone, Toby realised he was in a trance, staring at Sue, almost in another world. 'The baby's got no arms.'

Sue's hands flew to her face, her eyes wide and saucer-like. 'Oh my God, no.'

Neither spoke for several moments. It felt as if the earth had stopped spinning and time had frozen. Beyond the shock of what had happened to Sally, one thought screamed in his head.

Could this happen to us?

The next few weeks were going to be hell, the waiting, the worrying, expecting and fearing the worst. With both of them disabled, the haunting possibility of their baby being born with deformities hung heavy in the air and darkened those final weeks of Sue's pregnancy. They could only hope and pray that everything would be okay, but they had to face the reality that it might not be.

45

1987 moved into 1988 and the world was wrapped in a shroud of frost. It was now late January, a couple of weeks before Sue's planned caesarean, and Sandy had spent the day tidying and cleaning the bungalow in preparation for the baby's arrival. She was amazing, so incredibly helpful and had even helped Sue pack her hospital bag as well as cook and freeze a fortnight's worth of meals. Sue enjoyed having her around and she was lovely company. She was a good listener and never gave her opinions, just the odd wise comment. Ever since Sue learned that Sandy was Toby's mother, she had got closer to her, and their relationship had blossomed. She was the support that Sue had long craved.

It was still hard to think of her as Toby's mum. In her mind she'd always be a model or St Bede's charity worker. She was simply too glam to be a mum. Whenever she thought of Sandy, Sue always had a mental picture of her wearing some little fashionable outfit. Skirts and jumpers coordinating. Shoes matching handbags, a silky scarf toning exactly with her lipstick. A bit like one of those cardboard cut-out dolls they used to dress in paper outfits with folding tabs to fix them in place: a paper sundress for the beach, a fur collar for a winter walk, a polka dot dress for a party.

Sandy made them a delicious beef casserole, laid the table, and dished it up before heading home. They were about to sit down to eat it when the phone rang. Sue reached to answer it, surprised to hear Sally's voice at the other end. They'd sent a card and present but had heard nothing from the couple ever since their brief conversation following the baby's birth. It was a difficult and sensitive situation, hard to know what to do for the best, and they didn't want to be a pain by interfering. Martin had said they'd be in touch so all they could do was wait to hear from them.

'Sal, how are you?'

'Yeah, not bad, we've been through the mill and back, but I'm out of hospital now and settling into a routine of sorts. I'm sorry I haven't been in touch. You must be due any day.'

'Don't be sorry, not your fault, my God, you must have had a hard time. How's the baby?'

'Josh is doing well, he's gaining weight, feeding well. Can we come over, tomorrow evening? We can fill you in, it's easier than over the phone.'

They arranged for them to pop over the following evening, joking that the men could drink while they stuck to juice, as Sally was breastfeeding, and Sue hadn't touched alcohol since the start of her pregnancy.

HEARING THE BELL, Toby hurried into the hallway. When he pressed the button on the wall, the automatic door opened. Sally stood shivering in a large coat, bundled up against the chilly evening, and Martin was wearing his usual leather jacket, hands shoved into his pockets.

'Hi, come on in.' Toby stepped aside to let them in, shutting the door behind them with the back of his foot.

Sue came flying into the hallway to greet them. When she saw the baby, she gasped. 'Oh my God, he's tiny.'

Everyone peered down at the bundle in the car seat.

'Is there a baby in there? He looks like a little doll,' Toby joked. He'd forgotten just how small and delicate newborns were. Josh was almost hidden beneath layers of blankets, with only his tiny head, adorned in a pastel yellow knitted bonnet, poking out.

They all went through to the lounge, where coats were shed and draped over the settee. As Martin gently unwrapped Josh, careful not to disturb him, the baby let out a soft mewl like a tiny lamb. In that instant, Toby caught his first glimpse of the baby's hands. A peculiar feeling swept over him, and he couldn't tear his gaze away. It was as if he was looking at his younger self, a glimpse of himself as a baby.

Toby was eager to find out everything and many questions burned in his mind, but he held back. It was best to allow the conversation to unfold as he and Martin listened to the women rattling on about the baby's routine, sleep and feeding patterns. He raised his eyebrows at Martin when the women started talking about baby clothes and nappy sizes. None of it seemed important in the scheme of things. They were all carefully side-stepping the elephant in the room, and even the laughter felt forced. But then Martin made a remark and as everyone turned to look at him, the room's atmosphere felt like a candle flickering in a draught, fragile and uncertain.

'The first thing Sal did was ask for a pair of scissors.'

Toby and Sue looked at each other, confused. 'I don't know what they thought I was going to do with the scissors. The doctor just stared at me, so did the midwife, and all those student doctors crowding round the bloody bed. I didn't want them there, I wanted to be alone.' She looked at Martin. 'Did they think I was going to harm him, harm myself?' She glanced down at Josh, her eyes wet. 'Poor little mite. It's not his fault.'

A solitary tear rolled down her cheek and they were left speechless. 'All those beautiful matinee jackets Nanny knitted for you. Nanny didn't know.'

As Toby stared down at the raggedy edges of the baby's sleeves, he wondered with sadness how Sandy had reacted when she first saw his hands. Would she have bothered to alter his clothes if she had no intention of keeping him? Rona, in contrast, likely made him clothes. He'd ask Bill because somehow this detail about his early life mattered to him and gave his life a sense of perspective.

'What have the doctors said to you?' Sue asked. 'I thought it couldn't be passed on. That's what we were told, wasn't it, Toby?'

Toby looked at Sue and wondered if she was thinking the same. Was this a fluke, should they be worried about their own baby?

'Like you,' Sally said, 'we went to our GP and told him we were thinking of starting a family and he said that thalidomide couldn't be passed on to the next generation.'

Martin looked at Sally. 'And we rang the Thalidomide Trust right after he was born and asked them how it could have happened. You spoke to the director several times.'

Toby looked at Sally. 'And?'

'They reiterated the same thing, that it can't be passed down. But now, a couple of phone calls later, they're going down the route that I was probably misdiagnosed, and my impairment isn't due to thalidomide after all.'

'What?' Toby was stunned.

'They can't just change their mind,' Sue said.

'They said they'd probably given me the benefit of the doubt when I was assessed back in the early sixties, and maybe I should have been put on the Y list instead of the X list.' The X list was for all those children whose mothers could prove they'd taken thalidomide, by way of a prescription or other evidence.

Sue stared at Sally. 'Could they be right? What does your mum say?'

'I'm on the Y list,' Toby said. This was because of his circumstances. Keeping the secret had its consequences.

'She's furious, so are we,' Sally said. 'She rang the director and had a right go at him. She said, "are you accusing me of lying about taking Distaval?" She had proof for God's sake. Her doctor wrote a prescription, and she kept it. What more evidence do they need?'

'So, if they're now revising your case and saying you should be on the Y list, does that mean you're no longer a beneficiary?'

'My Trust money's safe, they reassured me that nothing will change.'

'I can't believe they're saying they might have got it wrong.' Sue shook her head. 'Those panels were made up of world-renowned doctors, leading experts in their field, they assessed each case, they examined, they tested. They were so thorough. We got asked to perform different tasks. It wasn't a quick process.'

'Exactly,' Sally said. 'My mum remembers asking the panel what they thought and them saying, "yes, it's obvious, we've seen many like your daughter". They also said I had all the classic features of thalidomide damage: problems with my ears, face not symmetrical, facial features. They could instantly tell. They were one hundred percent sure, they were the exact words they used, and you don't get surer than that. I was rubber-stamped thalidomide, and now they're saying I might not be.' She shook her head. 'Don't get me started, I'm furious.'

Toby couldn't believe what he was hearing.

Martin leaned forward resting his elbows on his knees. 'They should have said they were only ninety-five percent certain and that there was an element of doubt. Any lawyer would have advised them as much, surely?'

'If they think you might not be thalidomide, what about Josh? What's caused this? Bit of a coincidence, don't you think, both of you with the same impairment?'

'Yes, quite.' Martin tutted and sighed. 'It's a pretty big coincidence. All they could say was, "these things happen, there's a one in a million chance of it happening" and we just happen to be that one in a million.'

'So, we're that one in a million, but it just so happens my mum took the drug.' Sally looked exasperated as she glanced from Toby to Sue. 'The coincidence is way too high, it's like winning the Pools twice, do the number crunching, you get my point?'

'Basically, we're not getting anywhere, we've spoken to countless people in the past fortnight, no one is listening, doors are being shut in our faces, the more we push to be heard, we're hushed. I want to prove them wrong but I'm no scientist,' Martin said wearily.

As Toby listened, he began to wonder if Jasper could pick up the story. Press coverage was a powerful tool, and this was definitely a story the newspaper could explore.

But aside from this, Toby was desperate to hear Martin's

experience of the birth—how he felt as Josh emerged into the world. After all, he was about to go through the same experience, and both fear and excitement clawed at him. Maybe he would suggest they go for a drink one evening and have a proper chat.

46

A few days later, Toby and Martin met for a beer in The Swan Inn in the centre of Haslemere. It was a favourite haunt of Toby's and where he often met Dave and other mates, and occasionally Lucy or Mandy. Sometimes they ate in there, which was fine with certain friends, but Dave was the fussiest of eaters. At the wedding breakfast, Toby noticed him picking at his food and he tended to only like eating in the Wimpy. He couldn't tolerate the entire vegetable food group apart from potatoes, but his mate Steve was less complicated. Shovel any combination of three ingredients into his mouth and he was quite happy. He'd never taken Sue in The Swan though because access was too tricky—there was a step leading into the bar on the roadside and via the alley.

Inside, it was dark and welcoming with a chink of copper and warm low lighting and an array of colourful bottles behind the bar.

He'd always thought the whole point of pubs was to provide people with somewhere comfortable to gather and nurse unhealthy habits under the guise of catching up with others and putting the world to rights, but Toby always loved the ambience and chatter around him. It was a welcome escape from the bungalow and the drivel on TV. Sue was hooked on soap operas, especially *EastEnders* and *Coronation Street* and those theme tunes had burrowed deep into his brain, causing him to question his sanity.

Toby bought the first round. As he was a familiar face in the pub, the barmaid knew to pop a straw in his pint before Martin carried them over to a small table in the corner.

Toby took a sip of his lager. 'How's Sal?'

He smiled. 'She said we were off to the men's crèche. I think she likes me out the way sometimes, well, that's my excuse and I'm sticking to it.'

Toby looked directly at him. Men were good at masking how they really felt, Bill was like it too. But part of his job as a journalist involved putting people at ease so they felt comfortable sharing their story. 'I can't imagine what you've both been through.'

Martin slouched in his seat and rubbed his chin. He had several days of growth and Toby wondered if he was growing a beard or had simply given up looking after himself.

'Sal's a strong woman, a wonderful mum, but I do worry about her.'

'Oh?'

'No matter how much I keep telling her it's not her fault, she blames herself. Mostly she's coping but there are times when she breaks down in floods of tears and I haven't a clue what to do or how to help her. I wish I knew what to do, I just feel so helpless.'

He looked suddenly drawn, diminished somehow, and seeing him now, his defeated shoulders reminded Toby of Bill after Rona's death. His hair looked a mess as if he'd run his hands through it repeatedly, which he probably had.

'That must be hard.' Toby knew the guilt Sally was going through and however illogical it was, it wasn't going to go away. She had no control over how she felt. It was the most awful situation.

'Sometimes she screams at me, "why me?" and one time I caught her staring blankly at Josh, all ghostlike with a strange vacant expression. She scared me then. Then she turned to me and said she wished he'd never been born, that he'd have to go through everything she'd gone through, and it didn't feel right to watch him suffer. This isn't how it's supposed to be, Toby.' He sighed. 'It's meant to be the happiest time of our lives, we're parents.' His face was pained, and Toby had to look away, it was upsetting him and making him scared for his own situation.

'I can't imagine how you felt when you saw him. Everything that went through your head. I take it you were in the room––you didn't chicken out and hover in the corridor?'

'It started as a normal birth, she was in labour for maybe six, eight hours.'

He glanced at the nearby grandfather clock, pursing his lips, staring at the hands as if trying to gauge the timings.

'It's difficult to recall the hours leading up to the head emerging, they're one big blur. They don't matter.' He paused, staring almost through Toby, in another world. 'But after that moment––when the head popped out, then his shoulders and immediately after, tiny hands coming out of his shoulders, his body slithering into the midwife's waiting hands––time slowed, every detail of those moments is so strikingly clear.' He looked at Toby through glazed eyes. 'I couldn't quite believe what I was seeing, maybe I had it all wrong, I kept thinking, my mind's playing tricks on me. I knew I was very tired and when you're so exhausted you can't focus. It had been such a long day, I hadn't eaten or drunk anything, my head was all woolly. And there was blood and slimy stuff and the twisted umbilical cord, and I remember some things on a metal tray.'

He gave a wave of his hand. 'I couldn't take it all in, the angle of the baby's body, the medical people obscuring my view. I tried to focus, I thought I must be dreaming, time felt distorted, the room looked suddenly different, it was as if I was detached from reality. You ever been in that situation?'

Toby didn't know if Martin wanted him to answer, so he shrugged and let him carry on. 'It's hard to explain, it was the most peculiar feeling, I'm not likely to ever experience it again. But in the back of my mind, I knew what I'd seen. And that wasn't going to change. But what the hell was I going to say to Sal? I didn't know what to do, I couldn't cope, I just stood there not saying anything, not smiling, I didn't even go over to kiss her and tell her all those normal things like, "I'm so proud of you", and "we have a baby son". I couldn't tell her. I was a coward, I just wanted to leave the room, I thought I was going to faint or throw up.'

Toby listened intently.

'I ran into the corridor to get a drink from the machine, I couldn't get the coins out of my pocket, my hands were shaking so much and anyway, there wasn't enough coffee in the world to sort me out in that moment. I broke down. Every conceivable emotion hit me at once. We had a new baby, all those weeks and months of waiting and he was now finally here, it was a tremendous feeling of joy and excitement, but that wonderful euphoric feeling was marred, and I felt myself plummeting into this despair, but I knew I had to pull myself together for Sally. I remember thumping the bloody machine, and someone came and put their arm round me, maybe it was the doctor, I don't know, but he spoke to me, he persuaded me to go back into the room. He said Sal needed me, but I was a wreck, I was of no use to her.' He stopped talking, wiped his brow. 'I got back in the room, Sal was drowsy. They'd given her something. I think they wanted her to sleep.'

'And Josh, where was he?' Toby glanced at the young guy near their table who was constantly feeding coins into the one-armed bandit with its bright lights and spinning reels, and wished he would stop. The clinking of the coins and the whirring noise were drowning his thoughts, making it hard to concentrate.

'They were still cleaning him up, weighing him, I'm not sure. Then a while later our own GP arrived. By then we were in a side ward. The look of horror on his face, he was in complete shock. It was an odd coincidence that he was there. He said he just happened to be making a visit to another patient, but I reckon he'd been sent for. Sometime later I went to phone our parents, I knew they'd be waiting for the phone call, and I was dreading telling Sal's mum, this felt like history repeating itself. I knew she was bound to blame herself for this, for taking thalidomide thirty years ago. It was returning to haunt her.'

'And how did she take it?'

'She was completely stunned. Don't think she could quite believe it.'

'That must have been a hard phone call.'

Suddenly, Martin seemed brighter. He sat up, wide-eyed and leaning forward said, 'On a more positive note, do you remember Dr William McBride?'

Toby frowned. 'I don't know him personally, only of him, the doctor who linked our impairments to thalidomide?'

'That's right, the Australian fella. He's here on business

and talking to another thalidomide survivor who's recently had a baby with the same impairments as himself. It turns out, Tobe, Sally isn't alone. There are others, maybe five or six. He's on our side and passionate about proving the second-generation theory.'

'Oh wow, that's fantastic news. I wonder if Jasper and I could interview him.'

'I don't see why not, publicity is just what we need.'

'I'll speak to the editor first thing Monday.'

He furrowed his brow. 'McBride wants to meet us, but the hospital isn't keen, and neither is the Trust.' He threw up his arms, slapped his knees, and let out a sigh.

Toby was finding it hard to concentrate. A group in the corner of the pub had erupted into laughter and were clinking glasses. 'I expect the Trust probably doesn't want to pay money to all these additional people if the second-generation theory is proven.'

'I don't know, there's more to it than that. Some woman from the General Medical Council contacted us and told us not to build our hopes up. Apparently, the GMC are very dismissive of McBride's work and dismissive of him as a person. They said he's not been trained in research, he's just an obstetrician yearning for recognition as a scientist. But they would say that, wouldn't they, anything to get out of their responsibility?'

Toby was horrified. 'But he alerted the world to the dangers of thalidomide, he must know his stuff.'

'They said, at best he's just an alert practitioner.' Again, he threw up his arms in exasperation.

'Sounds like a cover-up to me.'

'They wouldn't tell me much, only that his recent work has been discredited. He was working with a Chinese doctor, conducting research into an antihistamine and claimed it caused birth defects. The drug company were in court several times before it was taken off the market even though there wasn't enough evidence to back up the claim that it had caused birth defects. The litigation costs were rising and the company eventually reached the point they didn't want any more negative publicity. Then, after all that, McBride was found to have manipulated his data. I don't know what to believe, Toby. I can't look at him as a fraud, I just want to meet the guy, after all he did make the connection with thalidomide. To us, he's the hero. He might have been wrong about one drug, but he could be right about second-generation thalidomide. If they ignore his work on this, how many more Joshes will be born? It could be a tragedy on a grand scale, just waiting to happen.'

Toby was worried for his and Sue's baby, it wasn't long now. But then a new thought came whipping through his mind and he felt a wave of dizziness wash over him.

'Antihistamine, you say? But that's as common as paracetamol and ibuprofen.' He was starting to feel panicked. Sue struggled with hay fever. He was certain they had some in the cupboard. She couldn't possibly be foolish enough to take something like that while pregnant, could she? 'How much truth was there to McBride's claims?'

'I've no idea, I'm not interested in antihistamine.'

'There must have been enough babies born with birth defects though for McBride to pursue his claim. After all, what would he gain from it otherwise?'

'Maybe.' Martin shrugged. 'Perhaps the lesson here is for women to steer clear of all medications during pregnancy.'

'Not so easy for some if they have a long-term condition.' Toby was filled with dread. He was desperate to know if Sue had taken anything for her hay fever, or any other medication. He downed his pint and stared at Martin. 'Sue suffers with hay fever. What if it's too late?' He got up all in a fluster and prepared to leave. 'And what if Sally took something too, have you considered that too? Are we missing a point here?'

'Hey, mate, I'm really sorry, I've been rambling on, I should have been more sensitive.'

He stood up and helped Toby with his jacket. 'Look, what happened to us is really uncommon, and I don't believe for one moment Sue would have taken anything untoward. Besides, the doctor will have warned her not to.'

Just then the door swung open and three giggling women burst into the pub, bringing a rush of cold air with them. Immediately recognising Lucy's distinctive high-pitched laugh, Toby looked over and went to greet her.

'Tobes,' Lucy said, rushing over and flinging her arms around him, hugging him tightly and planting a smacker of a kiss on his lips.

'Where have you been all my life?' She was grinning like a lunatic, and he was taken aback by her excitement to see him. He glanced over at Martin, who appeared equally astonished. Perhaps she was a bit tipsy.

Her friends waved to Toby from the background before heading to the bar.

She pulled away but kept her hands on his shoulders. 'How's Sue? When's the baby due?'

'Next week.'

'Oh wow, you must be so excited.' Her eyes were bright and full of life and twinkled under the lighting.

She frowned and gazed into his eyes with a look of concern. He couldn't hide his feelings from her, he never could. She could read him like a book, they'd always been aligned in that way. Sometimes it was as if she could see into his very soul.

She kissed him again. They were inches apart and staring into each other's eyes. He was oblivious to everyone and everything around him as a glorious feeling welled inside. Something flickered in him, maybe it was that effervescence she always exuded, but his heart soared for her and in that brief moment he wanted to melt into her and be carried off to a different time and place.

'Everything's okay, isn't it?' She'd noticed his shift in demeanour.

He turned towards Martin. 'Martin and I were just discussing things.' Toby introduced his friends. 'You remember his wife, Sally, she was bridesmaid at our wedding?' Toby went on to tell Lucy about baby Josh.

'I'm really sorry,' she said to Martin, then to Toby, 'it's easy to worry but worrying won't help Sue. Give me a bell sometime, we can meet for a drink.' She winked at him.

After Lucy headed to the bar, Martin stared at Toby with an incredulous expression. 'Wow, she's a little cracker, so how come you didn't end up with her?'

Toby felt his face flush. 'Mate, she'd eat me for breakfast.' He tried to be light-hearted but that brief hug had sent his longing soaring and he now felt the ache of her absence.

Martin laughed and gave Toby a nudge. 'Yeah, but what a way to go. And by the way, you better get rid of that lipstick on your cheeks.'

'Oh shit.' He tried to rub at his cheek.

'Lucy and I go back years. There's nothing Lucy and I have done that Sue could get upset about, just glad you can't get hung for your thoughts.' He laughed.

When Toby got home, Sue was sitting in bed watching TV. 'Nice evening?' she asked, keeping her eyes on the TV. How he regretted the day he ever agreed to have a television in the bedroom.

He mumbled an answer, and gave a cursory glance round the room before asking, 'Where do we keep the medicine?'

'You okay, Martin given you a headache?' Her gaze was still fixed on the TV, which annoyed Toby, he found it rude.

'The paracetamol is in the bathroom cupboard.'

Then he noticed the bumper bag of crisps by her side. Crisps were her latest craving, which wasn't good because the doctor had warned her to be careful about putting on excess weight. It looked as though she'd munched her way through the lot.

He sat on the bathroom floor sifting through the box of medication with his toes until he found the antihistamines. Opening the packet with his teeth, he found several tablets missing. He dashed back into the bedroom, his heart thumping.

'Have you taken these?'

'What are they?'

He dropped them on the bed and went to turn the light on. It was a struggle to see in the dim and flickering light of the TV. 'Hay fever tablets.'

'No, why?'

'You've not taken any, during the whole pregnancy?'

She turned now from the TV and stared at him looking dumbfounded. 'After what happened to us, do you honestly think I'd be that stupid?'

Relief washed over him. 'That's what I thought, but I just wanted to check.'

'Honestly, Toby, you astound me. I've been so careful. Anyway, you know I haven't taken any, I was really suffering with hay fever last summer if you remember.'

'What did you take for it?'

'Nothing. I leaned over a bowl of hot water doused with

Vicks. You're in your own world sometimes, Tobe, you must remember me complaining about it.'

He felt embarrassed that he hadn't remembered, but at least the panic was over. Or was it? He couldn't shake the worry that the baby would be born with impairments. After all, both he and Sue were affected by thalidomide, which surely increased the risks greatly compared to Sally and Martin.

Toby went into the bathroom to get ready for bed, pausing in front of the mirror. A cold chill of fear trickled down his spine.

The doctor had reassured them their defects couldn't be passed on.

But heck, doctors made mistakes. They were not infallible. Sue understood this truth, just as he did, yet the thought hung heavily between them, unspoken. It was a reality that neither dared confront.

The prospect of a little one who might share their fate was both a profound connection and a source of paralysing anxiety.

After the conversation with Martin, he just didn't know how he'd feel if the same thing happened to them. He was now full of dread and couldn't wait till the baby was born so that his mind could be put at rest. It had even put him off being at the birth. He would rather be told after the event than see it unfolding before his very eyes, confirming his worst fears.

47

As with every aspect of their lives, Toby and Sue had approached the entire pregnancy in a practical manner. Their whole lives they'd found innovative solutions and solved problems in a step-by-step way, and raising a child was no different. They'd thought through every detail from how they were going to feed the baby, how they were going to change its nappy to how they were going to lift it and take it for walks.

It was Saturday afternoon, the day after beer with Martin, and Toby's entire family were eager to call round with last-minute preparations ahead of Sue's scheduled C-section on Friday.

Bill and Patsy were first to arrive. Bill bustled in carrying the changing table he'd built, and Patsy had bought a sling for Sue to carry the baby in her wheelchair. Sue was very excited and followed Bill out onto the driveway to watch him take the new cot out of his truck. They'd bought it from Mothercare, but Bill had fitted new catches to make it easier for them to release the side and he'd extended the legs so that it was the same height as their bed. He'd also used his carpentry skills to make the Moses basket taller so that Sue could easily lift the baby.

'We're going to miss you when you move to Blackpool,' Sue said to Bill as she followed him back into the bungalow.

Patsy was standing by the front door, and she gave Bill a questioning glance, as if to say, *you haven't told them yet.*

'Don't you worry, love, we've no intention of abandoning you. We've decided to muddle along for the next year to make sure you're all settled and coping.'

'That's brilliant, Dad,' Toby said, stepping into the hallway.

'The things we do for you.' He shook his head in jest. 'You've got Patsy to thank for that decision.'

The look on Patsy's face revealed everything. She wasn't happy about it, she had her own family to think of and grandchildren she enjoyed spending time with, but what choice did she have? They needed Bill, that much was obvious.

Just then a taxi pulled up and Norman got out.

'What's he doing? This is supposed to be a family get-together, did you invite him?'

'I can't control when he decides to pop round.'

Norman bounded down the drive carrying the cot bedding she'd asked him to buy.

He focused only on Sue as he passed her the bedding, ignoring everyone around him.

'There we are, my sweet petal, I got the bedding you wanted from House of Fraser, and I managed to get a discount. I know the store manager.' He gave her a wink and looked as pleased as punch with himself. 'We go back years, Eddie and I.' Norman had told her this so many times that the story of how they met was getting boring. 'He was only too happy to help, he knows what a special lady you are to me.'

Toby, Bill, and Patsy stood to the side, aghast at his rudeness, and none of them seemed keen to engage him in conversation.

'Norman,' Sue said as he turned to go, 'you don't need to get a taxi round here specially. I could have called round sometime.'

He started to walk off and raised his hand in a wave.

'Nonsense, petal, you're worth it, shout if there's anything else I can help with.'

As they watched the taxi pull away, Sue was aware of Toby standing stiffly beside her. 'Rude bloody man, he can't even acknowledge me. Has he always been that ignorant? Do you have to invite him round?'

'I didn't and sorry, I know he can be a bit strange, but don't have a go at me. Just be thankful he doesn't live next door anymore.'

Toby mimicked Norman.

'Toby, you're so cruel but so good at mimicking him.'

'What an odd little man,' Bill said, shaking his head before going back into the house to set up the cot. Sue went to watch him, and Patsy took the bedding out of the packaging.

A short while later, Sandy, Jasper and Angela arrived. Sandy and Patsy busied themselves in the kitchen, brewing tea and slicing fruitcake to serve on plates before going back to the lounge.

'Now then,' Sandy said as she poured the tea. 'I'm going to come in every day and prepare the baby's bottles and I won't take no for an answer.'

One thing they hadn't yet done was employ a mother's help to assist them. Gill was still coming twice a day to help

Sue, so they were going to wait and see what additional help they needed.

Sue glanced from Toby to Sandy. They'd had this discussion before. She was going to feed the baby herself as it was more practical. 'That's really sweet of you, but I'm hoping to breastfeed.'

'Yes, I know, pet, and I'm really conscious of not interfering, but just in case for whatever reason you can't, and not every woman can, I just want you to know, I'm here if you need me and I'm happy to make up the bottles.'

Patsy leaned forward to pick up her cup. 'You're lucky if you can feed it yourself, I wasn't able to breastfeed. My eldest was a grisly baby, always hungry, and then they found he was losing weight and eventually they rushed him to hospital, where we found out I just wasn't producing milk.'

Bill glared at Patsy. 'Don't scare the poor lass.'

'It's just something to bear in mind, that's all.'

'Eventually we'll bottle-feed, but the midwife told us, breast is best.' Toby chuckled and went red. 'And I have to agree, I've always thought breast is best.' He winked at Sue.

'Cheeky sod. The only breast you'll be getting for the next two years is a chicken breast.'

Angela shot up. 'Toby, how rude. And I've got something for you, it was Mum's idea,' she said excitedly, pulling a doll out of a plastic bag. 'You can use this doll to practise on.' She smoothed its dress and dumped it onto Toby's lap. 'Here's a bottle too,' she added.

'How the hell will I feed it?'

'I'm sure we can work something out, Toblerone,' Sue said. She started singing, 'Toblerone, feeding your own.'

'It's another job I can get out of,' Toby said with a laugh, but he really wanted to be able to feed the baby.

Jasper took out his camera. 'Sorry, lad, but you playing with a doll calls for a photo.'

Everybody laughed.

Thank God my mates aren't here to watch. They would really take the mickey, especially Dave.

'Stop it, Jasper,' Sandy said, slapping Jasper's arm. 'Give the poor boy a break.'

Toby didn't like to tell them he'd been playing with one of Gill's daughter's dolls. He would never have heard the last of it. But he'd yet to find a solution to this feeding lark, he'd got more chance of feeding the carpet than the baby.

Everyone watched, amused, as he tried out different ways of holding the doll. He was happy to entertain and make them laugh. 'Why can't a baby be like a cat and lick the milk from a saucer?'

Sandy shrieked. 'Toby, you're so funny.'

'I wish I had big boobs full of milk, it would be so much easier. I'd just dangle the boob over the baby's face. Save the bother, let me hover.'

Bill let out a low rumbling laugh.

He tried several ways of holding the doll and its bottle. Whatever he did, it proved tricky. And then Sandy came up with the idea of getting some bottles with handles so that Toby could hold the handle with his toe like he did with mugs and cups, or slip several toes under the handle. That would give him full control of it, but they still needed a safe way for Toby to hold the baby.

Everybody pitched in with their ideas. Sandy suggested putting the baby on a pillow on the floor, Sue said it would be better on the settee.

'How are you going to bath the baby and pick it up?' Angela asked.

Impatient little madam. She wanted him to master it all,

but it was going to take time to work out the best way to tackle tasks, and some he'd never be able to do, at least not safely, and he was not prepared to put his child at risk just to prove a point.

'I'll pick it up with my teeth like a bear picks up its cub.'

Everyone gasped.

Toby laughed. 'Don't worry, it'll be perfectly safe, I know what I'm doing.' He leaned down and bit the doll's dress, scooping it up with its clothing between his teeth, and passed it to Sue. He chuckled. This gave new meaning to babies being delivered by storks. 'I won't be able to bath it, sadly, and Sue will need help if she's to bath it. That's one task we'll both struggle with.'

'You'll have to be very careful not to bite the baby,' Patsy warned.

Bloody woman, thinking of every disaster.

Angela, who'd sat on the floor peering intently at Toby as he played with her doll, hurried to the kitchen. He heard drawers being pulled open and the clatter of cutlery and wondered what the girl was up to.

She returned with a spoon and bowl and dumped it onto Toby's lap. 'Now try and feed my dolly some mashed banana.' Angela was twelve and now attended secondary school, but there was a childish streak about her. He was surprised that she was interested in him feeding a doll.

'Where's the banana?'

She waved at him dismissively. 'Just pretend.'

'That's cheating, I can't cheat.' He laughed. 'There's a banana in the bowl on the kitchen worktop. Go and mash it up and I'll feed you.'

'But I hate bananas and I'm not a baby, I don't want to be fed.'

'You do not hate bananas,' Sandy said with a laugh. 'Go on, do as Toby says, love.'

'Toby should do it, otherwise how will he get the practice in?'

Toby laughed. 'I don't need to prove myself, I'm quite capable of peeling and mashing a bit of banana.'

Angela huffed and stomped off to the kitchen bringing back a bowl of mashed banana with a teaspoon. Toby was now sitting at the dining room table. She put the bowl in front of him and went to hand the spoon to him, but he turned and grabbed it with his mouth then dipped his head and dived into the mushy mixture.

Once again everyone laughed and clapped and it felt like a game, but for Toby and Sue this was real life and feeding their baby was just one of the many challenges they were going to face. Toby was concerned about every aspect of parenting, yet beneath his concerns lay a fierce determination to be the best parent he could be, and he felt sure that together, he and Sue would navigate their own path.

48

While everyone's attention was on Toby, Sue sloped off to the bedroom to look at the cot. Bill had done a grand job, it was perfect, and she was so relieved that he wasn't moving away yet. He was such a practical man, useful to have around and they'd come to rely on him.

She stroked her bump and whispered, 'Little prawn, soon you'll be here lying next to me.' Excitement bubbled at the thought of finally holding her baby. She pictured a boy with a sheen of mousey hair and a scrunched-up face, his tiny fingers wrapping around hers. The smell of him, all powdery and milky, his soft skin next to hers, his chubby arms, legs.

The hardest thing to imagine was breast-feeding. The very idea of a small creature latching on to her nipples felt foreign and unsettling, like something out of an alien movie. She couldn't shake the discomfort she felt when she thought of this intimate act and found herself grappling with an odd resistance to it. Yet, deep down, she knew that breastfeeding was the most practical way to feed the baby. She just hoped that once it arrived, hormones would kick in to help her feel comfortable and make it easier to enjoy this special part of being a mum.

A wave of anxiety churned in her stomach, but she was trying to make a conscious effort to push those dark thoughts aside. After all, the likelihood of the baby inheriting their defects was quite low and she was determined not to let this worry overshadow the joy of their first child. It was hard though not to dwell on the possibility. How on earth would they cope with a disabled child? And how would she truly feel about it? What if she took one look at it and felt pure revulsion? Was that how her own mum had felt when she saw her for the first time? Until it was born, these feelings remained abstract, distant, and difficult to grasp. It was a bit like losing someone, not realising how much someone meant until they were gone or not knowing how strong your feelings were until they were put to the test.

This would be a huge test, that much was clear.

In the quiet corners of her mind when she imagined a disabled baby, a troubling thought surfaced: what if she rejected it like her own mother had rejected her? The idea terrified her. And then she thought of her mum, and sadness curled around her. Her eyes filled with tears.

How she longed to talk to her mother, really talk to her. She desperately wanted to understand, especially now that she was about to become a mother herself.

What had gone through her mind in those minutes, hours, days after her birth? She didn't know the catalogue of events, Pearl had never told her story or spoken about her feelings. Her emotions had been locked away all these years, as if she'd made a silent agreement with herself not to show an inch of vulnerability, not to admit to the guilt she felt. Sue hated that stoical façade she wore like a second skin. A hard, cold woman, Pearl had never been the mum she should have been, warm, loving and supportive. But a part of her wondered what pressures she'd been under at the time. Had others condemned her for taking Distaval? Did her dad blame her and never let her forget?

She leaned towards the cot and gripped the bars tightly, like a prisoner longing to escape. Yet, the freedom she craved wasn't from physical confinement, it was liberation from the emotional burdens and haunting memories of her past.

In the background, laughter rose from the lounge where Toby and his family were enjoying themselves. How she'd always longed to be a part of her own family, to be included in these sorts of gatherings—simple get-togethers, Christmases, barbecues, birthday parties—but they'd always excluded her.

She let out a sob. It wasn't fair, how could her parents treat her so badly? *They should be here too showing an interest in my life.* Perhaps, just perhaps, the arrival of their first grandchild would change her parents. Surely, they wouldn't want to miss out on those precious moments.

49

Monday morning arrived, casting a pale wintery light into Sam's office, bouncing across the walls, and making Toby squint. He was sitting with Jasper facing the editor's desk. Outside, a chill blanketed the city, and the windows had a frosty sheen. Sam, leaning back in his chair, was already indulging in his first cigar of the day, the rich aroma swirling into the air. Toby moved his chair towards a shaded area so that the sun didn't blind him, and glancing out of the window, he took in the view over the Docklands.

Cranes towered like sentinels over the ongoing regeneration. Steel beams and scaffolding created a patchwork of progress against the skyline and there was so much to interest him that he could have easily spent all day gazing out of the window. A cluster of tall buildings were going up, mostly for financial institutions. Soon they would pierce the sky, and their gleaming glass façades would reflect the sunlight in a dazzling display. It was a scene of ambition and achievement, all unfolding before his very eyes.

He loved his job right in the heart of London, the city's

energy invigorated him. There was a lot of flexibility to the role, and he had the perfect balance of working from the office and from home. When he was in London he covered local stories, and sometimes he went out with Jasper to interview people then wrote up the story at home.

They briefed Sam on recent stories and then Toby shared news about Sally and Martin's baby. He recounted everything that had happened, leaving out no detail, and ended with Dr McBride's upcoming visit and the hospital's negative reaction.

Sam sat in stunned silence as he fiddled with his moustache, absorbing the gravity of what he'd just heard. 'That's truly shocking,' he finally remarked. 'It would have to be an enormous coincidence for that to be a random fluke. It's a bit like a man who bumps into the twin he never knew he had, in an airport on the other side of the world, or a family of four dying on the same day of different causes or winning the Pools twice.'

'Yes, it does seem a remarkable coincidence, birth defects are so rare. We're having a hard time believing thalidomide doesn't cause second-generation defects. But the medical profession is adamant it can't. Is this worth exploring? I think it is,' Toby said. 'Their baby isn't the only one to be born with the same impairment as their parent. There are others out there, maybe five or six in the UK alone.'

'And McBride is working on the theory that thalidomide damage can be inherited?'

'Yes, but given his recent work and the way he was discredited, is he even a credible authority?'

'I think we should hear what he's got to say. I'll leave it with you both, shall I?'

Afterwards, Toby wasted no time in contacting

McBride's office in Australia and a meeting was set up. Meanwhile, for the remainder of that day and the next, Jasper continued interviewing Tory politicians for a piece about Margaret Thatcher's lengthy time in office, as she had become the longest-serving UK prime minister.

Toby was given permission to interview McBride in a side room at Great Ormond Street Hospital. Jasper had insisted Toby go alone. 'This is huge, lad, you're going to meet the man who made the thalidomide connection. He's going to enjoy meeting you, you aren't any old journalist, he will be so proud of you and I'm proud of you.'

Meeting McBride felt like such an honour but as he arrived at the busy hospital entrance and joined the throng of people spilling into the corridor, he couldn't help pondering what his life could have been had McBride made his discovery just a couple of years earlier.

Life is just a dance of fate and fortune, the interception of time and chance.

Sandy wouldn't have taken thalidomide and because she'd planned to have him adopted, he could be anywhere now, raised by entirely different people. He contemplated all the possibilities and wondered what opportunities he would have had. It was a bizarre thought that ended with him concluding that the life he had wasn't so terrible. He'd been given plenty of opportunities, and most important of all, he was surrounded by people who genuinely cared for and loved him, which was the greatest gift of all.

In the corridor he asked for directions to the department and went up several floors in the lift. After asking a few people, he reached his destination.

He recognised William McBride as soon as he saw him, from photographs he'd seen. He was wearing a pale insipid grey suit with a matching tie. His brown eyes were magnified behind thick glasses and his hair had been combed into a side parting. He had the appearance of a clever chap, the kind who knew his stuff, Toby thought. Highbrow, the type of fella who resided in an ivory tower, completely oblivious to the opposite sex or social events.

'Hello, really great to meet you,' Toby said as they approached each other. He clocked a momentary awkwardness in McBride's eyes, unsure how to shake Toby's hand. Sometimes people were relaxed and reached for his hand and at other times Toby would lift his leg and offer his foot. They were always amazed when he did this, which he found slightly patronising because for him it was a natural body movement and he thought nothing of it. But there was always laughter that followed. He knew this gesture must look rather bizarre to the able-bodied.

The awkward moment passed, and they turned and headed into the meeting room.

'At last, I get to meet you. I've read about your work and obviously I'm one of the ones affected,' Toby said as they sat down.

'It's always lovely to meet a survivor and find out how their lives have turned out. You're doing quite well for yourself by all accounts. Great career and you've recently got married.' He beamed at him and swept his fingers through his hair before reaching for his briefcase and pulling out a wad of papers.

'And our baby is due in a couple of weeks.'

'Oh goodness, congratulations, you must be very excited.'

'On my way up in the lift, it suddenly occurred to me, had you made your discovery two years earlier we may not be meeting now. It's very kind of you to take time out like this and at such short notice.'

They had a general chat about mundane things before McBride said with a laugh, 'Right, let's get down to business, what do you want to know?'

'I gather you're meeting close friends of mine, Sally and Martin. Sally's a thalidomide survivor and she's just had a baby with the same impairment. You think thalidomide could be passed on, it could be inherited, is that right and what evidence do you have for believing that? And on a personal level this is of great interest to me because, I'm now worried our baby could be affected too.'

'Yes, I completely understand your worries.' He furrowed his brow and tilted his head with concern.

'How far has your research come? How many others might be affected? There's a lot of confusion in my mind because all the science, without exception, seems to suggest it's not possible to pass on the defects, so what makes *you* think otherwise?'

'I'm working with a Chinese doctor on this, Dr Huang, and our tests are still ongoing, so it's too early to say.'

'Forgive me, doctor, if I speak out of turn, but you are very much the exception here in what you believe, have you ever wanted something to be true so badly that you'll do anything to make that happen? That sort of situation happens all the time, but we head down that path at our peril. Could that be the case, perhaps?'

'The findings of my research will be the proof, one way or the other. I have and I am devoting a lot of time and money to proving my hypothesis, that thalidomide can indeed be inherited. I established Foundation 41 back in the early seventies using my prize money for making the connection between birth defects and thalidomide. I've devoted many years of my life to looking at the causes of birth defects.' He raised his arms and sat back. 'I have no personal gain to make from my work, Toby.'

'You haven't really told me what your theory is.'

'It's too early to say.'

'Yes, you've already said that.' He laughed, not wanting to harangue the man but take the reins back. 'But what can you tell me, so far?'

'You're an eager young fella.' He smiled. 'I think that thalidomide causes malformations by interacting with the DNA of the dividing embryonic cell. If that turns out to be the case, it will explain why a few children born to thalidomide survivors––like your friend Sally for instance––have similar physical abnormalities to their parents. Part of the thalidomide molecule can bind to genetic material in rat embryos. If my tests turn out to show that thalidomide can bind to the DNA, it inevitably interferes with the genetic code. We think that possibly––and I stress possibly––thalidomide does the same thing in humans.'

'That's very interesting. Is there anything I can help you with? I'm in a good position to find things out, I have links both in the newspaper and in the thalidomide community.'

'Quite possibly, you could be useful. We'll certainly stay in touch.'

'Great.' Toby leaned back. Their conversation looped inside his head. He was happy with the information he had so far and thought he could bash out a short article.

McBride looked at him with a curious expression, as if he were holding back on something. Then he tentatively said, 'the problem is, some of the research I'm doing is being challenged and some are discrediting my work and don't like what I'm discovering. I've had this ever since I made the discovery of thalidomide. Drug companies don't like incompetency uncovered. There were a lot of raised eyebrows, how was it allowed to happen?'

He leaned forward, his words suddenly passionate. 'These were top level experts in their field, for God's sake, and they failed to pick it up. It's time the medical profession cleaned up their act. Our work has led to greater regulation, far more rigorous testing, but there's still a long way to go. And I'm very suspicious, the way they are all closing ranks and saying that thalidomide can't be passed down. Look at the history of the drug and how long it took them to make the connection. Everyone said no, they denied it for so long. It may well take the same length of time for the truth to come out about second-generation defects.'

'Yes, the medical profession is adamant.'

'I'm being blocked at every avenue. There's a lot of closing of ranks because they don't want another scandal.'

'And they don't want to fund another generation of thalidomides.'

'It's going to be a battle to prove my theory, and no doubt they will want to brush it under the carpet, pretend these children aren't being born.'

'That's how it's been all along, we don't matter because we're only a tiny number of people affected, and the NHS and government have so many other causes. I guess it's a bit like the threat of an asteroid, there's always a bigger one out there somewhere in the solar system.'

Having mingled in political circles over the years as a member of the Young Conservatives, Toby understood. 'Indeed. Every new scandal requires financial help, another drain on resources and that's before the government has dealt with other unexpected situations, like a war or a looming recession or whatever. So many demands on government and massive reluctance to take on new issues.'

He tutted. 'And nowadays everyone wants compensation. It's the same the world over.'

'Yes, we're becoming a litigious society.'

On his way home, Toby reflected on his conversation with McBride. While it had been engaging at the time, he now doubted its substance. The next day, he met with Jasper to talk it through and think about the piece he was going to write. Jasper was much more enthusiastic.

'You did well, lad. You've got to remember that not every article has to be about a monumental event like the moon landings or a ground-breaking discovery like penicillin. It's about the discussions we have, their potential direction, how you engage your readers, and what they glean from your words. Generating interest is much more important. If it gets people thinking, that's all we can ask for. Never give up just because someone tells you it's not worth it.'

Toby realised there was still much to learn and to make it to the top he had to be tenacious, but he had a passion that drove him, wasn't afraid to ask awkward questions and he had an inquisitive mind and hated taking no for an answer.

50

Sue hadn't slept a wink. The baby was pressing down on her bladder, and she'd had to get up several times in the night. It was quite a struggle sitting up and transferring to her wheelchair and invariably she'd get to the loo just for a tiny trickle. It was very frustrating, and she couldn't wait for the baby to be out. She didn't have long to wait. In a few hours' time, her baby would be in her arms.

Gill came early to get her washed and dressed. As she prepared for her scheduled caesarean at 10am, it felt oddly like heading to a dentist appointment for a tooth extraction, but it also felt as if all her Christmases and birthdays were arriving at once.

A little after seven, the phone rang, startling them all.

'That better not be the hospital ringing to cancel,' Sue said with a laugh as Toby dived in to answer it.

'I think it'll be Martin. The press has been bothering him.'

'Oh. You didn't say.'

'Martin, everything okay, mate?' Toby asked. He hadn't

finished dressing, and he was standing in his underpants and t shirt. It was a funny sight. To think how shy he'd been months ago around Gill, now he didn't seem to care if she saw him half-naked.

Sue wheeled over, straining to listen to the conversation. Martin was jabbering on, and it was hard to make sense of what he was saying.

'I'll ring you later, Sue's going into hospital today, but please, please, don't do anything rash, you might come to regret it, these tabloids, they're a law unto themselves.'

This time, Sue caught his words. 'I'm really sorry, I forgot it's today, good luck and keep me posted.'

'What's that all about then?' she asked, turning, and wheeling over to the table where Gill had just put a plate of hot buttered toast. It smelled delicious. She was about to pick up a slice before remembering she wasn't allowed to eat anything until after the caesarean. 'No.' She let a mock howl. 'I'm so hungry.'

'Oh blimey, I'm so sorry.' Gill looked all flustered. 'Toby, you need feeding up, tuck in.'

Toby sat down. 'I don't have much appetite, Gill, I'm worried about today.'

Gill laughed. 'Sue will be doing all the hard work. Honestly, you men, my husband was just the same. In fact, he sloped off for a pint just before I was rushed into theatre.'

'No wonder you asked him for a divorce,' Sue said with a tut before glancing over at Toby. 'I won't be letting you sneak off for a swift half, that's for sure. I'm relying on you to look after my handbag, these hospitals, they're teeming with thieves.'

Toby took a swig of his tea and stared out of the window. 'I'm worried about Martin and Sally.'

'This is meant to be our day, you shouldn't be worrying about them.'

'Sorry.'

'You still haven't said what's going on.'

Gill went out of the room and returned holding Toby's trousers. 'You might want to put these on.' She held them up for him, laughing and he stood up to put them on before nipping into the bedroom to use his aid to pull up the zipper.

'*The Sun* have been in touch. They want to write about Martin and Sally. I just think they're going to sensationalise the whole story. They need to think carefully about the implications.'

'Depends how much they're offering.'

'They were told to name their price.'

'Jeepers.'

'What they need to consider is the intrusion on their lives. If they agree, it won't just stop at one interview and one article, they'll be followed, hounded, and poor Josh, think of his privacy, of their privacy as a family. They'd be famous, people would recognise them wherever they went. It would be awful. Can't say I'd like it myself, however much money I was offered.'

'True, I hadn't thought of that. That's a big dilemma.'

A short while later, Gill helped them into the car. They'd recently bought a blue Mini Chairman which had been adapted by Gowrings Mobility of Newbury and as they drove along, a song by the Pet Shop Boys blasted out from Mercury FM and they sang the words.

After parking the car and getting out, they headed towards the hospital entrance, and minutes later were buzzed onto the ward.

As they entered, they were greeted by a cheerful nurse

carrying a clipboard. 'Mr and Mrs Murphy, welcome. I'm Olwen and I'll be looking after you today.'

Sue had to smile, it felt like the welcome you'd receive at a restaurant or a cruise ship. It was hard to believe she was about to go into theatre for surgery. If a waiter had appeared with a tray of drinks, she wouldn't have been taken aback.

Another couple were sitting off to the side of the corridor. The woman was heavily pregnant. Sue sensed their eyes on her and Toby, and then the woman leaned in to whisper something to her partner.

Three other nurses were standing at the workstation looking at paperwork. They glanced up and smiled.

'This is the special couple, Mr and Mrs Murphy,' Olwen said by way of introduction.

Sue flinched. She didn't want to be referred to as the "special couple", it felt horribly patronising.

The nurses suddenly seemed interested in them, and Sue was certain that wouldn't have happened if they had been able-bodied.

One of the nurses put her glasses on and stepped towards them. 'Oh, you're the thalidomide pair.' It was such a dehumanising description and Sue felt her hackles rise. 'We'll be taking extra care of you, my love.'

She didn't want to be singled out for special treatment.

Then, out of the corner of her eye, she clocked the other couple looking on, all interested, before whispering. This time she heard what the woman said. 'How would she even get pregnant?'

Sue looked straight at her with daggered eyes and said, 'Same way as you did.'

The nurses all looked embarrassed, and Olwen turned to Sue. 'Let's take you down here.' She pointed the way.

As they headed down the corridor, the pregnant woman

said, 'How on earth will they look after a baby? Bloody ridiculous.' Sue felt so angry, but she resisted turning round and making a cutting remark. It wasn't worth it.

'We'll need to do some routine checks first, I'll ask you to pee in a pot, then after the checks, we'll prepare you for surgery and get you shaved.'

'Shaved? How do you mean?'

'Where the baby comes out.'

'But I'm not having a normal delivery.' It seemed a bit unnecessary.

'We always shave down there. It's routine.'

'After that, you'll be given an enema,' Olwen added.

'Jeepers, what else will you be doing to my poor old bod?'

'You'll have a catheter inserted just before you go in, which you'll appreciate for the first couple of days, not having to get up for the loo.'

After the preparations, Sue was taken into theatre and introduced to the obstetrician and the anaesthetist. They were both middle-aged men.

The obstetrician explained that he would be making a ten- to fifteen-centimetre cut at the bottom of Sue's abdomen, just at the top of her pubic hairline, big enough to deliver the baby.

'The hospital's obstetricians wanted you to have the very best care, so our obstetrician today has come all the way down from Birmingham. He's got years of experience. We've also got three trainees with us today. Do you mind if they join us?' Olwen asked.

Sue was a bit wary and wondered if they were expecting to deliver another baby with birth defects. She glanced at Toby to gauge his opinion.

'That's okay, but will I be able to stay?' He'd decided he did want to watch the birth.

'Yes, of course,' Olwen said. Toby was already gowned up.

The three trainees, dressed in white coats, entered. They didn't say anything and hovered in the background.

'Now,' the obstetrician said, 'are you absolutely sure you want to be awake for the birth?'

'Yes, we've discussed all this, I want that magical moment watching it come out.'

'You won't be able to see much because we'll be putting a sheet up, but you will be fully awake, and you'll be able to hold your baby.' He hesitated. 'I'm going to just insert the catheter.'

Sue was attached to various machines which monitored her heart rate and blood pressure as well as the baby's, and all she could do was lie back and stare up at the white ceiling. With lights blinding her, she glanced down to see them pegging a green sheet, as if erecting a tent across her belly. It was a wall looming in front of her, dividing her body in two and blocking her view, turning her lower parts into a crime scene. And now, everything that happened beyond that wall of green was a complete unknown and felt both scary and mysterious. She had always felt vulnerable because of her disability, but now, as she lay on the operating table, that vulnerability felt even more intense.

Suddenly a sharp pain shot through her body, and she screamed in agony.

'What's that?'

The obstetrician glanced over the sheet, his face mostly obscured by a mask. 'I'm sorry, I've just inserted the catheter.'

'Couldn't you have done that after the spinal block, then I wouldn't have felt it?'

The trainees looked at the anaesthetist with quizzical faces. 'Yes, I could have done, but it doesn't usually hurt.'

Sue was sobbing, feeling as if she needed to apologise for her pain which was overwhelming and greater than anything she had experienced before, despite prior surgeries to remove a few toes and a foot bone.

While she was still recovering from the shock of the pain, now subsiding, the anaesthetist, calm and focused, prepared to give her an epidural, explaining each step. His hands felt steady and reassuring as he held her back.

'Please stay very still,' he instructed. She realised the importance of not moving and thoughts raced through her mind as she stayed stock still in an awkward position. What if she moved? What if the needle slipped? She held her breath, glad she wasn't about to sneeze or cough.

It seemed to be taking an age. She wondered if it was a complicated procedure. She felt a scratch, then an electric-shock type of pain shot down her spine. When he stood back, she thought it was all done and expected to feel her lower body go numb, but it didn't. He stepped over to the obstetrician and trainees, lowering his voice as he spoke, but she didn't understand what he was saying. He had a heavy accent which made it difficult, and she thought she heard the odd Latin word. She wished he'd speak to her first. What was going on?

After a few moments, he turned and spoke to her. 'I'm having difficulty inserting the spinal block. I can call in another anaesthetist to assist but that might be some time, or we can give you a general anaesthetic which will put you to sleep. Either way, the baby doesn't suffer.'

In that moment, she hadn't anticipated the wave of

unexpected relief that washed over her. She glanced at Toby to see that he was as surprised as she was. He knew how adamant she'd been throughout her pregnancy about wanting to be awake during the birth. Hearing the baby's first cries, holding him, smelling him, that special moment, but now, with exhaustion settling into her bones, it didn't matter, she just wanted an easy, pain-free delivery. The thought of surrendering to sleep sounded so enticing.

As soon as she'd agreed to the procedure, the anaesthetist held her hand and before administering the anaesthetic through the IV, he smiled at her and said, 'it will feel like a nice gin and tonic.'

Everything went black.

Sometime later, she heard Toby's voice and background noise. People talking. Was she dreaming? She felt too groggy and comfortable to move or open her eyes. She just wanted to sleep, but Toby was being persistent.

The baby, she'd had a baby. Still, she couldn't move, she didn't want to move.

'We've got a little girl, it's a girl.' He kissed her cheek, but she felt like a slab of meat and couldn't respond and still hadn't opened her eyes. He must have left her then because she drifted into a deep sleep, waking hours later when a nurse spoke to her.

She opened her eyes. She was in a side room by herself and beside her in a plastic cot lay a gremlin-like creature with a pinched face and a scabby head. Toby was standing by the cot with an adoring look on his face. He came over to her and as he leaned down to kiss her, she saw tears welling in his eyes.

'She's perfect, Suekins, just perfect. She's got ten fingers and ten toes, just perfect. We made her, we did it.'

Tears were streaming down his face, and he looked tired.

She wanted to share in the joy and hold the baby, but she felt so groggy and disorientated. More sleep was what she needed most, but she felt guilty about this and forced herself into a sitting position before she was tempted to drop off again.

'I'll ask the midwife to put her in your arms. I wish I could do it myself, but it wouldn't be safe.'

He went out into the corridor to find a midwife, who came in and gently lifted the baby and put her into Sue's waiting arms. She immediately started crying and Sue was worried she was holding her wrong.

'You could try feeding her.'

'Oh hell, what do I do, how do I feed her?' She felt suddenly panicked and unprepared, and needed to be shown what to do. Luckily the midwife showed her how to cradle the baby and coax her little mouth open so that she could latch on. It felt strange having someone lift her boob and manipulate it into place as if it were an inanimate object, a piece of machinery with a set of instructions and training manual. She soon got the hang of it though and the baby latched on.

'She won't get any milk yet, but she will get colostrum which is very nutritious, and it's good to get her used to feeding, it helps the bonding.'

Sue stared down at the baby in her arms, a rush of love so overwhelming washing over her. It was hard to believe this cute little baby had come out of her body, there was a disconnect. She'd been asleep, she hadn't witnessed the birth of her child.

'We still haven't decided on a name yet,' Toby reminded her. 'We can't call her Prawn.' He laughed.

They'd discussed various names but gone round in circles unable to decide. Sue wanted to name the baby after a character from her favourite soap, *Neighbours*. Charlene or Kylie for a girl and Scott or Jason for a boy. Toby hated the programme and loathed the idea of naming a child after one of its characters or the characters' real names. He didn't particularly like Kylie Minogue or Jason Donovan. The people he admired were politicians, but he had no intention of naming his child Margaret after Thatcher or Norman after Tebbit.

The name Heidi was growing on Toby, but he hadn't suggested it to Sue. Jasper had given him the idea because he'd been chattering about their German friend Heidi recently. Claudia, finally ready to share her story with Jasper, had invited him over to Germany. Under Mikhail Gorbachev's leadership in Russia, his policies of Glasnost and Perestroika were beginning to impact East Germany, and although it was still a communist state there was a loosening of restrictions particularly with regard to travel, and East Germany's borders were slightly easier to cross. With the situation getting a bit easier, Claudia hoped Jasper might be able to help find Heidi's parents. Jasper was keen to hear her story and write about it at the very least but how much he was able to do to find them, he wasn't so sure. Apparently she'd kept a diary and she was going to let Jasper read it.

'Do you like the name Heidi?'

'That was my favourite film when I was a kid. Yes, let's name her after Shirley Temple.'

The idea had backfired, he didn't want his kid named after anybody on TV. 'I wasn't thinking of the film, I was thinking of our friend Heidi. It's such a beautiful and unusual name. You don't hear it much. For me it carries a sense of sadness that her mum never got the chance to call her that after they were separated by the Berlin Wall.'

Sue frowned at him. 'We should choose a name for happy reasons not sad ones. But I do like the name. My mum gave me such a boring name. Just about every other girl of my sort of age is a Susan. I want her to have something different.'

'I think Heidi would be very honoured we're naming our baby after her.'

'Heidi it is then,' Sue said, beaming.

'I'll give her a ring later.'

'And the middle name?' Sue asked. 'What about Nicola?'

Toby hesitated then said, 'Yes, that's nice.'

SUE STAYED in hospital for two weeks learning how to feed and care for the baby. She couldn't understand though why they'd put her in a side room away from the other new mums on the main maternity ward. It was lonely all by herself and she desperately wanted to chat to them, ask about their experiences as well as make new friends. She felt completely isolated. She hadn't paid for a private room or requested one.

On the second morning, she asked the nurse why they'd put her in this room.

'Why am I in here? I'm just a mum like everyone else.'

'But you're our special mum,' the nurse said with a smile as she went to the cot to pick up Heidi.

'I don't need to be treated any differently though.'

The nurse picked the baby up and brought her to Sue, gently lowering the child into her arms. Sue pulled at her nightdress and prepared to feed Heidi. The baby latched on like a barnacle.

'We decided you'd be better off in a private room.' She leaned in, her voice falling to a whisper. 'Some mums can be judgemental. We didn't want you overwhelmed and upset.'

'I don't want to be separated just because I'm disabled, I just want to feel normal, I can handle any negative comments and questions.'

She put her hand on Sue's shoulder. 'I know you can, and I admire your strength, but it's also important you don't face unnecessary stress. This room is quieter, most mums would love the chance to be alone.'

Sue bristled, thinking her comments felt patronising and designed to make her feel guilty for being ungrateful. She turned to the baby, feeling tearful. She didn't want to continue the conversation.

'You're doing a wonderful job, dear, and we're here to support you. I'll pop back a bit later.' She left the room in a hurry and Sue watched her stride down the corridor like a gazelle.

Between feeds and visitors, Sue slept. One night, at around midnight, Heidi woke crying. Before Sue had the chance to lean over and lift her out of her cot, a nurse she'd never seen before dashed in, lifted her up and went to take her from the room.

'What are you doing?' Sue asked in alarm, dazed from sleep.

The nurse stopped by the door and turned. In the dim light, Sue's vision was foggy. 'Taking her away to feed her.'

She blinked rapidly, feeling completely disorientated and confused. So far, nobody had taken her baby out of the room to bottle-feed her. They all knew she breastfed, and only came in to lift Heidi from her cot.

Something doesn't feel right.

Suddenly she felt vulnerable. 'She's mine, I feed her.'

'No, we'll do it, you're still recovering, you need rest.'

'I'm breastfeeding, I don't want her bottle-fed. I decide what's best for her.'

Ignoring Sue's pleas, the nurse turned and hurried out of the room.

A cold chill of fear trickled down her spine and panic rose inside her. She'd read about women sneaking into maternity wards, disguised as nurses, to steal babies. Had the woman taken her baby? How did she know who to trust? She couldn't remember seeing the nurse's name badge, but she did remember what she looked like. She was short and a bit dumpy.

With panic pulsing through her, her heart hammering in her chest, she glanced round for the red cord and gave it a yank. A yellow light on the wall started flashing and an alarm rang. It was a relief to know there was an alarm because she couldn't simply slip out of bed and hotfoot it down the corridor, and even if she had legs, they'd stapled her abdomen and that part of her body was extremely sore.

Another nurse came in and glanced down at the empty cot before reaching over to turn the alarm off. 'Everything okay?'

'My baby's gone, someone's taken her.'

The nurse didn't look at all concerned. Instead, she smiled reassuringly. 'Yes, that was Jane, she's feeding Heidi to let you sleep.'

'Well, I'm wide awake now and I want to feed her. She had no right to just take her like that.' Sue should have felt relieved, Heidi was safe, but all she felt was burning rage. How could a nurse blatantly go against her wishes?

A few minutes later, Heidi was returned to Sue's arms. As soon as she was back home, she was going to put in a complaint to the hospital's management. She wondered how frequently nurses went against a mother's wishes. Once again, she felt isolated, she needed to share what had happened with the other new mums.

The day before Sue was due to go home, a group of nurses popped into her room asking for a chat.

'Everyone is amazed at how well you've coped giving birth and looking after your baby.'

'I'm just doing what every other mum is doing, I'm no different.' She felt embarrassed. What were they singling her out for this time?

'We'd really like to video you with Heidi to show other mums who express concerns about this or that.'

One of the nurses was holding a camcorder. 'In our eyes, you're somewhat of a celebrity.'

Sue laughed and felt herself blush. 'Coping here is one thing, but I've no idea how I'll get on at home.' As soon as she'd said this, she regretted it. She didn't want to look incapable and risk her baby being taken into care. She'd read about that happening to disabled parents and it was her greatest fear. She was all too aware though that her biggest challenges were yet to come when she returned home, and she was terrified she wouldn't be a good enough mum. What if the baby was sick and she couldn't help her? What if Toby dropped her? How would they cope when the baby became more mobile?

'Maureen, the social worker will be coming to visit you later to discuss and assess your needs and see what additional help you might need. She's lovely, she's here to help you and make sure you have the necessary support. You might not get all the support you need though as resources are limited.'

'Cutbacks,' Sue said, raising her eyes and tutting.

'And I believe the Thalidomide Trust and Thalidomide

Society offer assistance.' Her voice rose at the end of the sentence as if her statement was more a question.

'Yes, they're brilliant and there's a lot of sharing of ideas through both organisations of what works, what doesn't.' She thought of a special spoon Sally was going to use to wean her baby. It had been made in the workshop at St Bede's. Roehampton Hospital in London had also developed specialised equipment and adaptive tools to assist disabled parents.

Friends and family came to visit her in hospital, bringing gifts: cuddly toys and knitted outfits, grapes, chocolate and more grapes. And Lucozade. Why did people always bring Lucozade when they visited someone in hospital? There were cards, flowers in vases crammed along a ledge, their perfume intense as it dispersed into the air and made her sneeze.

It was lovely to see Jasper, Sandy, and Bill, but when her parents appeared unexpectedly, their visit caught her unawares. From her bed, she watched with dread crawling through her veins as they entered the corridor and trotted towards her room. After their initial disapproval of her pregnancy, she was determined to prove them wrong and show them she could be a good mother. Their scepticism had dampened her spirits and because of that she'd really struggled through her pregnancy, asking herself over and over if she was doing the right thing, but now the baby had arrived, she wanted to show her excitement and desperately wanted them to be excited for her. The baby needed its grandparents, how lovely it would be if they embraced the role.

She should have realised, baby or no baby, they weren't going to change. They were the same selfish people they'd always been, evident the minute they walked into the room, with the stiff and starchy manner she was used to. When they didn't head straight to the cot to coo over the baby like normal grandparents, her heart sank. Her mother dramatically slammed her handbag onto the table at the bottom of Sue's bed and then with a heavy sigh, she whined about her parched throat and how she'd felt trapped in the car for what had seemed like an eternity.

'I need a cup of tea,' she complained.

'The café's on the fifth floor, but it's closed at this time.' How she wished it was open. They'd only just arrived but already she wanted them gone.

Pearl tutted and huffed. 'Unbelievable. Don't they realise people travel halfway across the country to visit family? What kind of a hospital doesn't have a café open when you need it? I can't believe they don't serve a cuppa somewhere in this place.'

Her dad raised his eyebrows to Pearl and shook his head. 'I did tell you to bring a flask. You're not the one who had to drive. All those roadworks and endless traffic lights, it's a terrible journey.' Then he looked at Sue. 'You could have chosen somewhere easier to live. The things we do for you, and as for the parking round here, it's a nightmare. Took me an age to find a space. We cannot stay long as they charge by the hour.'

'Nice to see you too,' Sue said sarcastically. The only nightmare was her parents.

Her mum looked straight at her and with a haughty laugh said, 'How did it go, I do not want all the gory details, just how long did it take and how much does she weigh?'

She briefly glanced at Heidi before looking back at Sue. 'Does she have all her bits or are any missing?'

'She is fine, Mum, perfectly normal, what were you expecting, a horror story like me?'

Sue spat it out, appalled at how unkind her mum could

be. If she could disown her own parents, she gladly would. They were going to be nightmare grandparents and if they kept their distance, that would be fine by her.

Her dad went to the window and peered through the Venetian blinds. 'Grey out, looks like it's going to rain.'

'When are you going home? I expect it will be a while before they let you out. You will need to show you can cope and that will take a while.'

Sue bit her lip. There was a coldness to her mother, there was no warmth, no empathy, it was as if she was an empty shell that spoke.

She went to look in the cot. Heidi was asleep. Any other grandma would have reached to touch or kiss her, or asked to pick her up. 'You poor little mite, God help you.'

Her dad turned from the window and shook his head in agreement.

'What do you mean?' She was close to tears but sniffed them back. 'It's not her fault she's got grandparents like you.'

Sue couldn't bear it. Their visit was much worse than she had expected. She chastised herself for thinking it would be anything else. They just didn't have it in them to be loving. She wondered what they would be like when the twins had children. They'd always treated them differently. She knew she couldn't sit by and watch them all play happy families.

'At least she's not got your looks, Mum.' She hated being nasty, it wasn't in her nature, but she'd been driven to it. 'She looks more like Sandy, Toby's ...' She cut off just in time when she remembered, as no one knew.

'Just like who?

'If you've got nothing nice to say, you may as well go.'

'Yes, well,' her dad said, his hands deep in his pockets as he stood there jangling coins and looking bored, 'we can see you when you get home. We don't want to have to pay an extra half hour on the parking.' He checked his watch and looked impatient.

As he passed the cot, he glanced in and asked, 'What name have you chosen?'

'Heidi.'

Her mum looked incredulous. 'After the film or the sitcom, *Hi-de-Hi*?' She laughed.

Her stomach sank like a balloon deflating.

'I hope you're not expecting us to babysit when things get tough. We've brought our children up and had our fill of babies.'

'You've already told me that, Mum.'

The visit was over as soon as it had started. It had been such a horrible experience. As soon as they were gone, Sue burst into tears and felt incredibly low. With streaming eyes, she gazed at her baby, who was sleeping peacefully, so blissfully innocent. The room felt heavy with the chill of her parents' disapproval. The whole time they'd been here, Heidi had been oblivious to her grandparents' cold presence in the room. And then, in that unexpected moment, Sue was overwhelmed by a powerful wave of love—pure and unconditional, and all-consuming—that left her breathless and weakened. The rush of love was quickly followed by fierce protectiveness welling inside her, a strong determination to shield her child from all that was destructive and bad.

She sat there, crying, and feeling completely crushed. Her parents were horrible. Anyone could see how awful they were and yet a part of her always had to question her feelings and her reaction to their comments and behaviour. She'd always been filled with self-doubt, and she was tired of being this way. Now, here she was blaming her hormones for her tears, what mothers often referred to as the baby blues. Why did she always question herself and yearn for their approval? They were never going to be proud of her, she was searching for something that just wasn't within their capacity.

Just then her mother swept back into the room and went to grab her handbag. Sue hadn't even noticed she'd forgotten it. She stared at Sue and looked shocked that she was crying.

'Pull yourself together, life's not all about you, you've got a baby to think of now, it's too late for tears, you should have thought of that before you got up the duff. Now you'll find out just how difficult it is to bring up a child.'

Sue rounded on her and let out a mirthless laugh. 'That's a complete joke. You did not have the burden of bringing me up. That was far too beneath you. The doctor told you to go home and have another. And so you did.' She clicked her fingers. 'And just like that, my replacements were born. I shall be a proper mum to Heidi.' She gave a sarcastic laugh.

Pearl didn't answer immediately but seemed to process Sue's words. Something passed over her face; was it regret, guilt or shame? Her face softened and she glanced over at Heidi. For a brief moment, Sue wondered if she was going to make the grand apology, the one she'd waited for her whole life, but it didn't come.

'Look, love, it's not too late to have it adopted or fostered. I know you think you think you can cope, but trust me, you don't have a clue, even for a normal parent it's hard, and Toby's not going to be a lot of use.'

Sue was appalled, especially considering her mother seemed to be softening. How wrong she'd been. 'I really didn't think you could be that ashamed of me, thank God

Toby's family are kind and supportive. I don't know what has made you so cruel and unkind.'

'Oh, don't be such a drama queen, you're being ridiculous.'

Her heart was hammering so hard, she tried to bat down the humiliation welling inside and was relieved when her mother left.

SUE HAD BEEN HOME for a week. It was early evening, and she had just finished feeding Heidi. They were all snuggled on the settee, the soft glow of the lamp casting warmth across the lounge. The baby lay peacefully between them wrapped in a pink blanket, a tiny miracle that had transformed their lives.

'Mum and Dad laughed at her name,' Sue said.

'Sod them, she's our child. If they don't have anything nice to say, they should stay quiet. We like the name.'

'Do we though? I'm not sure. When I think of Heidi, it's the film I think of.'

'We can't change it now. I've already told German Heidi.'

'What did you do that for?' She wanted to send out proper baby announcements.

'I just wanted her to feel good about herself. She was so chuffed. Must be terrible to be separated from your parents and spend your entire life hoping for a reconciliation.'

'Yes, we've both had our own experiences to understand what she must have gone through. All of our stories, they're interwoven and our sorrows are united.'

'That's very poetic, for you.'

'Ha ha. I can be quite philosophical.'

'I wonder if she'll ever find her parents.'

'I guess it depends if the wall stays up,' Sue suggested.

She leaned down and gave the baby a kiss on her cheek.

'She's doesn't look like a Heidi. She looks like a Nicola.'

'I suppose we could have Heidi as her middle name.'

'Yeah, I like that. Nicola Heidi.'

They were silent for a while, the TV droning in the background, and in that silence they sat and gazed at their daughter. Sue was mesmerised, it was hard to look away, she was just such a gorgeous little thing. Her heart was filled with such pride and love, she felt she would burst with all the emotions.

'We've come a long way, haven't we?' Toby said, turning to look at her and smiling so wide it seemed to take over his face. 'I know it's been hard for you dealing with your parents but look at what we've achieved. My career, your career, this lovely bungalow we've made our home.'

'And all the protests we've been on. One day the world will accept us, we just have to keep making a noise.'

'I have a dream,' Toby chuckled. 'That one day this nation will rise up.' He was good at putting on an American accent. 'We'll rise with a powerful voice that won't be silenced. One day our abilities will be celebrated, not overshadowed by our challenges. The future will be about understanding and acceptance because we refuse to be defined by our limitations.'

'Oh 'eck, Toblerone, I can feel another speech coming on.'

He nodded. 'One day, I want to give a speech at the biggest protest you've ever seen, on Westminster Bridge or outside Number 10.'

'Watch this space, kiddo,' she said, looking at the baby and blowing a kiss. 'Your dad's got fire in his belly and passion in his heart.'

'I've got fire in my pants too,' he said, teasing her. That was the last thing on her mind right now, and he knew it.

'I feel so happy,' she said. In that moment it was as if something swirled between the three of them, floating like champagne bubbles. Something opened up inside her in the deepest most untouched part of her heart that for years had been hers alone.

Everything felt perfect; what could possibly go wrong?

THE END

The story continues in book 7, **Every Child's Fear,** *to be published in Spring 2026.*

AUTHOR NOTE

Thank you for purchasing *Every Couple's Fear*, which I hope you enjoyed. If you have a moment, please would you kindly post a short review on Amazon. Reviews are always appreciated.

Every Couple's Fear is part of a series called 'Every Parent's Fear.' The other books in this series can be found on Amazon. Here is the link: https://amzn.to/3GfEAN4

You might also enjoy my blog at https://joannawarringtonauthor-allthingsd.co.uk/ I enjoy writing articles from time to time, particularly after travelling, I'll write up my observations and on other issues which hopefully will be interesting for you, the reader.

OTHER BOOKS BY JOANNA WARRINGTON

To stay up to date on my latest releases, please follow me on Amazon. Here is the link: https://amzn.to/442iLuu

You might also enjoy *The Baby Hunters*, the story of Kathleen's escape from incarceration in an institution for "fallen women". This is part of a series called 'Every Family.'

PRAISE FOR *THE BABY HUNTERS*

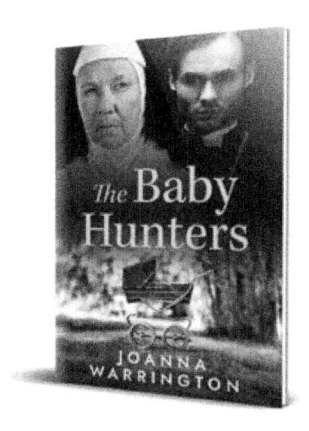

"A well plotted story, exposing the cruelty and hypocrisy Catholic priests and nuns are capable of." Reader Review

"What eye-opening stories these poor young women experienced. I could not put the book down." Reader Review

"This story highlights how cruelly young girls were treated in Ireland in the 1970s." Reader Review

"Great story, loved the book, really hard to put down, looking forward to the next two books. Best read in a long time." Reader Review ☆☆☆☆☆

In 1974, the shadows of the Magdalene laundry still haunt Kathleen as she daringly escapes from a life of oppression. Now she's on the run, the priest hot on her trail. As the priest's attention shifts to other lost souls, the consequences are nothing short of devastating.

Meanwhile, a famous American actress and her wealthy husband have arrived in Ireland to adopt a baby and discover an unexpected offer they cannot refuse. Will it turn out to be a dream come true or a nightmare waiting to unfold?

Enter the O'Sullivans, a struggling Catholic family in Belfast battling the weight of poverty and the turmoil of the Troubles. With a fifth child adding to their financial strain, and ostracised by their Protestant neighbours, their house is about to be petrol-bombed. The couple face a momentous choice—hope the conflict will pass or leave behind everything they know for a new life. Desperation drives Mrs O'Sullivan to come up with a plan that offers the family a glimmer of hope, but at what price?

Inspired by true events, this is a powerful story of joy and sorrow uncovering the profound and catastrophic effects of the Irish Troubles, the Catholic Church's practices in Ireland and the systemic abuse by those in positions of authority.

For fans of *Philomena*, the book that inspired the Academy Award-nominated film, starring Judi Dench and Steve Coogan.

Here is the link to **The Baby Hunters:** https://amzn.to/3S3C3Ip

The Catholic Woman's Dying Wish

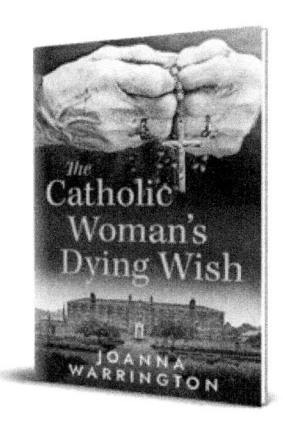

My Book

A dying wish. A shocking secret. A dark, destructive and abusive relationship.

Forget hearts & flowers and happy ever afters in this quirky unconventional love story! *Readers say: "A little bit Ben Elton" "a monstrous car crash of a saga."* Middle aged Darius can't seem to hold on to the good relationships in his life. Now, he discovers a devastating truth about his family that blows away his future and forces him to revisit his painful past. Distracting himself from family problems he goes online and meets Faye, a single mum. Faye and her children are about to find out the horrors and demons lurking behind the man Faye thinks she loves.

Every Family Has One

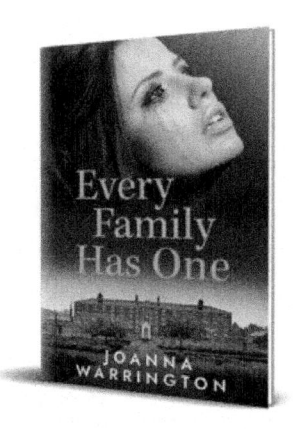

My Book

The harrowing story of a 14-year-old facing betrayal by a trusted family priest in a close-knit 1970s Catholic community.

Imagine the shame when you can't even tell the truth to those you love and they banish you to Ireland to have your baby in secret. How will poor Kathleen ever recover from her ordeal? This is a dramatic and heart-breaking story about the joys and tests of motherhood and the power of love, friendship and family ties spanning several decades.

Slippers on a First Date

My Book

Inspired by real events! Donna's love life is a mess. Years of online-dating have left her self-esteem in tatters. Now 56, she can boast a list of failed relationships longer than a grocery bill.

When her spiteful daughter Olivia makes a scathing remark about her mother's love life, Donna sets out on one last quest to find Mr Right. Is it too late to find lasting love, or will she just repeat the same mistakes?

It's 2020 and England is in lockdown, presenting a whole range of new challenges for daters.

Donna's forays into the world of dating lead her on a series of calamitous adventures involving an unwanted gift, faking her identity, and getting arrested. And finally, her job as a nurse is on the line. When things go horribly wrong, Olivia decides to take matters into her own hands.

The love that Donna has always searched for isn't the type of love she needs. Her journey reveals a few home truths and ultimately she discovers that real lasting love has been staring her right in the face all along.

Don't Blame Me

My Book

It's every parent's worst nightmare

When tragedy struck twenty-five years ago, Dee's world fell apart. With painful reminders all around her she flew to Australia to start a new life. Now, with her dad dying, she's needed back in England. But these are unprecedented times. It's the spring of 2020 and as Dee returns to the beautiful medieval house in rural Kent where she grew up among apple orchards and hop fields, England goes into lockdown, trapping her in the village. The person she least wanted to see has also returned, forcing her to confront the painful past and resolve matters between them.

Holiday

My Book

Lyn wakes on her 50th birthday with no man and middle age staring her in the face.

"For readers who enjoy British humour." Readers Favorite. Determined to change her sad trajectory Lyn books a surprise road trip for herself and her three children through the American Southwest and Yellowstone. Before they even get on the plane, the trip hits a major snag. An uninvited guest joins them at the airport, turning their dream trip into a nightmare.

Amid the mountain vistas, secrets will be revealed, and a hurtful betrayal confronted.

This book is more than an amusing family saga. It will also appeal to those interested in American scenery, history and culture.

Time to Reflect

My Book

A BRITISH AUNT AND HER NIECE SET OFF TO EXPLORE MASSACHUSETTS AND RHODE ISLAND. IN THIS CALAMITY-RIDDEN TRAVEL TALE THEIR RELATIONSHIP IS CHANGED FOREVER.

It's a trip with an eclectic mix of history, culture and scenery. Seafood shacks. Postcard perfect lighthouses. Weather-boarded buildings. Stacks of pancakes dripping in syrup. Quaint boutiques. Walks along the cobblestone streets of Boston, America's oldest city—the city of revolution. Throw in plenty of disagreements and you have all the ingredients for a classic American road trip.

Everything is going well, until a shocking family secret is revealed. In a dramatic turn of events, Ellie's father joins them and is forced to explain why he has been such an inadequate parent.

An entertaining but heartfelt journey through Massachusetts from Cape Cod to Plymouth, Salem, Marblehead, Boston and Rhode Island.

Weaving between past and present, this emotional and absorbing family saga is about hope, resilience and the healing power of forgiveness.

You might also enjoy reading my series about the lives of four women and their complicated relationships and challenging family life. This is a collection of four books which are also sold separately. **'Can We Sync Or Will We Sink?'**

"Light-hearted read about four women's lives." Reader Review

Here is the link: https://amzn.to/3GghFBf

Printed in Dunstable, United Kingdom